Brett

Thanks for the
ride & your
interest!!
It means a lot!

3:41

A
NOVEL
BY

DENNIS AIDEN
LOCKHART

TO
JOAN

There is a point in every race when you have to decide whether you are going to go for it or if you are going to let the race come to you and, you know, hope that things work out for the best, but I'm not that kind of runner, or person, so I generally try to take the situation by the balls—most times, when I want to be aggressive during a race, I flash in my mind that classic picture of Roger Bannister crossing the tape as the first person to ever break four minutes for a mile, and that usually charges me up—and I remember this one time, it's a mile at Fresno and we're about ready to hit the half and I'm in pretty good position—this was the days before all those big screen jumbotrons or whatever they call them, where the runners can look up and see how they're doing and where everybody else is in the race—so we're coming up to the half and they're calling out the times and they're at 1:55, (which is fast, because, for some reason, there were some really good runners in this race) and I'm third, thinking to myself that that's a pretty good split, since I hadn't been training that hard lately because I had had a cold for the last week and was eating almost nothing but chicken noodle soup, like, three times a day, because they always say that chicken soup is the best thing for you when you have a cold, but soup does not have many carbohydrates for energy—well, the noodles have carbs, but there aren't that many noodles, and I tried that double-noodle chicken noodle soup that Campbell's made, because it had a lot more noodles, but it was more like a casserole than a soup, and so I went back to regular chicken noodle soup, because then you can use the store brands, which, although they are not quite as good as Campbell's, are not bad, and a lot cheaper—so I would mix two tablespoons of corn starch with some of the broth from the soup, add some frozen peas and maybe an egg white (without the yolk, because that's all fat) and brown rice for some extra protein and carbs, and, presto, you have a Chunky soup for about eighty-five cents—and so that's all I'd been eating for the last week, and I'm hitting the half in 1:56, thinking to myself that so far, so good, and wondering if I should start pushing it on the third lap, because that's when I usually make my move, not like the Kenyans—the Kenyans wait until the last lap to make a move sprinting to the end and looking like Usain fucking Bolt at the finish—and then see if anybody else has got the balls to go with me when there's still 660 yards to go, but this time I really didn't know if I should or not, maybe just let the race take care of itself, you know, when I thought about the Gospel where Jesus tells the story about the master who gave each of his three servants a talent and left town and the one servant invested it and made ten, the second one invested it and made five, and the third one pussied out and buried his one talent in a hole, and when the master came back, he praised the two servants who invested and increased what they had, but he really got pissed at the servant who just tried to save the one talent he had, who was too afraid of failing to try and succeed, and threw him out in the street, and I figured that that applied to me here, and by this time we were halfway through the third lap, almost exactly 660 yards from the finish—I never talk in that meters bullshit if I can help it, although it's hard not to if, for example, you're running a 1500 meters instead of a mile, but even then I try to break it down into yards, just to piss off the suits—and I'm still in third, ten yards off the pace, feeling pretty good, thinking we're still running about the same pace—a 1:56 half is 58 for each 440, which is a 29 for a 220—so I'm figuring we are right around 2:27, with a lap and a half to go, and if I jack it up right now I can do the next 220 in a 27, which would get me to the 1320 at 2:54 with a 440 left, and that should really piss off everyone else in the race, who are just trying to go through the motions on the third lap while waiting for their Big Finish, so I just take it up a notch, pass the two guys in front of me, who each give me a look out the corner of their eye like "Are you shitting me?" and cruise around the curve, heading into the last 110 of that lap balls-to-the-walls—well, not really, since I still have about 550 yards to the finish, but, you know what I mean—and I really feel like a machine, legs turning over smoothly, breathing easy, just like that old Jag I used to have, a '67 XKE—that was the last year for the enclosed headlights, because the Feds made them replace them in 1968 (halfway through 1967, actually) with headlights that stuck out, which really ruined the smooth hood contours of the XKE (the government is always messing around with people's lives)—and I started to think about that as I was finishing the third lap, waiting for the bell for the last lap, which you love if you're leading and hate if you're fading—

expecting 2:54, and I got a 2:52, which really surprised the hell out of me, and I almost wanted to stop and go over to the timer and say "Are you shitting me?" but I just kept on trucking, and the people in the stands—there was only a couple hundred of them because this meet was no big deal to anyone—were trying to get me to run faster, and I knew why they were doing it—they didn't care about me, they just wanted to see a record (American, meet, whatever)—so they could brag to their friends that they were so smart by going to this jerk-off track meet everybody else ignored, and now they had a lifetime memory while their friends just went to the mall or something, and that's how people really are, you know, only thinking about themselves even when they try to appear as if they are cheering you on—but I said to myself that these people were dreaming, because the world record then was like 3:45 or something, and even the American record was under 3:50, and I might get the meet record—big fucking deal—but to get anywhere near a world-record time I would have to run like a 54 flat for the last 440 after I had just run a 56, with the chances of me being able to do that not real good, although the chances of me leaving a lung on track if I tried were excellent, but, what the hell, I would do what I could—maybe not the servant who made ten talents, but the one who got five, still not bad—and down the backstretch I was dying to look around and see where everybody else was, if they were fading or holding on, and the looks on their faces, because I knew they were just shitting—I hadn't run this good since the first three laps of the Olympic Trials—but turning around while running is a great way to fall down and like I said before, we didn't have jumbotrons in those days—not that this crappy-ass meet at some junior-college football stadium would've had one anyway—and so I had to just imagine how those guys were reacting, and what Judy would've been thinking, if she would still ask what happened, seeing me nail these other bastards, and as I ran I even fantasized for a moment or two that I was stomping on the divorce papers she had served me, and a guy on the backstretch with a stopwatch called out to me as I passed him that I was at 3:21 with a half-lap, 220 yards, to go, and I realized I had just run a 29 for the last 220, and if I could keep that pace, I would be under 3:50, close to the American record, and a personal best for me, someone who was supposed to be over the hill and at the bottom of the valley, and something to make everybody who wrote me off shit in their pants, assuming I could keep up the pace, but I felt strong and as I rounded the final curve to the finish my body seemed to be working almost independently from my brain, as if I was just along for the ride, which was okay with me, but I couldn't figure out what was happening, and I didn't even try to dig in for the last 100 yards—which is actually the way you are supposed to run, nice and relaxed, because I remembered that story about Bill Bowerman, the guy who helped start Nike, when he was the track coach at Oregon and he told all his sprinters to line up and run relaxed, at three-quarters speed, and they all ran their personal bests—and all I could think about was that maybe all that corn starch had given me extra energy, and I was still trying to figure it out when I crossed the finish line, running through some cheap-ass red ribbon that must've been left over from somebody's birthday present that they stretched a couple of feet across the track, with the ribbon wrapping around my body and face, when some guy runs up to me, shoves a stopwatch in my face and screams at me, "3:50.7... 3:50.7!" and then some other guy, I guess he was a reporter, asked me how I did it, and I just said "Corn starch", jogged around the track, got on my bike, and rode away.

That's all I remember.

Hardman Runs 3:50.7

Tim Hardman comes out of nowhere, runs the fastest American mile of the last two years, and then disappears back into the obscurity from whence he came.

New York Times News Service

(NYT) **Fresno, CA** Running the kind of race that he seems to undertake every few years—in other words, just often enough to make people think he might still have the goods, but not often enough to make them believe it—Tim Hardman once again proved that he is not just yet ready to become the answer to the trivia question: Which American miler disappeared just before achieving his full potential? A 3:50.7 will do that. What it will not do, unfortunately, is propel Hardman back to the front ranks of American milers, a position that seemed so firmly his before the last Olympic Trials, when he blazed around the track for three and a half laps in record time and then collapsed, enduring a death march on the last half of the final lap, collapsing again at the finish and having to be resuscitated right there on the track.

No one has ever doubted Hardman's talent, only his methods of employing it. Had he been able to continue his torrid pace in those Trials for the last 200 meters, he would have broken the 1500 meters world record by two full seconds; if he had backed off somewhat, he wouldn't have made history, but he would have made the U.S. Olympic team. Instead, he did neither, breaking not records but, instead, the hearts of all those who had such high hopes for him.

And today's performance shows that those hopes were justified, then and perhaps even now. What it doesn't show is that he has yet been able to harness that talent in any meaningful and sustained way. He could just as easily, assuming he even races again in the next three months, run fifteen seconds slower the next time he sets foot on a track. Nobody knows—including, it would seem, Tim Hardman.

In fact, even setting foot on a track is a major production for Hardman these days. He wasn't officially entered in this all-comers meet today at Fresno City College, a warm-up for the very important Modesto Relays next week. Hardman basically rode his bicycle up to the starting line about twenty minutes before the race and asked if he could run. For better or worse, almost everybody in U.S. track knows who Tim Hardman is, and so, even though he could produce no proof that he was registered with the U.S. Track and Field Association, those in positions of authority at the meet essentially shrugged their shoulders with a collective "Why the hell not?" He stripped down to some gym shorts and a t-shirt, put on his spikes, and jogged around the track and infield, warming up. He looked good—nothing like the stories and the rumors about him getting ready to enter a Howard Hughes look-alike contest—and his stride was as beautiful as ever. The man is an athlete—below the neck he is the complete package, but, unfortunately, above the neck seems to be another story. The race itself was classic Hardman. It is unknown if he was aware of the quality of some of the entrants in the race—Paolo Rubiano from Italy and the Irishman Pat Ryan, two finalists from the 1500 meters in the last Olympics, were in the field. Hardman might have recognized them, assuming he still pays any attention to the sport when he is away from the track itself, but it is doubtful that he knew why they were there. This race was simply to be a glorified workout for Rubiano and Ryan. They had just arrived in America three days before, and the purpose of this race was simply to get them ready for next week at Modesto, nothing more and nothing less. Of course, you have to understand that what we regard as a workout and what they regard as a workout are two completely different things. Rubiano and Ryan alternated the lead for the first two laps, setting a scorching pace, blistering through the half-mile at 1:55. The plan was then to cruise through the third and fourth laps, saving their closing energy for next week. The two Europeans seemed comfortable in the lead and unaware that Hardman was only about ten yards off the front. Had they seen him, they probably wouldn't have known who he was, since Hardman's fame, such as it is, has never spread much beyond our shores. It now may, because when Hardman charged past the two on the backstretch of the third lap, he definitely got their attention. Rubiano and Ryan glanced at Hardman as he passed them and then at each other, the looks on their face suggesting that they didn't know who this was, or why he was doing this. They continued at their own pace, while Hardman charged to the front, as has been his MO for the last seven or eight years. Hardman continued pushing himself right to the finish, being rewarded with the best time in the mile by an American in the last two years. Perhaps, in his mind, he was making up for the disaster at the Olympic Trials.

The problem is figuring out what exactly is going on in Hardman's mind. This reporter has always given any gifted athlete—and, make no mistake, that is an accurate description of Hardman—the benefit of the doubt in almost everything they do in their chosen field. They are so finely-tuned, both physically and emotionally, that they always seem to be on the edge of catastrophe. It is a very fine line, one that Hardman seems to have crossed, in both directions, on numerous occasions. This was amply documented when this reporter asked about the race, and Hardman gave a two-word reply—"Corn starch"—then jogged over to his bicycle, put on his jeans and sweatshirt and, still wearing his track spikes, pedaled off into the late afternoon sun.

The melodramatic part of all this—I am loathe to call it tragic—is that Hardman's performance and the time it produced are not likely to be recognized in any official capacity. Hardman has not been tested—or located—for so long that, in these days of rampant cynicism about dramatic improvement by unknown or unsupervised athletes, there is little chance his time will ever be anything more than footnote. Were he, of course, to suddenly avail himself of the opportunity to be tested for performance-enhancing drugs, this might change, but that is not likely. Nothing really is at stake here but Hardman's reputation, which needs a great deal more than one good drug test and the course record at some all-comers meet to repair the damage done to it. Hardman's cycling off into the distance doesn't seem to indicate an inclination to cooperate with anybody—or any *body*—about anything. It is generally assumed, given his erratic behavior over the last few years, that he has been under various degrees of psychiatric care, with the prescription drugs such a regimen would involve, those drugs undoubtedly precluding a clean test or, at the very least, a clean bill of health.

The discussion about Tim Hardman has always come down to this: He has great talent; what will he do with it? We are no closer to that answer now than ever.

--Randall Miller

The strange thing is that all I remember about that race in Fresno is the race itself and none of the stuff that went on before and after it, like where I was staying, or who I was staying with, or why I was even in Fresno because I can't think of anybody I know who lives there, although when I was running for UCLA we had a meet against Fresno State one time and I think I got friendly with a couple guys on their team but that meet was down in LA at Drake Stadium on the UCLA campus, so it isn't like we all went back to those guys' place afterwards for a couple beers or something, although they probably did tell me to look them up if I was ever in Fresno—I'm just guessing here—and maybe that's what I did, but I can't for the life of me remember anything like that and I don't even have any idea where the bicycle came from or even whose it was and I really don't think I would've ridden it all the way to Fresno—that's a long way from southern California—although, it's not impossible since I'd had a lot of free time on my hands, but it's more likely I would've driven, except I don't think I could've afforded the gas, since I was then only getting $600 a month on SSI, or maybe these guys drove me up to Fresno, I stayed with them, used their bike to get to the meet, then they drove me back down there to my home in the desert afterwards—so, yeah, it could've happened that way and I could've stayed with those guys and they told me about the race, and maybe they were even in it, and maybe that's how it all came about even though I don't remember any of that but you can sort of deduce certain things if you know one thing is true, like if you are alone in a house in the middle of the night and the room you are in is the only room in the house with the lights on, even if you don't remember it you can pretty much assume that you went into that room and turned on the lights yourself, although it's possible, I guess, that the lights were already on, but, you know, why would lights be on in a house in the middle of the night if you were the only person in the house and you didn't turn them on, see what I mean?

I just don't remember any of it.

I sort of have a problem.

I forget things. Lots of things…all the time. I will remember everything I did today, but tomorrow it will be gone from my memory. It's as if it never happened. I know it did, but my mind can't prove it. Short-term memory loss is what they call it. You don't want to know what I call it. Like the analogy about the lighted room in the house in the middle of the night: I have to make certain assumptions about what has happened previously because I don't remember, which I guess could be considered a form of amnesia. But, I know what I'm doing when I'm doing it, since I've never gotten in any trouble or wandered away from my house and out into the desert like you hear about happening with people who have memory problems, and I think I'm in the best running shape of my life, if I can judge from my workouts, which I don't remember but which I make long notes about. I just know that I can still run really fast and really far, although a mile is as far as I want to run competitively. I can remember almost every detail of every race I have ever run, back to my first 660 race as a junior varsity runner as a freshman in high school (I ran a 1:30, not terrible but not real good, either, but every 220 was 30 seconds flat, which my coach said was a phenomenal sense of pace for a kid who had never run in an organized race before, and that really pumped me up and I remember that in the next race I ran the first 220 in 30 seconds, the next one in 29, and the last one in 26 seconds, a 1:25, and won the race, and then the coach put me on the varsity for the next race, and I ran the 880 and won in 1:59 and the coach was going out of his mind and he entered me in the mile for the next meet, and I won with a 4:28, with a 67 second split on each lap and I think the coach wanted to adopt me and I knew right then what I was going to do for the rest of my life) but I can't remember what I had for lunch yesterday. I'd rather have it this way rather than the other way around, I guess, since it all seems to be working out for me—so far, anyway.

I live in a very small, old house in the high desert of Southern California, about fifty miles north of Palm Springs (or a hundred miles east of LA), near a place called Landers. Really, it's out in the middle of nowhere, which is a pretty good metaphor for the way my life feels sometimes. I'm in control of what I do right now, and I guess I was in control of everything I did yesterday, although I don't actually remember anything about yesterday. But, I take notes if something is important enough. Also, I got a video camera from someone a long time ago, and I tape something if it seems worthwhile. (I forgot who gave it to me and they, whoever they are, haven't come and taken it back.) And, from what I see on my tapes, everything seems pretty normal, like I'm just going about my business, doing normal stuff, under control, especially my workouts, which are really good and probably better than when I was in college and had a big-time coach and you wouldn't think anything is unusual, because in fact it's all pretty boring, which is the best part because that tells me that I'm doing okay, sort of like an animal…yeah, pretty much like an animal in that I seem to move from place to place with some sort of logic that is probably more instinctive than thought out, even though some of the conversations I have with myself on tape about stuff I didn't even know I knew very much about are pretty intense and intelligent and I am sort of getting the idea that even though I try to keep up with things as much as possible, what is really important to me is mostly running and family stuff from the past. Even though I don't have any memory of what happened yesterday, everything I do, according to my notes and tape, seems to be rational and sensible, which tells me that I know what I'm doing when I'm doing it, even if I completely forget about it the next day, so I guess I can live with that.

I use that video camera all the time. I'm always taping…everyday. Not all day, of course. Just here and there. Sort of like a diary. Most of it is pretty boring. I just want to make sure everything is okay. If something is unusual, or really interesting, or will help me from one day to the next, I'll save it on the tape, but the things that seem ordinary I will probably erase, since I don't need reams of video tape covering every second of my life. (Someone once said you can read the transcript of a day's video in a few minutes, but it will take a day to view a day's worth of video.) The thing is, when I got this video camera it was pretty high-tech but now it's like an antique, kind of bulky, and I'm wondering how much longer they'll be making the kind of blank VHS cartridges I need, although that may not be a problem after tonight, but, in any case, it's just good to have those tapes with me, and I kind of wish I had had that video camera for what happened with me at the Olympic Trials, to help explain some things for me, because I think a lot of what I'm going through now can be traced back to what happened then, like passing out at the end of the race and having a doctor tell me afterwards that I was clinically dead for about thirty seconds while I was lying on the track, before they got my heart pumping again, and I've never really told this to anyone before, but I remember drifting up out of my body and looking over the whole scene as they worked on me, just like other people have described it when something similar happened to them, and I remember thinking to myself— or to whoever I was when I was outside my body— "Holy shit, this is actually happening!" and watching the doctor, the officials, and Judy stand over me, and Judy asking the officials if I was going to make it, and one of them saying that my life signs were coming back and Judy saying that she was asking if I was going to make the Olympic Team, and one of them shaking his head and she muttering under her breath about what a waste of time this had all been, and then when I came back to consciousness the first face I saw was Judy's, and her first question to me was not "How are you?" but, instead, "What happened?"—as in "What happened? Why didn't you qualify for the fucking Olympic Team?"—and I've never been the same ever since then, and I don't know if it's because I was clinically dead for half-a-minute or so and maybe suffered some brain damage, even though I thought you normally got about four minutes of no oxygen to the brain before that started, although we're not usually talking about someone who just ran 1500 meters in 3:35, so maybe my brain was needing a lot more oxygen right then and thirty seconds was a critical amount of time, or maybe it was just the shock of seeing how Judy reacted to all of this—we were supposed to be one of the All-Time Great Couples, you understand—

that blew my mind, or some combination of the two, I don't know, but what I do know is that my life has never been the same since, and, although life hasn't been bad judging from the few things I can remember since then— the blockage of memory took a couple years to fully develop—from what I see on the tapes, I really divide my life into two parts, before the Olympic Trials and after...and try to remain positive...as long as I remember how.

CBS-TV TRANSCRIPT

Brian Palmer: The runners are now coming onto the track for the finals of the 1500 meters. The first three finishers make the Olympic team... simple as that.

Charles Johnson: Well, actually, the fourth-place finisher will go along, too—as an alternate.

B.P.: Just along for the ride, huh? How many times does an alternate compete?

C.J.: You're right, not too often...but it does happen every once in awhile. In Atlanta, a couple of alternates got to compete because of training injuries to athletes who had qualified.

B.P.: Okay, so the first four will get to go, but only three, and probably the first three, will compete.

C.J.: Right.

B.P.: We've spent some time during the prelims profiling most of the major competitors in this race, but there is one, Tim Hardman, who we haven't talked about, and he has at least an outside chance to make the team.

C.J.: Yes, he does. How good of a chance really depends on which Tim Hardman shows up, the one who will stay up at the front and try to steal the race from everyone, or the Tim Hardman who just sort of blends into the crowd and tries to finish near the front. Tim Hardman is very difficult to predict.

B.P.: He has had some outstanding times, Charles.

C.J.: Yes, he has. And he has also had some dreadful performances, where it looked like he was just going through the motions.

B.P.: Difficult to understand.

C.J.: Yes...very. He was that way at UCLA, and even in high school. He set the California high school record for sophomores, running a 4:05 mile as a fifteen-year-old. The next year, as a junior, he never broke 4:15. Then, as a senior, in his last race, at the state championships, he won with a 4:03. UCLA gave him a track scholarship, and, in his first race as a collegian, he broke four minutes, at 3:58.7. He spent the rest of his college career chasing that time, and won a few championships for the Bruins, but he never ran any faster than he did his first year.

B.P.: And yet, here he is, in the Olympic Trial finals hoping to make the U.S. team. Does he have a chance?

C.J.: I don't think anyone knows, Brian—including Tim Hardman. Six months ago, no one would have predicted that he would even have been invited to the Trials, let alone qualify for the finals, until he ran that 3:53.5 in San Diego six weeks ago.

B.P.: The fastest time by an American this year.

C.J.: ...or last year. Basically, they *had* to invite him off that performance, even with his history of up-and-down outings.

B.P.: Is there a concern among American track officials that if Hardman does qualify for the team, there is a chance that he will go in the tank, for lack of a better term, at the Olympics?

C.J.: There certainly is. That will be in the back of everybody's mind if he qualifies for the team. But, we live in a democracy. Everybody who merits a chance gets one. However, if he does qualify, I can guarantee that the coaches here will be spending a lot of sleepless nights trying to figure how to extract from him the performance that he may indeed be capable of.

B.P.: We shall see. The eight runners line up at the start, there's the gun, and they are off. Hardman sprints to the front, and sprint is the right word...He must've run that first fifty yards in about six seconds He looked like he was shot out of a cannon.

C.J.: That's not really a good sign. His nerves probably got the best of him there. He looks tight...he looks nervous.

B.P.: He also looks very fast. On the backstretch of the first lap he already has a ten-yard lead on the field, with Maldonado leading the other seven runners. Is Hardman running this first lap too fast?

C.J.: He just hit the first 200 meters in 24. That is scary fast...and probably very stupid. He could jog through the rest of the first lap and still have a great time, which would indicate he is heading either toward a meet record or the intensive care unit.

B.P.: Hardman increases his lead coming around the second curve of the first lap. Does he look as if he is slowing down, Charles?

C.J.: If he is, it's imperceptible to me. It is also foolish. The goal here is not to break any records or run your competitors into the ground, the purpose is to make the team. You save your best race for the Olympics, not the Olympic Trials.

B.P.: Coming up to the end of the first lap, Charles.

C.J.: 43.5 for the first 300 meters! Unbelievable!

B.P.: As he heads into the first turn of the second lap, he seems to have doubled his lead over Maldonado, to at least 20 yards, with Brown and Wilson together another ten yards behind. Can he continue this pace, Charles?

C.J.: Well, the question to me is, why would he want to? If you win by a hundred yards or a hundred inches, you still make the team. It seems to be all or nothing for him.

B.P.: Which will it be?

C.J.: Let me see his split at the 500 meters and I'll tell you...1:13.5. He just ran the last 200 in 30 seconds. He's calming down.

B.P.: He must have heard you.

C.J.: He probably just heard his heart and lungs screaming for mercy.

B.P.: He still has the big lead, even though he's slowed down.

C.J.: Well, the others, especially Maldonado and Wilson, are very experienced runners and they know almost for certain that they do not have to catch Hardman, that he will come back to them.

B.P.: Well, it hasn't happened yet, as he comes around the curve and down the stretch, he looks to have lengthened his lead. Is he speeding up again?

C.J.: I don't think so. I think the others are just holding back, waiting to reel him in. They are very clever, saving their energy...1:39.5! This is unheard of! He just ran that last 200 meters in 26 seconds! No one can run the first two laps that fast and finish the race. *No one.*

B.P.: What are you saying?

C.J.: We are either witnessing one of the greatest performances in the history of human sport or...

B.P.: Or what?

C.J.: I'd rather not say.

B.P.: That sounds ominous.

C.J.: It is. Humans are not designed to run this fast, this early, at this distance.

B.P.: Halfway through the third lap, six hundred meters to go, his lead is still approximately twenty yards.

C.J.: 2:09.5—that last 200 was in 30 seconds again.

B.P.: Is he slowing down or just coming to his senses?

C.J.: Hopefully...both. He just needs to maintain a reasonable pace the next lap and a half and he qualifies. He doesn't need to prove anything to anyone.

B.P.: Except maybe to himself.

C.J.: Exactly. The on-going opinion about Hardman is that his toughest opponent, his toughest competition... will always be Tim Hardman.

B.P.: His lead seems to have shrunk by about five yards, but he still looks strong and confidant.

C.J.: Tim Hardman has never lacked confidence. It just has often been misplaced.

B.P.: We are now coming to the finish line for the bell, signaling the beginning of the last lap. He is raising his fist and shoving it into the air. I don't know if that is a gesture of defiance or triumph, but it looks very serious.

C.J.: 2:34.5! He just ran that last 200 meters in 25 seconds! I'm speechless!

B.P.: Maldonado, Wilson and Brown have pulled away from the others, but they are not going to catch Hardman.

C.J.: This is unreal! He is starting his kick on the backstretch! 3:00 flat with 200 meters left to go! If he runs anything under 30 seconds for the last 200, he will shatter the world record. This will rank right up there with Bob Beamon as one of the—

B.P.: HE'S STOPPED! HARDMAN HAS STOPPED RUNNING! HE IS ON THE GROUND1

C.J.: He looks like he's in pain and—

B.P.: Now he's up and starting to run again as first Maldonado, and then Brown and Wilson pass him at full speed...he's trying to regain his pace, but he looks as if he's running in place as Raymond Darkisian passes him for fourth. Hardman has now gotten back to his previous pace, but...

C.J.: It just won't cut it. He's trying to catch up with them while they're running away from him.

B.P.: Here comes Hardman!

C.J.: I can't believe this! He won't reach the first three, but he might catch Darkisian and make it as an alternate.

B.P.: Here comes Hardman! He is sprinting, his arms are flailing, he looks like he is swimming through the air.

C.J.: He might just make it.

B.P.: They come to the finish and Hardman is...fifth. He collapses just past the finish line. Charles, that did not look like the fall of someone who was exhausted, that looked the fall of someone who was shot.

C.J.: He just fell into a heap, as if his body had just stopped functioning. There was no momentum to his fall—he just dropped where he was standing.

B.P.: Have you ever seen anyone drop like that before?

C.J.: No, not on a running track, but...

B.P.: Then, where?

C.J.: I've seen guys like that drop on a battlefield...and they don't get up.

B.P.: Hardman looks as if he has been suctioned to ground, face down, motionless. Those of you who are bothered by this sort of thing should maybe look away from the screen for the next few moments, as one of our cameras at the finish line takes a better look. I don't know if he is moving.

C.J.: I...uh...can't tell if he is breathing.

B.P.: Let's cut back to a farther angle as they roll him over. Paramedics are pounding on his chest and checking his pulse. I think that's his wife Judy running to the scene and leaning over her husband. She seems to be shouting something at him, as if to wake him up. She looks frantic. Have you seen any movement, Charles?

C.J.: Nothing...nothing at all.

B.P.: Well, ladies and gentlemen, for three-and-a-half laps, Tim Hardman was tempting fate by seeming to push his body to extreme limits, heading for a time that would have not merely broken but shattered the existing world record for 1500 meters. Instead, what we have ended up with, as Charles cautioned us during the race, is the torrid pace that

Hardman set indeed coming back to haunt him. We can only hope that what we are seeing lying on the track and being desperately attended to is simply an exhausted athlete and nothing more than that. Can you remember anything like this happening before?

C.J.: Well, in the 1984 Olympics, in the women's marathon, a Swiss runner weaved her way around the Los Angeles Coliseum for the last lap, and then collapsed, but she was fine in a few minutes; back in the Sixties, before my time, US runner Max Truax collapsed in the 10,000 meters during a US-Soviet Union meet, but he was okay, too.

B.P.: Can you speculate on Tim Hardman's chances here?

C.J.: No.

B.P.: Uh...silence has come over the crowd as the medical technicians continue to attend Tim Hardman. There is never an easy way to handle something like this, is there?

C.J.: No...there is not.

B.P.: It is eerie, the quiet that has filled the stadium...a stadium that a minute or two ago was rocking with cheers and enthusiasm.

C.J.: I think it was the way he fell, as you said, as if he had been shot...as if his systems had all shut down.

B.P.: Well, perhaps this would be a good time to take a commercial break and let—

C.J.: He's moving—I saw a leg move!

B.P.: Let's get a camera back down there...yes, he is moving ever so slightly on the ground, rolling back and forth on his hips. His wife seems to be relieved, putting her arms out in front of her and then folding them on top of her head. Hardman is now standing up, slowly rising to his feet. You can hear the crowd break into a loud cheer for him as he walks away from the track. He motions for the crowd to calm down, but they continue to cheer. He sits on a chair...slumps on it, really. Are those tears, Charles?

C.J.: Probably.

B.P.: The important thing is that Tim Hardman is all right. He did not qualify, but neither did he...well, we'll just leave it at that. Let's take a break, and when we come back we will feature the women's 110-meter hurdles, which, hopefully, will have less drama than we have just witnessed. Stay tuned.

I was born in L.A....
...not around L.A...
...not close to L.A...
...but, *in* L.A.

That's real important to me. It's always kind of bothered me when people say they're from L.A. and they live in, like, Anaheim or someplace in Riverside County, and to me it's kind of like they're trying to grab some of the cache or whatever of being from L.A. when they're not. The reason I feel it is so important to me that I tell you exactly where I grew up, or why it was in L.A. proper, not just around L.A., is because my life for the last few years has been so imprecise that, to me, it's important to nail down every item of any consequence I can recall about my past. As I said, I remember the first twenty-three or so years of my life as well as everybody else remembers theirs, maybe a little better because I keep concentrating on them to remember how my life was then, my daily routine, for some kind of clue as to what I should be doing now. I know that trying to pattern your life when you're in your mid-thirties on what your life was like when you were in your early twenties is not realistic, but then neither is much of my life. So, I just sort of grab at whatever works.

So, anyway...I was born in L.A.

I grew up by the beach—I grew up *at* the beach—in all sorts of ways...emotionally, physically and maybe even spiritually. Emotionally, the beach was an escape for me, a place where exciting things could happen, where I could free myself to be whatever I wanted to be, rather than being dragged down by some of the stuff that was happening at home. Physically, the beach was where I first realized I was a pretty decent athlete. Most young kids discover this playing basketball, football or baseball. I did it through body surfing. I was very good at it right from the beginning. I never really cared very much about swimming (more about that later) but body surfing only required a couple strokes before you caught the wave. The way I could maneuver my body through the waves showed me right away that there was something going on here, that I had complete control of what my body did and I could put it to very good use. I don't remember ever being awkward...ever.

L.A. is not a beach city. Most of the beach areas in Southern California are their own municipalities—Redondo Beach, Manhattan Beach, Long Beach, and so on. The city of Los Angeles is, like, about 460 square miles, but not much of it is beachfront—mostly just San Pedro, Venice, and Playa del Rey. I grew up in Playa del Rey, which is why, I think, I became a runner, because Playa del Rey has a wide beach, where you park your car on the street, then go down a hill or path and it's at least a quarter of a mile to the water, and so when I got to the sand I would run as hard as I could in the sand to the water, and I was always running back to my parent's car for something—we lived at the beach, but not *on* the beach, so it was still a mile from our house, a short drive but a long walk, especially if you had been body-surfing all day—so I would probably put in two or three miles a day running hard on the sand, and when I was running back to the car with someone else, they would always be out of breath, and I kept chugging along, and soon it became pretty obvious that running back and forth from the water was actually accomplishing more for me than what I was doing in the water, and so I started just running along the beach—I'm talking when I was about ten years old—and I would be running next to much older and stronger guys and try to race them without it being a race, but I never gave it much thought, because my Dad was in the hospital by then and my mom was too busy trying to keep everything together to worry about anything else, so the fact that I was becoming a good distance runner was pretty much a distraction for everyone else but me, and for me it was just a source of entertainment—yeah, running was that much fun—and an easy way to burn off the energy and frustration after a visit to my Dad at the hospital, wondering if he was ever going to get better—he looked okay to me but everybody said he was very sick—and watching my mother try to deal with everything and making a very hard job of it, so running was really an escape, which, I guess, is not exactly an epiphany to anybody who reads many sports biographies, since most great athletes, at least the ones from poor backgrounds (which is the majority of them, I would guess) used sports as an escape from their oppressive environment, and that was me, too, although I lived in a decent house, always had enough food, went to a Catholic grade school, and generally wasn't deprived of very much of anything except my father's presence and my mother's attention—well, now that I've said it, that actually sounds like quite a lot—but I really needed that running, much more than I realized at the time, and I had no idea of what it would lead to over the next twenty-five years, not that I would have necessarily changed anything if I had known what was in store for me, because it was fun and I was good at it and I felt pretty good about myself afterwards. Running got me to where I am today...and, hopefully, where I want to be tomorrow. It made me somebody when I was too shy to be anybody. It made me a star at Venice High School (I really wanted to go to a Catholic high school, because my religion has always been real important to me, and if my Dad had still been around I'm pretty sure that I would have, but he was in the hospital by then, and my mother said we couldn't afford to send me to a Catholic high school—I think what she meant was we could not afford sending me to a Catholic high school and also be able to buy all the things she wanted—so I went to Venice High instead, which probably worked out better, at least for my running, because they had a great track coach) and got me a track scholarship to UCLA.

NEWS FROM VENICE

FIFTEEN YEAR-OLD RACES TO FUTURE

Fifteen year-old Tim Hardman is becoming something of a celebrity because of his running ability. "He is not just good," says his coach at Venice High School, Ray Robbins, "he is fabulous." That may be something of an understatement.

Tim, who just turned fifteen, last week ran the fastest mile by an American high schooler in almost ten years when he clocked a phenomenal 4:05 in the state championships. What makes this performance even more impressive is the fact that Tim only started running the mile seriously less than one year ago.

"My first race was as a freshman on the junior varsity," remembers Tim. "It was a 660. I did okay, ran the same pace the whole race, and the next week I ran five seconds faster and won the race."

After that, Coach Robbins took notice:

"I decided to bump him up to the varsity for one meet, just to see how he would handle the big boys. I put him in the 880, and decided to let him sink or swim."

Tim did not sink.

"Actually, I won the race...kind of easy," says Tim, sheepishly. "It was a 1:59.2, which was pretty strange, because I didn't think I'd last the extra half lap, but I actually got stronger coming around the final turn."

"Let me tell you how strong he ran," adds Coach Robbins. "He hit the 660 two seconds faster than his time at that distance the week before, and he still had half of a lap to go. He ran that 220 in 28 seconds. Just an amazing performance, only four seconds off the school record—as a freshman!"

So, when did he move up to the mile?

"A couple weeks later, Coach asked me to run a mile in a meet. I'd been doing some longer distance workouts, so I said sure, why not," said Tim, nonchalantly.

And how did that work out?

"I ran a 4:28, which was okay."

"He ran a 67 on each lap, which is an incredible sense of pace for such a young runner—remember, he was only fourteen at the time," said Coach Robbins.

And how did young Tim feel about the first mile he had run?

Tim laughs.

"Actually, I didn't think it was ever going to end. It was twice as long as the races I'd been running before this, and halfway through the third lap I realized I still had a lap and a half to go, or as long as I had been running in races a few weeks before that on the junior varsity."

So, how did he maintain his pace and energy?

"I just tried to think I was at the beach, running through the sand," he said, smiling at the memory. "That last run through the sand after having been in the water all day is really tiring, and you really have to dig in, so that's what I thought about. It worked out."

Yes, it did. And, speaking of running through the sand, that's what Tim credits with giving him all the running prowess he now possesses.

"The beach is the best," said Tim. "There's no place like the beach, for running, exercising, or just forgetting everything else. Without my running at the beach, I'd probably be reading this newspaper, rather than being featured in it."

Tim grew up a few blocks away from the beach, in Playa del Rey, and he credits the wide beach, necessitating long runs to and from his parents' car, as being critical in giving him the leg strength and endurance he now has.

"Without the beach," he said, "I'd just be another runner." He thought about that for a moment or two. "In fact, without the beach, I might not even be a runner at all." He paused. "I'm glad my folks moved to the beach when I was a little kid."

Ask Tim how proud his parents are of him and he turns a bit quiet.

"Yeah, my mom's real proud. She can't go to any of the meets, because she's working two jobs 'cause my Dad's been in the hospital for awhile, but she reads about me in the paper. She's always got the latest articles on the door of the refrigerator, and she's starting a scrapbook."

Asking Tim about his father does not much bring much information or enthusiasm.

"He's been in the hospital for awhile. I don't know what's wrong with him, 'cause he looks okay, but they say he needs to stay in a little longer."

Does his father know all about his son's exploits?

"Well...yeah," said Tim, slowly drawing it out, "I tell him whenever I go to see him, and he smiles, so I guess he appreciates it. He used to take me to big-time track meets like the Colisseum Relays when I was younger, so I thought he'd be more excited when I told him what I'd been doing, the times I'd been running, but...well, he just smiled."

Had Tim told him about the 4:05 yet?

"No, I only go out to see him every couple of weeks, so I haven't been back since, but I'll be sure and tell him and show him the newspaper clipping."

Does his father have a collection of his articles about Tim, too?

"I didn't see one. Maybe they've got it hidden away."

There was a silence and Coach Robbins spoke up.

"His Dad hasn't been able to come to any meets yet, but I'm sure he'll be there next year."

Tim smiled at that.

Does Tim think about his Dad when he's running?

"Yeah...all the time. At the state championships last week, the backstretch of the last lap was tough, and I started thinking about how I could tell my Dad I won if I kept pushing...so I did"

Was Tim thinking about a record time in that race?

"Well," he said, pausing to collect his thoughts, "I knew I was running fast, and I was in front, but I didn't know by how much..."

"A lot!" interjected Coach Robbins.

"...and I only heard one of the splits—2:01 something at the half—because people were screaming too much for me to hear the time at three laps. I just kept pushing—I just wanted to win. I didn't really know how fast I was running, but I know the fastest guy wins, so, I wanted to be that guy."

Was he surprised at the time?

"Yeah...kinda...." He paused. "I mean, I mostly just wanted to win. I've got two more years—I'm just a sophomore—for worrying about great times, so I just wanted to win. Actually, when the race started I just wanted to place in the top three, since there were some pretty good runners in the race, and they were all seniors. So, yeah, I was happy with the time, but I was more happy at winning. Faster times will come."

I asked Coach Robbins what he thought Tim's potential was.

"No one knows," he answered, "including Tim. He is still a work in progress."

I asked Tim if he felt an undue pressure on him now, because of his performance.

"Well, just the pressure I put on myself. I really don't care about what other people think. They don't know what's going on inside of me."

I asked Coach Robbins if he thought a sub four-minute mile was possible for Tim while he is still in high school, something that has only happened twice in America, and not in the last twenty years.

"Anything is possible with Tim," said Coach Robbins. "It is all up to him."

And so, what does Tim see in his running future?

"Well, I expect to get stronger and run faster. That's it."

And does he expect to see his father in the stands, cheering him on as he sets new records?

"Oh, yeah," said Tim, a big smile on his face. "Oh, yeah."

--Andy Franklin

Running also got me Judy. She was the California girl that even California girls wanted to be. Fabulous personality, great smile, long blonde hair brushed back over her ears but always falling forward to frame her face...oh, my God, that face...golden eyebrows so soft they seemed to be made of silk, hovering above eyes of UCLA powder blue which looked over cheekbones that, a couple hundred years from now, will still be things of wonder, separated by a perfectly-upturned button nose that Michael Jackson would have killed for, just above thin, aquiline lips with enough of a blonde, fuzzy ledge to let droplets of water, orange juice or whatever dangle with gravity-defying balance on the edge, just waiting to be licked off, and finished with a softly-chiseled chin begging to be snuggled into a shoulder.

I had been interested in a few girls before, but nothing was even remotely serious until I saw her in an English class in Royce Hall at UCLA and realized she was the girl of my dreams. I also immediately realized she was probably the girl of everybody's dreams, *everybody* meaning guys with a lot more money and class than me, so I stayed my distance. We exchanged glances, but I didn't think anything of it. I figured she was way too beautiful, way too cool, to be interested in a runner. I was certain she must have a boyfriend, probably a football player, although I never saw her with any guy, either in class or around the campus— okay, so I followed her around a bit, but it wasn't like I was stalking her or anything (well, maybe a little). I never approached her. As it turned out, I didn't have to, she did all the heavy lifting. All I had to do was say yes. Within a week, I had met all her best friends and within two weeks I had met her parents. They were... *polite*. (I even managed to drag my mother out to meet them, and I thought it went well, everybody seeming to get along, which was a major accomplishment for my mother.) Suddenly, I was half of the best couple on campus. I didn't look at other couples...they looked at us. And every time I thought it couldn't get any better, it did...until it finally didn't, but that took years. And those years were wonderful.

The Daily Bruin

What's Bruin...

(from p.3)
and on the wagon....That couple we see all over campus holding each other's hand with a death grip is none other than our own Judy Hamilton and Bruin track man Tim Hardman. They probably don't notice that everyone is looking at them because they spend all their time looking at each other. We are surprised that we haven't seen them skipping across the campus together, because they look that happy. Since we never miss anything, we noticed that Tim, the jock from Venice High hoping to repeat as NCAA 1500 meters champion for UCLA, is wearing one of those cute (we were going to say "quaint" but that might be considered a

pejorative) little "A" pins that the Catholic Newman Center hands out to those among us who pledge themselves to abstain from sex until after getting married. It has also been noted that Judy is not wearing one of those pins. That must make for some interesting conversations on a late Saturday night. We can only assume that until she gets a ring Judy will not know for certain if runner Tim really has the endurance to go the distance....

Let me explain what is happening in my life right now, and how I get by from one day to the next. I leave notes for myself every night for the next day, and then I videotape a message to myself about those notes, because, you know, sometimes words on a page just aren't enough. How do I remember to do this? Because I leave a note to myself, like, *don't forget to remember...*

And how did I remember to start leaving notes to myself in the first place ? Well, as I mentioned before, this memory-loss thing took a couple of years to develop, although I was fairly certain early during this period that something either was or was not happening. I suppose if I had pursued this with doctors and everything, maybe something could have been resolved, although I'm not certain what that would have been or what it would have involved. In any case, I didn't. The reasons mostly involve my marriage dissolving. That was really dominating my life. I had gotten some appearance money for races, and I had managed to get some money under the table for interviews—don't let magazines try to tell you they never pay for exclusives—and Judy had a good job as a financial consultant, so money was not a problem. But everything else in my life was. My marriage was falling apart, which meant I didn't have the focus to train—or to even, on some days, leave the house for a run around the track—which, in turn, meant that I didn't compete in races, which really had been my main contact with the outside world. Everyone assumed I was so depressed about my failing in the Olympic Trials that I had just curled up in a ball. Well, that's pretty much the way I did act, but it wasn't because of the Trials thing, except in the most obvious of ways. I was just incredibly unhappy about my relationship with Judy unraveling. As I said, I probably should have sought some medical advice when the memory thing started, but my experience with my Dad and the way the doctors screwed around with him and his condition pretty much obviated the chance of me seeking any psychiatric advice. Would it have helped? Maybe…maybe not. Who knows?

What I do know is that I would have been better informed about what was happening to me. Whether or not it would have changed anything is debatable, given what I've been able to discover about my condition during the interim between then and now. In fact, if I had known then what was was going to happen to me now, that could have combined with my disintegrating marriage to really send me over the edge. Ignorance may, you know, sometimes be bliss.

Basically, what I have is referred to as MCI. (Weren't those the initials of some telephone company a few years ago?) MCI stands for *mild cognitive impairment*, which is, as you might conclude if you have even the slightest awareness of the science of memory loss, something of a precursor for…uh…Alzheimer's disease. Well, golly, that's something to look forward to, isn't it, boys and girls? So maybe that's what was wrong with my father all those years ago when they kept him in that hospital—they called it a hospital but I realized later it was just a sanitarium because I never saw anybody with any injuries or recovering from an operation—and he never seemed to get better or get worse but he never came home again, ever, and so maybe it's just as well that nobody told me when I was in my mid-twenties that I was starting a downward spiral into Alzheimer's disease, although I'm not certain that most people at that time, including me, even knew what that was or what it meant, although if you had mentioned senility, I'm sure that would've gotten the message across loud and clear, but maybe that would've made all the difficulties with Judy seem not so bad—I mean, if you are being told that you are in the process of losing your memory, maybe the prospect of losing your marriage does not seem quite so catastrophic, and maybe we could have worked it all out, because maybe we would've had something to bring us more together—I'm just speculating here—rather than all the other stuff, although I have never been sure exactly what that "stuff" was; maybe—maybe—we would've gotten back together, rather than just living in the same house, sleeping in the same bed and even, believe it or not, having sex without hardly ever speaking to each other (you haven't lived until you have had great sex with someone you already know intimately but with whom you never speak a word or even utter a sound during the entire sexual act, and then afterward roll over and fall asleep without even acknowledging your partner's existence) and gradually drifting apart in a manner that all divorced couples say "just happened" and that all divorced couples know happened because at least one of them, and probably both of them, wanted it to happen, and maybe Judy would still be with me today, instead of my videotape machine and my notes, to remind me of what happened yesterday, what is supposed to happen or it is hoped will happen today, and what to prepare for tomorrow. MCI, from my research, seems to be diagnosed when a person has evidence of memory loss, but is still able to think and function as a normal person on a daily basis. Also, there is an absence of diagnosed dementia. I'm not exactly sure what un-diagnosed dementia is, although that's probably what you have before they make it official. I keep checking my notes everyday to see if anybody's taken me to the doctor and had me diagnosed, but, so far, so good—with dementia, I mean. Actually, what I have, technically speaking, is amnestic MCI , which is what they call it when memory loss is the predominant symptom. That, as far as I can tell, is the situation with me. Again, I don't know if anybody has hauled me off to the doctor—I was going to say "without my knowledge", but that wouldn't be true since they, whoever "they" might be, would probably have my complete agreement; I just wouldn't remember unless I had written it down, although you would think that something like that would be important enough for me to write down if it ever happened, so I can only deduce that something like this has never happened.

Judy,

You don't know me or my name. We have only met once or twice here at UCLA, so you probably wouldn't remember me, but I remember you and how sweet a person you were. And that is why I am sending you this note. I want nothing but happiness for you, because I think you deserve it. But I think you deserve someone much better than Tim Hardman. I have read several articles about the two of you, and while you both seem very happy, I wonder if that is because you do not know the whole story. Tim uses girls. I know that he proclaims how he won't have sex until he is married, and maybe he is technically being honest, but I don't think he is really telling the truth. I went out with him once before you two started dating, went back to his place, and the next morning, Sunday, he made me give him oral sex three times. (I asked a friend about claiming date rape, but she said my never actually saying "no" when he told me to suck him off would probably go against me.) He came on my face the first time and made me leave it on while I did it two more times, and the last time he rolled over on top of my face and shoved it so far down my throat that I almost choked. And then he told me I had to leave right away. I was still coughing up his cum as he pushed me out the door. I see him at Royce Hall all the time, and he looks away from me. Maybe he treats you better because he didn't just pick you up for the night, but I think you should know what he can be like. The next day after this happened, a girl friend of mine told me she saw him at St. Paul's that Sunday morning and he was taking Communion, right after he kicked me out. How can that be? You may love him, but I think he's an asshole and a hypocrite. I wish you all the best. I do not wish you Tim Hardman.

A Good Friend You Do Not Know

I guess I should go off on a sidebar here because I'm sure when I mentioned that I researched about MCI, you probably assumed that I just clicked on to my computer and checked out the information, but...I don't have a computer. Never have and never will. I seem to remember Judy having a really expensive one, but not me—ever. It's too easy for anyone, especially the government, to check up on you if you use a computer. I must've read some article about this one day, because I have a ten-minute segment on one tape of me explaining all the bad things that can happen. I'm sure that computers can do good things, too—it's like medicine; any medicine that is strong enough to go good things is strong enough to do bad things, as well (ying and yang, you know)—but the possibility of bad things occurring, like the government keeping track of everything you do, everything you say, well, that's too much for me. I don't know where I got the information, but I must've read something pretty serious, because I look real concerned on that tape.

I don't have a cell phone, either. (I have a regular phone, but the only time I use it is when Judy calls. We have a system: she lets it ring twice, then hangs up, calls back again, lets it ring once and hangs up, then calls again...and I answer, because I know it's her. That's the *only* time I answer my phone.) Judy really loves her cell phone. I've never understood the appeal of anyone and everyone being able to get a hold of you anytime, anywhere. Of course, that would be a real problem for me now, since I would never remember any conversations I had the day before, and if I had to write down something about every phone call I made or received, I'd have a notepad the size of *War and Peace*. Plus, there's also the whole thing about the government being able to track you down or listen to your conversation. They can eavesdrop on you anytime they want. I know that for a fact. You just can't be too careful. I think that is true for everybody, and even more so for someone in my situation. If the government wanted to accuse me of saying something criminal on the phone yesterday, there is no way I could argue with them. I wouldn't have a chance. The government always wins anyway, but this would be even worse than usual.

I also have a back-up plan for my notes, in case somebody tries to steal them. If all my videotapes and notes were stolen, I would be completely screwed. What would I do? I could probably function a day at a time all right, but any kind of day-to-day continuity would be lost. The only thing that frightens me more than that is dying, and then you don't have to worry about anything. If I lost all my tapes and notes, I would literally be lost at sea, alone in the middle of everything. (I should be able to dredge up some literary reference for that—four years of English Lit and a B.A. at UCLA—but I'm drawing a blank.) My only solution in that case would be to do the one thing I consider only slightly less appealing than dying—asking for someone's help. Look, I probably do need help anyway, with this kind of Rube Goldberg-set up I've got for keeping up with things (hey, does Rube Goldberg count as a literary reference?) not exactly being the optimum, but it's the best I could come up with, and it works, and to switch to any other system would sort of mean starting all over again, (which is kind of what I do every morning, anyway, but that's another story). Asking for someone's (or some group's) help would expose me to whatever ideas and motives they would have for helping me. I would be completely at their mercy. I'm not helpless. I'm in great physical shape, function pretty good on a daily basis in terms of personal awareness and mental activity—I took an IQ test that was in some magazine and, according to my notes, did pretty good, scoring a 130, not a genius but definitely above-average—and, as far as I can determine from my notes and tapes, my life isn't that different from anyone else's—I just don't remember any of it.

Tuesday morning

Jude—

*Your father and I have been trying to
decide which is more depressing, the
decreasing frequency of your visits home
or the increasing concern we feel for you
after you leave and go back to school. The
fact that we do not seem to have much
input into the decisions you have been
making about your life might just be
selfishness on our part. However, the
decisions you have been making lately do
cause us some concern. First of all, let me
say that both your father and I like Tim.
He seems to be very genuine and sincere,
and the fact that he is an athlete means to
us that he leads a good life. We appreciate
the fact that he is Catholic, but we think he
is a little too extreme when it comes to
religion and seems very intolerant of other
people's beliefs. When the Tuttles told him
that they were Episcopalian and he said
that while the Catholic Church can trace
itself back to the sacred heart of Jesus
Christ and the Anglican Church can only
trace itself back to the sweaty loins of
Henry VIII, your father and I almost lost
our closest and dearest friends. And please
do not ever have him bring his mother,
however much he loves her, across our
threshold again. She may be the most
unpleasant, not to mention over-dressed,
person we have ever met.(She also has the
worst face lift we have ever seen.)*

*We understand that you feel very strongly
towards Tim, and we respect him as your
choice, but we never understood what was*

wrong with Paul Costello. We thought you were going to follow him to USC. His mother tells me he just made the reserve football team there, and says he always asks about you. (He is majoring in pre-Med and is going to become a dentist, she says.) We always thought you and Paul made the perfect couple. We have nothing against UCLA. It is a fine school. As an alumnus, your father could have helped you to get into USC, but, again, we respect your decision. However, to choose a university to attend simply because you liked the boys there seems very silly to us. If you remember, USC was seriously considering giving you a volleyball scholarship, while the UCLA coach showed no interest at all. We are sad that your volleyball days seem to have ended. At one time, we thought you might make the Olympic team.

Let me say again that we have nothing against Tim. He does seem to get his name in the newspaper with some frequency, and from what we can gather, has a bright athletic future ahead of him (something we thought was in your future, too) and has a chance of perhaps making a living at it for a period of time, as long as he does not suffer any injuries. If that should happen, you will have to depend on his degree in English Literature for him to get a job. Are you going to end up being the wife of a teacher? With all due respect, Jude, we raised you with higher expectations than that. The business degree you could have gotten from USC would have opened many doors. What can you get at UCLA?

We are not trying to scare you, and we are probably just being too protective of our

*only child, but please understand, darling,
that we have only your best interests at
heart. We like Tim. We do, however, have
some concerns about his family, since we
understand that his father has been
hospitalized with a mental condition. We
are not rushing to any judgment, but we
really think that you should investigate the
implications of this if you and Tim should
decide to continue and expand your
relationship. We are not trying to scare
you, but you remember what happened to
the Murrays' boy when he married that
girl whose father was having seizures,
don't you? It goes without saying
that we do not want something like that to
happen to you. It is not Tim's fault that
there may be a defective gene that he has
inherited from his father. This does not
mean, of course, that Tim would have the
same problems. We just want you to be
aware of things, that's all.*

*Jude, we just want to smother you with our
love. We are not worried about you and
Tim. We like Tim. If Tim makes you happy,
then we are happy. Our only concern is
that you could rush into something that
you would later regret. All we want is
what is best for you…all we want is for
you to know what is best for you.*

*All our love,
Mother and Dad*

Asking for help from a person or an organization would
be the worst because I would just be turning myself over to
them, lock, stock and barrel— they would have some kind of
plan for me (they always do) and I'm sure they would smile

and say all the right things, but you know for sure that when you are in that kind of situation, you are at their mercy, which is what I fear most because they feel that they know exactly what it is you need, and they will shove it down your throat if they have to, never wiping that beatific smile off their face—and you know the first thing they would do is get rid of my notes and videotapes, or at least edit them so that I would think that everything is absolutely wonderful and, for them, it would probably would be, because that is who they would be doing all this for, to validate all of their theories and beliefs and hunches and everything else, and if they're wrong, what the hell, they meant well and...*we learn by our mistakes, don't we?*...so that the next time they have to deal with some sort of situation like this they may not know what to do, but they will know what *not* to do...which is just as important in the long run, isn't it?...because...*trial and error is an important part of the scientific process, isn't it?*...and if you never made mistakes, then you would know for certain that you are doing it all wrong, because there are always mistakes, and if the mistakes negatively affect someone's life—as long as it's not theirs—that is just the price that has to be paid in the furthering of knowledge and...*yes, it is unfortunate* if *mistakes are made, but that's just the way things happen sometimes....*

So, anyway, I have a Plan B for remembering things— well, actually, I guess it's a Plan C, since the daily notes are Plan A and the videotapes are Plan B. Just in case someone manages to somehow get hold of my notes and videotapes and hide or steal or erase them, I also have a secret stash of notes where no one would ever go—in my underwear. I go into the bathroom sometime during the end of the day and scribble just the basic, really important stuff, in as few words as possible, on a small piece of paper from one of those pocket- spiral notebooks, and then I rip the page out, so there's no trace of it, like there would be in a regular notebook where you tear out the pages, but, as you might imagine, this could get pretty bulky, so every few days, according to my notes, I take them and hide them around my home, leaving little clues in my regular notes about where they are, clues that would only make sense to me, and I know that this all sounds really secret-agent, but it's worked so far. The main thing is, I want to be in control of my life as much as is possible. I understand that this is an imperfect world, and I am one of its shining examples, but I am not trying to make my life perfect, just manageable. I know…that sounds awfully simplistic. I really want more out of life than just being able to make it through every day intact. And my running is still the most important thing in my life right now, for two reasons: it dominates my life, and I can dominate it. Running is the one thing in my life over which I have complete power. I decide when I will run, how I will run and where I will run.

For awhile, after I got married, my relationship with Judy was just as important to me as was my running. That is probably why, when the marriage started having problems, my running nose-dived. It was an important lesson for me: decide your priorities, and then separate them. I tried to put my running and my marriage on top together. You can't do that. They are two different worlds. For a time, I lost both worlds. I have managed to salvage one of them.

Right now, at this moment…running defines me. I am Tim Hardman, and I am a runner. That is all you need to know. The rest is soap opera.

Sports Illustrated

THE RUNNER AND THE STUNNER

Tim Hardman and Judy Hamilton are
the All-American couple

Ken and Barbie actually do exist. They live, not surprisingly, in Southern California. Surprisingly, they do not, given this day and age, live together. "That's not gonna happen until we get married," says Tim Hardman, a four-minute miler for UCLA and a bit of hottie according to most of the girls around Westwood. Judy Hamilton, a hottie according to any red-blooded male who has eyes, agrees completely. "We can wait. We've got our whole lives to live together. We want to experience as much of the college lifestyle at UCLA as we can. We expect to be married for a long, long time. There's no rush."

Tim saves his rushing for the track, where he is the odds-on favorite to win the 1500 meters, the metric equivalent of the mile, at next week's NCAA Championship in Tucson.

Tim does not like the term "metric mile".

"I hate the name and I hate the distance. A mile is 1760 yards...the 1500 meters is...well, I don't exactly know how far it is and I don't care. All I know is...it's not a mile. I'm a miler. I run the mile. I run the 1500 meters only when I have no choice." This is as serious as Tim gets during the entire conversation.

After next week, Tim will be able to choose for himself what distances he runs. He is no longer a Bruin academically, having gotten his degree in English Literature at a graduation ceremony in Pauley Pavilion with 5,000 close personal friends; after next week, he will no longer be a Bruin athletically. The NCAAs will be his last race at UCLA. Tim has enjoyed his time as a collegiate athlete ("I wouldn't have traded it for the world") but he cannot wait to enter the world of professional track and field. Because of the higher level of competition?

"Because of the money!" Tim says with enthusiasm as he and Judy start laughing.

"It's time to start planning for the future," says Judy—*Jude* to her friends and family—sounding wise beyond her years, but running her fingers through her long blonde hair like a teenager. "Tim's getting a shoe deal with Nike, and the advance money from that could make a down payment on a nice little house in the Valley, where I grew up."

Tim winces at this. Is he unhappy at the prospect of living so close to his in-laws?

"Oh, no...not at all. They're great people."

"They've loved Tim since the first time they met him," says Judy, who added, blushingly, "just like me."

"But...I grew up by the beach," adds Tim. "The San Fernando Valley is a lot of things...but close to the beach is not one of them. Until we can afford it, buying by the beach will have to wait."

Tim's love for the beach—could it be any other way for a Ken?—goes back to his earliest days, running on the wide beaches of Playa del Rey. "It's about a quarter-mile from the car to the water, and I used to run back and forth all the time to get stuff, and, before I knew it— presto!—I was a runner."

"Tim has worked very hard for everything he has," gushed Judy.

Including her?

Tim and Judy fell into each other's arms, laughing.

"No, that was a slam dunk!" she squealed.

"If it wasn't love at first sight, it was real close," added Tim. "Actually, she made the first move."

"I did," said Judy, sounding proud of this. "I saw him...I wanted him." She stopped, for a dramatic pause. Then, "I got him!" She paused again. "Some girls on campus were jealous of me, making up stories, trying to turn me off Tim. No way!"

Tim and Judy smiled at each and embraced. They look like a team.

"We *are* a team," says Judy, with Tim nodding in agreement. "We talk after every one of Tim's races, about what happened, how things could have been better, how we could have done things differently...."

We?

"Oh, yeah," says Tim. "We're in this together. Judy makes a lot of valuable suggestions. She's a lot smarter than me—I'm smart enough to know that—so I pay to attention to what she says. She can analyze a situation. I'm too much in the middle of everything."

Is this because of Judy's business-oriented approach to things (she has a double major in finance and accounting)?

"Probably," says Tim, looking at Judy for approval, which he gets.

Judy was something of an athlete herself in high school.

"I played some v-ball at Birmingham High, but that was a long time ago. This is more important.

She doesn't miss it?

"Well, yeah...but, first things first. Play time is winding down. It's starting to be grown-up time, time to start acting like an adult pretty soon. I've got one more year to be silly before graduation, but Tim..."

She looks at Tim and they both fall laughing into each other's arms again.

"...Tim starts being an adult next week."

And then what?

"Oh, lots of world records, tons of money, unending fame and fortune..." joked Tim. Then he became a little more serious, for the second time in the conversation. "I do have a particular time I want to run—I set it up in my mind five years ago.

A world record time?

"Oh, yeah."

Something spectacular?"

"Oh, most definitely."

What is it?

"Oh...I couldn't tell anybody."

"He won't even tell me," protested Judy, playfully, "and he tells me *everything*."

Why?

"Well, it's kind of way out there, and if I don't make it, it would be kind of embarrassing."

Does he expect to get that time?

"Oh…most definitely," he said, repeating the same phrase again, with emphasis. "It will be something special when it happens."

And then what?

"And then a house with a white picket fence and a little boy and girl as happy and as beautiful as their parents," interjected Judy, trying to sound lightweight, but more serious than she intends as she says it. Obviously, Tim has his dream and Judy has hers.

They look at each with straight faces and then burst out laughing. "Just your average suburban family," says Tim, trying to be mock serious and not succeeding.

Ken and Barbie in suburbia? What about Malibu?

"Oh, that's the beach house!" adds Judy, and they again break into laughter as they hug each other.

…JoBeth Anderson

The interesting thing about my parents is what I remember of them. I have some pictures of our family when I was growing up, but I don't have any images of them from the last fifteen years or so. Of course, my Dad died awhile back, so that takes care of that, and I don't have any memories of what he looked like at the funeral. I didn't videotape him in the casket—according to my notes, I wanted to, but, apparently, everybody else thought it was a terrible idea. Everybody but me, of course, and I guess I was just coerced into not doing it, although I really regret it, because seeing him at the mortuary, all laid out, was the most time I had spent with him in about fifteen years. In my notes, it says he looked kind of emaciated, and you know that mortuaries always try to make the deceased look as good as possible, so if he looked that bad even after they spent all kinds of time on him, trying to make him look at least okay, then I can only imagine what he actually looked like when he died, and so maybe it's better, in some ways, that I didn't take my camera with me and videotape him in the casket because I would always have that image in my mind, rather than the one I now have, the one I remember, which is of a guy who was kind of funny, always laughing, and who was always ready to do something with me, which I think probably had something to do with the fact that I was his only child, and so he doted on me, but I don't think he spoiled me, because I can remember plenty of times as a kid when I would get punished, sometimes severely, for doing something that he did not agree with, but by "severely" I don't mean anything physical, because I don't think he ever...I don't remember him ever hitting me in any way, even a little slap on the back of the head or something, because that was what my mother would do, although sometimes it wasn't just a little slap, but that's another story which I don't want to go into right now, because I'm talking about my Dad, which is a lot more pleasant and brings up a lot more enjoyable memories, like when we would go different sporting events, such as the Colisseum Relays that I talked about before, but also football and basketball and baseball games, and he even took me to Hollywood Park and Santa Anita a couple times, and I actually picked some winning horses once in awhile, which really made him laugh, and that's the picture I have most of him in my mind, and in all the photographs of him and me when I was a kid, he always seems in a good mood, which made it real difficult when he was hospitalized and I would visit him once or twice a month—I wanted to go more often, but my mother would say it was too far away and every couple weeks was the best we could do, and, yeah, it was kind of far away, but he was my Dad—because he just didn't seem the same, although he looked pretty much like before and would still smile when he saw me, at least for the first few years, but it was kind of an empty smile, if you know what I mean, as if he was just smiling because he had visitors and was happy to see anybody, and the fact that he was being visited by his only son, with whom he had spent so many good times, didn't really have anything to do with it, which was hard for me to deal with then and hasn't lessened over the years, and even though the visits that I can remember of going to see him never really lived up to their billing, so to speak (I was going to see my Dad and it should have been great, but it never really was) I would go back to those visits now in a second if I could, to be in the same room with my Dad, because just being there with him triggered all kinds of memories of the good times we had had together, although I must admit that the last few times I visited him, right after graduating from UCLA, most of the joy had gone out of the visits, because it was becoming obvious to me that he wasn't really sure who I was, which was okay in a way, because I knew who he was, but I was still a little uncomfortable with the entire situation, and—and this is hard for me to say—I kind of felt embarrassed for him, because I knew what a vibrant person he had been in his life, and how much fun he was to be around when I was a kid, and now he was just sort of lying there, smiling at me without seeming to be sure who I was, and me standing over him, telling him that I loved him and how my life was going and wondering if this was registering with him at all, and— and this is really the hardest thing of all for me to admit— feeling like it was my obligation to visit him, whether I wanted to or not, it was expected and, you know, it became like a job, and every time I would sign in at the front desk of the hospital before I could go up to his room and see him I really started to feel like I was punching in a time card, like at a job, which made me feel pretty uneasy, but I couldn't *not* visit him—that was unthinkable, and, yeah, I know, everybody has the same problems and the same inner conflicts in this kind of situation, but I don't care about other people, this was about my Dad, although as far as my mother was concerned if we just showed up for Christmas and his birthday that would have been enough, because she would go up to the room with me, on those occasions when she visited him with me— I don't think she ever visited him without me—and she would hang around for a few minutes and then I would look around and she would be gone, and I wouldn't see her until I got back into the car, which would have been okay if she had been sitting there dabbing her eyes because she had been crying or something, but she was generally listening to the radio, smoking a cigarette—yeah, that's right, I was a big-time runner and my mother was a smoker—and looking like she didn't have a care in the world, which always bothered the hell out of me, and on the ride home after the visits I would always be trying to figure out a way to ask her why she acted the way she did on those visits, but I never did, although this assumes that even if I had managed to summon enough imagination and courage—my mother could be a scary woman—to ask her such a question, she wouldn't have just taken a long drag on her cigarette, given me one of those withering looks that she was famous for (and which usually reduced me to complete and obedient silence) and never said a word or even acknowledged that the question had been asked, and so those drives back home from visiting my Dad at the hospital were more like funeral processions than anything else, and I was never so happy as when I would get home, jump out of the car, change my clothes and go for a long—and I mean *long*—run, just to get the hell out of there and away from her, which didn't seem to bother her at all, since she would never say anything when I left or when I came back, and there would be silence for the rest of the day in our house, and, yeah, I know you're probably thinking to yourself that my mother was just grieving for my Dad in her own way, but I'll never believe that, because I think she was really upset at him for becoming sick, and I don't mean in the psychological way that people get upset with someone because they have been left alone and have to place their anger somewhere, but I really think my mother took this personally, that my father had dumped this all on her because he didn't want the responsibility of raising a family anymore, and it was easier to just *veg* out at a hospital, and I can remember several times after our visits to the hospital suggesting to her that my Dad seemed to be better, and she just rolled her eyes—as if saying, "Oh, please…" —and then changed the subject to something completely different, usually about how hard her life was at the moment, which was a favorite topic of discussion with her (in fact, as I remember, that seemed like the only thing she ever talked about) and, yeah, I admit that she did have a difficult life, supporting a family by herself, but it wasn't as if this was a really big family or something, like she had six kids or something, there was just me, and I really think she could've made it all right—not great, but okay—on one job, but then she wouldn't have been able to make the payments on the house (houses anywhere near the beach have never been cheap) and we would've had to have gotten an apartment somewhere, and she also liked nice things, such as a new car every two or three years and clothes and everything, and those things were important to her, and I know that for a fact because she said it in almost those exact words: "I want nice things; I deserve them; I work hard", and there was no way she was going to get that working as a secretary for an insurance agent, so she took a night job, too, and, yeah, I know it was a lot of hours, but it wasn't like she was scrubbing floors for eight hours or some other back-breaking manual labor, she was just the night-supervisor at some six-bed rest home, where all the elderly patients went to bed at seven-thirty and, heavily-sedated, slept right through the night, occasionally not waking up the next morning (or ever again, but that was the morning shift, not my mother's problem) and I think my mother's most difficult task on that job was staying awake herself, because the couple times I visited her at this job, she seemed ready to nod off, and for all I know she may have, but what I remember most is that she never seemed in the least happy to see me and she almost seemed to resent my visiting her, as if I was intruding upon her life, which always gave me the idea that she took that job not just to be able to buy things but also to get out of the house and, more specifically, to be away from me, although maybe here I'm getting into pop-psychology bullshit, since she never, as far as I can remember, ever said a negative thing about me, but, on the other hand, I can't actually remember her saying many, or any, positive things to me; we were just sort of there in the same house together, and, to be perfectly honest, I really started to think of her, as I got older, as my big, bossy sister, rather than my mother, which might sound quaint and even a little charming, but it never was, and thinking of her as a sister is not a compliment, because I get the impression although I never had a brother or sister that siblings often tolerate each other's existence only until they can get away from each other, and I know that when I enrolled at UCLA and got a place to stay, there were no tearful goodbyes when I took my last personal items from the house because she wasn't even there when I moved and she just left a note telling me to be sure and lock the house, but there were no words of sadness at my leaving, words of encouragement for my new adventure or even a mention of when we might be getting together to do something...anything...just "Make sure the house is all locked up!!!", which was her style, all the exclamation points being used to make certain her point was highlighted just in case I somehow did not understand the importance of fully securing an empty house from possible intruders—and she didn't even sign it.

There is just one thing about this I do not understand:
I miss her.

I'll tell you an interesting story:

Years ago, I was talking to some guy who told me that about six months before then he had been in downtown LA for some reason—you have to understand, in LA, people only go downtown if they have to, and some never go there at all; I know some people who grew up in the San Fernando Valley, the furthest western parts of which are about thirty five miles from downtown but are still within the city of Los Angeles, who have never been to downtown LA—anyway, he's in downtown LA in the middle of the day for some reason or other, finds himself on some deserted side street, and, out of nowhere, this guy comes up to him, sticks his hand in coat pocket as if he has a gun, and robs my friend. (The guy telling me the story wasn't actually a friend; I'm just calling him "my friend" to differentiate him from the other guy, the robber...understand?) Anyway, as robberies go, this was no big deal. My friend wasn't completely sure whether or not the guy actually had a gun or was just faking that he had one—my friend says it was probably the latter—but who's gonna take a chance for a few dollars? So, my friend hands over all the money he has on him, the robber tells him to turn around and not look back for a minute, and, a minute later it is all over. The guy is gone, and the street is once again deserted. Pretty routine, one would say, unless, of course, one was the one who had been robbed. My friend told me that when he filed a report about an hour later when the police finally showed up, he was still nervous and almost hyperventilating as he gave them the information. The two patrol officers, on the other hand, looked incredibly bored, he said, and one of them actually stifled a yawn while taking down the information, and they said they would be in touch with him if anything developed, saying it in such a manner that he was positive that they were positive that nothing would ever develop.

And, nothing ever did.

About four months later, my friend is driving through downtown LA, and is stopped for a traffic light at Sixth and Broadway. It is a Sunday afternoon, lots of people walking around, and he is sitting in his car, watching the people walk in the crosswalk in front of him and waiting for the light to change. Suddenly, he sees the guy who robbed him crossing in front of him. And the guy is not alone. He is walking with a young woman and holding the hand of a little boy. They look like any young family out on a Sunday afternoon, except this is the guy who robbed my friend. My friend stares at the guy to make certain it is him—it is—and, in the way that we all seem to know when we are being stared at, the guy realizes my friend is looking at him and he looks back in my friend's direction, their eyes momentarily locking. And then my friend does something strange:

He waves.

He told me he couldn't understand then why he did it, and still didn't. The guy's stare seemed to be ambiguous—maybe he had committed so many robberies that my friend's face was just one of many that looked vaguely familiar to him, or perhaps he knew very well who my friend was but managed to steel himself against expressing any emotion, because he quickly looked away and kept on walking with the woman and child. The light changed, my friend drove on and, of course, never saw the guy again—and never went downtown again, either.

My friend couldn't understand why he waved, but I do. It took me years to figure out why it might make sense—it was one of those ideas percolating in the back of my mind that popped up every once in while, just enough to pique the interest, and then disappeared again. I don't remember how many times I have thought about it in the last ten or so years, since something like that is not significant enough to make it into my notes or on my tapes, but I thought about it today when I was remembering my mother. He waved to the guy, the robber, because they had a bond. Not a particularly positive one (for my friend, anyway) but a bond nevertheless, and one that only the two of them could possibly share. It had been a unique experience, at least for my friend, that they had shared, and his wave was an admission of that. It is probably something related to the Stockholm Syndrome that I studied in a psychology class at UCLA, which described a hostage situation that took place over several days after a botched robbery attempt in Sweden, wherein the hostages— some of them, anyway—emotionally bonded with their captors (I think one or two of them even got married) and regarded the police not as their potential rescuers but as the common enemy. And so, again without trying to get into the pop-psychology trap, I think I miss my mother for the same reason my friend waved to the guy who robbed him. There was a relationship. I know the picture that I have painted so far of my mother doesn't seem terribly attractive, much less positive, but the fact is that she was and still is my mother, and all that implies, and it is just about impossible to talk about my life in any detail without bringing her into the discussion, even if I don't want to, because even when she wasn't physically present, she was always there, lurking in my subconscious, and the question I have always asked myself—and I do get into this in my notes and on my tapes—is whether I love her now, did I love her then, or if I have ever loved her, and I really have not been able to come up with an answer—it is almost like wondering whether or not you love air, not in the sense that you can't do without it but because it has always been there. Does that make any sense?

Does it make any sense that I would miss my mother, considering that she was absent from my life much of the time when she was a part of it, and that since I moved away from home to go to college, I have probably only seen her ten or fifteen times total, and none, as far as I able to discern, in the last ten years (in other words, not since things started to go south with my memory)? I have about five or six mentions in my notes over the years about plans to either visit my mother or for her to come and see me, but that is all. There are no notes about the two of us ever actually getting together, and I'm certain that it would have been important enough for me to write down or videotape something about it, so I can only conclude that it never happened, for whatever reasons. It would be conjecture on my part as to why we have never spent any time together, and I really would like to see her, even if it was only to *see* her, to make some sort of connection because she is the one real link to the life I can completely remember. Meeting her would be pretty strange after all these years, for sure, but I wouldn't try to make it uncomfortable for her, although I certainly could do that, asking her why we never visited my Dad more often at the hospital, why she never once came to watch me run in a race, why she would always take down those newspaper clippings of me that I would attach to the refrigerator door with a magnet, or why she tried to throw out the scrapbook I made for her one Christmas of my clippings, a present for her that I spent weeks making just right and which she scowled at when she unwrapped it and asked me what she was supposed to do with it, as if this was one of the great disappointments of her life, and just tossed it aside and walked out of the room with disgust when she saw there was nothing else, like a piece of clothing or some jewelry, for her, which is what she always wanted because, to be honest, she was a really attractive woman—almost beautiful; in fact, if she wasn't my mother, I would've called her beautiful, but I don't think sons ever refer to their mother that way, because "beautiful" kind of implies other things like desirability and, well, sex—and she knew it, and I'm pretty certain that she felt her looks demanded that she be given a better lot in life than being stuck with a husband in the hospital and having to work two jobs to support a family, because I know for a fact that she had usually managed to get by in most situations by being best-looking female in the room, any room, and the stares she would get from the other women only confirmed that for me, because if you have ever been walking with a very attractive woman and stayed back a couple paces it is truly an amazing thing to watch the attention they attract, and not primarily from guys, who tended to be discreet about looking at my mother, but from women, who would do everything but stop and look her up and down, with a look on their face that was not all pleasant or approving, and it got even worse when my mother got a boob job (I'm guessing here because no one ever actually confirmed to me that she had breast implants; all I know is that she went to a hospital unannounced one time for a couple days, when I was old enough to take care of myself, and when she suddenly re-appeared, she looked different although I couldn't figure out in what way, since I never spent any time whatsoever looking at my mother's chest) and from that time onward, she got even more attention than usual when we would go anywhere, especially from other women, and she would seem to have a very satisfied look on her face as we would walk through a mall or any place with a lot of people around, as if she was putting on a show—and I think she probably was, in her mind—because I always remember her as being over-dressed no matter where we went (but without looking trashy because my mother actually had pretty good taste, so she would always look classy) although we never had the kind of money to go to the places to eat or stay at that her looks and taste would dictate, so we would walk through a Ramada Inn, for example, and she looked like she should be at a Ritz-Carlton—and would be walking as if she *was* at a Ritz-Carlton, which was pretty funny, because we got excellent service from everyone, since her behavior and attitude, I guess, looked as if they demanded and expected it, and the interesting part of all this was that, as far as I know, and I feel pretty confident in saying this, my mother never messed around at all, with anyone—in fact, she hardly went anywhere with anyone, except me—acting as if she was too good to share her company with anyone else, which, now that I think about it, seems to be a pretty good description of a diva, and yeah, so maybe my mother was a diva, which might sound like a bad thing or at least an unattractive trait, but I think she used it as a form of protection because (and here's the really strange thing about my mother) I don't think she was unfaithful to my father even once, despite all those years he was in the hospital (I can't prove it, of course, but just knowing her and her attitude toward everyone else makes me feel that I'm right)—and by "strange" I mean that she could have easily gotten any guy she wanted, but, as far as I can tell, she never made the slightest effort to do that, and, yeah, I know you could always say that I wasn't watching her 24 hours a day, so maybe she could've slipped away, or maybe she wasn't always at work, like she was supposed to be, but I think I would've noticed some sort of change in her if that had happened, but, as I remember, she was always the same.

What that means to me is that she was faithful, as far as I am able to determine. What that doesn't mean, as far as I am able to determine, is that she was necessarily a pillar of morality. She may have been—I mean, we always went to Mass and Communion every Sunday (and she wouldn't have gone to Communion if she was having an affair or messing around, since she would have to go to Confession and I know that she didn't go to Confession very often, because she always told me she didn't have much to confess)—but I don't think that's why she remained faithful to my father. I kind of have a theory about this. The two main women in my life, my mother and my wife, have both been beautiful women. Judy was a fox—long blonde hair, angelic face, legs up to her neck—one of the best-looking girls at UCLA, which has always been a babe-factory (an awful lot of *Playboy* centerfolds have attended or claim to have attended UCLA...for a little while, at least). I was kind of a stud then—big-time athlete in pretty good shape—and Catholic, which was important to Judy. So, it was pretty easy to make a move on her—but we never had sex until we were married, which actually wasn't as difficult as you might think, since most of my energy went towards running. And we made a great couple. (We were supposed to be on the cover of *Sports Illustrated* one time together as the All-American couple, but they changed their mind at the last minute and put on some hockey player instead, and all we got was some dopey one-page article, with a couple of crappy pictures, near the end of the magazine. But the point is, we were an all-time couple.) Guys would look at Judy and try to keep their tongue in their mouth. Half the UCLA football team tried to date her and wondered why she was going with some dorky runner. I know that's true, because she told me. One day, I walked with her past the football team during practice, them looking bigger than ever in their pads and me looking smaller than ever in my running shorts and a tank top. Practice almost came to a full stop. Guys were staring at her, dropping the ball, missing tackles and everything. The coaches were pissed. It was hilarious. I didn't mind. They just saw her as a beautiful woman and probably a great lay. But I knew the truth about beautiful women. I mean, I knew the truth about beautiful women and sex. Basically, it's not that big of a deal to them. I understand I'm generalizing here, but I remember asking a couple guys at UCLA what their experiences were with beautiful girls—sexually, I mean—and they would say how beautiful they were and how cool it was to be around them, but when I asked what they were actually like during sex, these guys would roll their eyes and go back to talking about how beautiful the girls were. So, here's the deal as far as I can tell with beautiful women and sex: to them, it's mostly about biology. It's how you produce offspring, generally beautiful offspring. For everyone else—guys and non-beautiful women—sex is about love, pleasure and fulfillment. Beautiful women have mirrors for that. They can tumble around with some guy in bed for a little while and have to clean up afterwards, or they can do their hair and make-up for an hour, looking at themselves in the mirror all the time, and end up looking even more beautiful than when they started. *Easy choice.* My mother and my wife both spent a minimum of an hour in the bathroom every morning getting ready for the day, apparently washing their face one pore at a time. Most guys' idea of a quickie is *wham-bam-thank-you-ma'am*. A beautiful woman's idea of a quickie is taking out her compact and looking at her little mirror at the most inauspicious moments—in the middle of a conversation, during a meal, or, apparently, whenever they want to look at themself. As far as I can remember, and I'm pretty certain I would remember it, my wife never took out a mirror to check herself out while we were having sex, although we did always try to have a mirror in the room—mostly my idea, since having sex with a beautiful woman may not be as emotionally fulfilling as one might expect, but it still makes for a hell of a visual experience—and she never objected. However, she did, on occasion, ask me not to mess up her hair during sex (maybe she had something important to do once she was finished having sex with me—like looking at herself in a mirror).

So, anyway, that's my roundabout way of saying that I don't think my mother ever messed around with other guys: it just wasn't that important to her. She didn't need anyone else's validation. I could have used some of hers, but that's another story.

Remember that race in Fresno that I was telling you about a little while ago, and how when I thought about my wife and the divorce papers I dug into the track with my spikes during the last lap? I could just as easily, one would think, have substituted my mother and her attitude for Judy's. I could have, but I didn't. My mother had much more of a negative influence on me than my wife (and hasn't made up for it since then the way Judy has) and she certainly disappointed me a whole lot more than my wife, but mothers sort of get a free pass, don't they? And wives almost never do. Judy's still a part of my life, since I see her on my tapes every once in awhile (she looks more beautiful than ever) and on those tapes we always seem to be having a good time, and she always looks happy, and I've never been able to find one bad thing about Judy on any of my tapes or my secret notes. Sometimes, I kind of find myself wondering why, if things all are so good between us, how come we're not back together again. That makes sense, doesn't it? You know, I don't actually know why we got divorced. I mean, I know it said on the divorce papers "irreconcilable differences", but that could mean almost anything, and usually does. She really pissed me off at the Olympic Trials that time, and I know that the next few years after that, as much as I can remember of them, were not a time of much happiness between us, but I can't find anything anywhere in my correspondence with myself that shows her to be anything but the most trusted and important person in my life. Maybe she just doesn't love me anymore—maybe we're just good friends. A couple of the tapes I have show her hugging me and holding on to me in a way that I don't think many friends do. Of course, I don't remember any of this, and have to rely completely on the videos and a few pictures I have of the two of us together. And I know that we all, sometimes, believe what we want to believe, and I really want to believe that Judy still cares about me, and not just because I have this MCI thing and everything that comes with it. I mean, she's the one who put me out there and sees to it that everything is taken care of, enough to make me feel there is a lot more than just pity going on here.

The Santa Monica Evening Outlook

HARDMAN READY FOR
OLYMPIC TRIALS

Coming off of a 3:53.5 mile in San Diego two weeks ago, Tim Hardman is packing his bags for the Olympic Trials next weekend. Was he surprised to be invited to the Trials?

"After the time I got in San Diego, they had no choice...they *had* to invite me. Nobody's run that fast in America in two years."

Does that say more about how well he's running right now, or how poorly everyone else is running?

"Both," said Hardman. "I'm doing well right now. My workouts have been exceptional. I could've run even faster at San Diego, but no one there pushed me. I expect to run much faster at the Trials."

How much faster?

"That's a secret. You'll know soon enough."

Just then Mrs. Hardman, the former Judy Hamilton, walked through the room. Did she have anything to add?

"No," she said. Her lips were smiling but her voice was not. She walked out of the room.

Getting back to the subject at hand, I asked Hardman about why he has been so up-and-down in his performances lately. Until two weeks ago, he hadn't run faster than a 4:05 in a year.

"I can't explain it. I go out and try to win and run fast every time. Every time I get on the track, I expect to win. Sometimes it just doesn't happen."

But his workouts have consistently been good?

"Yeah, I've been training by myself, at Santa Monica City College, and people who've been watching me have really been impressed."

How long has he been training at City?

"I don't remember. It's been awhile, but I don't remember how long."

Any predictions about his future?

"Well, I've been checking the long-range forecasts for the weather during the Olympics and also trying to decide what colors go best with gold."

Hardman had only the slightest of smiles as he said that. He followed his wife with his eyes as she silently walked back through the room again. He watched her walk out of the room, shook his head, then suddenly gave a thumbs-up.

"It's all good," he said, with a half-smile.

What this all comes down to is one thing: control. I have control over what I'm doing right now, but it is all day-to-day. There is no planning. That old saying about today being the first day of the rest of your life is a statement of fact for me. Every day is a life unto itself. I know enough about how to live my life from the years before my memory disappeared that I can still function normally, but there's no spontaneity unless I...uh...plan it in advance. I suppose that for some people this doesn't sound like such a bad life. For one thing, there are no regrets in my life. You can't regret what you can't remember. My tapes show nothing but positive things happening. The fact that I can find nothing in my notes or tapes but flowers and sunshine—you know what I mean—leads me to believe that either I have the greatest life of all time or else I'm just erasing everything I don't like. I mean, what else could it be? Nobody has nothing but good things happen to them all the time. My life seems to be good. I'm in good shape, my workouts, according to my notes, are really going well, and I've spent the last two days in a great room of a very beautiful hotel, sucking down as many expensive carbohydrates as possible to get ready for tonight. Life at this particular moment is very good. I just checked myself in the mirror—all those years with Judy must've rubbed off—and I've got some serious biceps, so my weight training must be working. My notes say that I do body-weight training—push-ups, pull-ups, chin-ups, whatever-ups—everyday, but the notes are kind of lacking in detail. Just the facts. See, here's the problem with me doing notes and tapes on myself: I think that writing about oneself is vulgar.

I tried to keep a journal while I was at UCLA because when I started hitting some fast times, an agent told me that if I wrote down all my thoughts and everything, that might make a pretty good book if I ever broke the world record—you know, a sort of behind-the-scenes look on how it all happened—and so I did that for a few months, and when I read the stuff back, even though some of it had just happened recently, I had already forgotten some of what I had written about, and it was almost as if I was reading about another person, except that I wasn't reading about another person, I was reading about me, and when I realized how fascinated I was about myself, I tore the pages up and threw them in the trash and never wrote another word, because it just seemed a little too self-centered for me, even though the idea made a lot of sense and some wonderful pieces of literature—not that I'm saying this would've necessarily been even a piece of literature, much less a wonderful one (and I know all about Samuels—Pepys and Johnson—and all the others from my English Lit classes)—I just couldn't convince myself that this wasn't one step above jerking-off, and so even now when I'm doing a tape or writing some notes to myself, I try to make it sound like I'm talking about some other person—some other terribly uninteresting person about whom the less is said the better—

just putting down the bare details, and almost never including anything about how I feel and judgments about what kind of a workout it was, etc., with the result being that I end up knowing what I did, but not how I did it, what it felt like while I did it, or if I felt like doing it again, and I know that this is not the most productive or insightful way to record things, especially since this is my only way of remembering anything, but I also know that if I did start writing down everything about how I felt, what the weather was like, what my reactions were, etc., I'd have a small book everyday, and that is mostly because of one other fact:

I really like me.

A lot.

I always have.

I've always thought I was the coolest guy around. Maybe it's because I was an only child, because I worked really hard to be a good runner, or because I felt sorry for myself…but I've always had a high opinion of myself. I've always thought the world would be a better place if more people were like me: I look good, I'm religious, I'm loyal to people, I work hard…and *yada yada.* Everybody thought I was lucky to get Judy. I thought she was lucky to get me. I never told her, of course, because, well, a good person would never do that.

I'll tell you how cool of a person I am:

I am not remotely pissed off at what has happened to me and my life the last six years or so. It has been a struggle, and I can only assume that there are people helping me who are getting nothing out of this but the satisfaction of doing so, but I just take it a day at a time. I have never once screamed out, in the middle of the night, the day, or whenever, about what has happened to me. *Why me*? Who knows? It just happened. Everything happens for a reason. Maybe God thought I was too full of myself and decided to cut me down a couple notches. That's cool. I handled the success in running pretty easily, so maybe God said, Let's see what kind of balls he's got when things don't go so well. Hey, I'm still here. Still cool. It all seems to have worked, although I have no idea how. It just has. I'm willing to take it at that. I've heard of a situation that golfers call "paralysis by analysis", when a person is so consumed with investigating everything that they never accomplish anything.

Hey…it happened. Get over it. I did. It could be a lot worse…it can always be worse.

Like I said, I've had this beautiful hotel room, great food, great views of the San Francisco Bay, nobody bothering me. Am I supposed to be depressed? I understand that refusing to feel sorry for oneself is the opposite of the more obvious side of a giant ego—feeling sorry for oneself all the time. To never feel sorry for yourself, I guess, is a way of saying that you are above the petty complaints that most people dwell on or in, because you are much better than most people and, as such, are able to rise above the muck and conduct yourself in a manner that is consistent with someone whose personal philosophy and outlook is much more evolved, much more thought-out, and, basically, greatly superior to pretty much everybody else's on the face of the earth, which, I would say, is a fairly accurate— actually, it is a *completely* accurate—depiction of how I view myself, being able to take a situation that would really be a killer for most people and turn it into a positive, something that not only manages to motivate me in what I do—running—but also makes me feel as if I have some reference points for the rest of my life, which, to me, is a pretty substantial thing, since I have absolutely no fucking reference points in my life whatsoever—I am out here on some island, a new island everyday, with my only connection with the real world, with reality, being some electronic images on a video camera screen and half-assed notes stashed in my underwear, which is not the foundation for building any kind of a life, although that is exactly what I have managed to do, which sort of reminds me of when I was a kid and made a skateboard for myself when all I had to work with was a crappy pair of roller skates and a piece of wood, and that skateboard, which I still have somewhere, is a pretty good symbol for what my life is today, everything sort of patched together but working just fine, and even though I don't know what kind of life I have, living day-by-day, everything seems to take care of itself. When I go to sleep at night, I'm usually pretty excited about tomorrow, even though I understand that tomorrow I will have no recollection, other than what I have recorded, of what has actually happened today. The only constant in my life is running, which I have been doing for the last twenty-five years. It is an on-going thread that's not particularly difficult for me to maintain since I have been training most of my life, which is both a good thing and a bad thing; good because I can rely on what I did earlier in my life, when I was subject to the greatest training and competitive pressures, to form a training schedule just for today that I know will work with what I have been doing up to today and what I will be doing after today, but also bad because it means that I am using the same training techniques that I did fifteen or twenty years ago, and I have to assume that training and running protocols have changed during the last ten years, but I am really loathe to try and find out what they are, because you have to assume they were not conceived in a vacuum, and then you would have to read up on what led to these innovations, going back further and further, almost like peeling an onion—for example, high-altitude training became fashionable for distance runners because of the bad things that happened to athletes at the Mexico City Olympics in 1968 who were not used to competing at such altitudes and the good things that happened to athletes, such as the Kenyans, who were; a US Olympic Training Center was set up for athletes in the mountains in Colorado, and I remember I got to go up there once before the Olympic Trials for about three weeks, and it was something I will never forget, especially my lungs straining for oxygen the first couple days after I got there until I got used to altitude, after which time I had the best training of my life, and which is why I took off like a bat out of hell during the Olympic Trials final that time, with the problem being that I never really practiced a finishing kick at that altitude, which meant that the only thing that could happen was what actually happened, that I ran out of gas with a half-lap to go, because I was so pumped up about going on long runs and building up my endurance during the training that I forgot about preparing for the final kick, which is mostly about strength and which I had mostly ignored up in Colorado, a strange situation for me since I would always spend time in the gym with weights in LA, because when you are running you need good upper body strength so your shoulders and chest don't sag near the end of the races when you're tiring a little, compressing your lungs and reducing your oxygen intake at the very time you need it most, so I always emphasized strength training for my upper body, but when I got up to the Olympic Training Center, I was so jazzed about being able to go on long runs and not feel worn out afterwards—sort of like a weight-lifter suddenly taking steroids and not feeling weak after a tough workout—that I forgot the basic regimen that I had developed and let it all fall out of context.

Context...

...that's the word I've been rummaging around in my mind to try and describe what I need.

Context...

...the one thing in my life that I do not have. Look, I've got enough awareness of what my life is about that I think I really could exist on a day-to-day basis without all these daily memoirs. In fact, I tried it once for about a week—uh, according to my notes—never taping or writing down anything and, well, I'm still here, so it couldn't have been that disruptive. I have sometimes thought, and mentioned in my notes, that it wouldn't be terribly difficult for me to live as an animal, working pretty much with a stimulus-and-response MO, rather than using a rational thought process to guide my activities. (We do that in sex, don't we?) And, running isn't all that cerebral, either—race strategy tending to go out the window about the same time somebody in a race does something you didn't account for, such as sprinting in front of you, and you just try to run faster than them and beat them to the finish, accepting compliments afterwards on what a smart race you ran when you know full well that you didn't have a clue what you were doing out there except that you wanted to run faster than everyone else. (Race strategy, if the truth be told, basically comes down to your workouts: if you are a strong runner, you concentrate on pace workouts to develop running strength, especially when you are tired, to build up your resilience; if you are a strong finisher, you work on speed and try to develop a killer 220 time. When you step on the track for a race, how you run is a product of how you trained. Any last-minute instructions from the coach are mostly for the purpose of making him feel important, whereas in actual fact you could just as easily be getting instructions from your grandmother, since last-minute instructions before a race are like a fart in the wind—a momentary unpleasant distraction quickly scattered to oblivion and forgotten. I mean, what the hell, you've done all your training for weeks and months on end and now you're going to suddenly change everything three minutes before the race?) On a superficial level, stimulus-and-response looks pretty interesting, all innovation and spontaneity. But, to me, it also looks like constantly moving from one crisis to another. No thanks....

DEPOSITION

Site: Offices of Clark, Wilson and Delaney, Attorneys-at-Law
Administrator: William Delaney
Recorder: Elizabeth Wiley
Case: Hardman vs. Hardman

William Delaney: For the record, we are conducting this deposition in the matter of Hardman vs. Hardman. Please state your full name.
Judith Hardman: Judith Ann Hardman.
W.D.: And you are seeking a divorce on the grounds of irreconcilable differences from your husband, Timothy Richard Hardman?
J.H.: Uh...yes, that is true.
W.D.: Is your marriage irretrievably broken?
J.H. Well, I...uh...would...uh...say...
W.D.: A yes or no, please.
J.H. Yes...I think so.
W.D. You are not certain?
J.H.: I am certain we should not remain married.
W.D.: Does your husband, Timothy Richard Hardman, agree with you on this?
J.H.: Uh...

W.D.: Yes or no, please.

J.D.: Well, we haven't really discussed this—that's one of our problems, we don't communicate anymore.

W.D.: You have not discussed a divorce action with your husband?

J.D.: Well, not in so many words, but...

W.D.: I need a complete answer to the question, Mrs. Hardman.

J.H.: No, we have not discussed getting a divorce.

W.D.: Did the two of you discuss a separation?

J.H.: No.

W.D.: Has your husband been served with legal documents of any kind that would lead him to believe that you are seeking the dissolution of your marriage?

J.H.: Uh...

W.D.: Mrs. Hardman, again...please answer the question.

J.H.: No.

W.D.: Does your husband know this deposition is taking place?

J.H.: No...he thinks I'm at the doctor.

W.D.: He has no knowledge of any of this?

J.H.: No...none.

W.D.: When will you tell him?

J.H.: Well, that's just it, it doesn't matter if I tell him or not. He is having some memory problems, and what I say to him today will mean nothing to him tomorrow.

W.D.: Is he mentally ill? Can he be declared mentally-incompetent?

J.D.: I don't think so.

W.D.: Has he been observed by a physician or psychiatrist?

J.H.: No.

W.D.: Is he having fainting or dizzy spells?

J.H.: No.

W.D.: Is he--?

J.H.: He's not sick—he just can't remember things from one day to the next, and it has changed him and it's changed our marriage and I just can't go on like this anymore, and I know that I am probably a bad person for not wanting to stand by him—you know, "..for better or for worse..." —but I just can't take it anymore.

W.D.: We are not here to judge you on—

J.H.: His father has Alzheimer's, and I think that he is starting down that same road, and I love Timmy, but I can't handle it.

W.D.; Do you need to stop for a minute?

J.H.: No...I'm okay.

W.D.: What is your occupation?

J.H.: I'm a financial planner.

W.D.: So, you are self-employed?

J.H.: Yes.

W.D.: What is your annual income before taxes and expenses?

J.H.: You mean, gross income?

W.D.: Yes.

J.H.: I suppose about $75,000, more or less.

W.D.: You're not certain? You're a financial planner and cannot give an accurate amount of your annual income?

J.H.: I'm a financial planner, not an accountant. I deal with concepts, not numbers.

W.D.: What is your husband's occupation?

J.H.: He is an athlete—a professional athlete.

W.D.: In which sport?

J.H.: Track and field. He's a runner. He runs the mile.

W.D.: Any other events?

J.H.: No, just the mile...and the 1500 meters, which they call the "metric mile", but he really hates that term.

W.D.: What is your husband's annual income?

J.H.: You mean, this year, or, in general?

W.D. Whichever is the most accurate assessment of his earning capabilities as a professional athlete.

J.H.: Well, this year, he hasn't made anything at all. He hasn't run in any races. He only ran in two races last year. He used to make more money than me, from endorsements and appearance money, but those days are gone.

W.D.: Would it be accurate to say, then, that his days of earning an income as a professional athlete are finished?

J.H.: Well, I don't know. I mean, he's still in shape, and if he wanted to race, he could probably do all right, and make some money, but not like before.

W.D.: I repeat, would it be accurate to say that his days of earning an income as a professional athlete are over?

J.H.: You don't understand how hard it is for me to answer that question. I've never known Tim as anything but an athlete.

W.D.: You say that he has run no races this year and only ran two last year, with almost no income. Does he train?

J.H.: Now? No.

W.D.: So, he is not at present an athlete. Is he retired?

J.H.: No, he just—he just needs help.

W. D.: What type of help?

J.H.: Every type—spiritual, emotional, psychological...you name it, he needs it.

W.D.: You're certain of this?

J.H.: Uh, yeah...pretty sure.

W.D.: And yet, neither you nor anyone else, according to your statement a few minutes ago, has provided him any access to such help?

J.H.: I thought you were supposed to be on my side---you're my attorney.

W.D.: Depositions are not about taking sides—they are about finding the truth, as a means of preparing a legal strategy.

J.H.: Okay.

W.D.: So, to repeat, neither you nor anyone with access to your husband has provided any kind of assistance to help him?

J.H.: That's right.

W.D.: And...why is that?

J.H.: Tim has a real aversion to doctors ever since what happened to his father. I doubt he would follow any advice.

W.D.: You know this for a fact?

J.H.: Well, we've been together a long time, and I think I know him pretty well, and I'm certain he wouldn't follow our advice.

W.D.: Because...?

J.H.: Because he doesn't think there's anything wrong with him. He is so upset about the problems with our marriage.

W.D.: I thought you said that he did not realize how serious the problems were with your marriage?

J.H.: No...what I said was that he does not know that I am planning to divorce him. He thinks things are bad, but not that bad.

W.D.: You are certain of this?

J.H.: He more or less said so just yesterday. He was complaining that we never do things together, and that's why we're having problems, and that's why he wasn't training or running, and that if we were like we used to be, we would be better and so would he.

W.D.: And it is your opinion that he believes this?

J.H.: Oh...completely. He obsesses about how things are going bad between us.

W.D.: And, in your opinion, are they?

J.H.: Oh, yeah. We just sort of occupy the same house—that's about it.

W.D.: You are not functioning as husband and wife?

J.H.: How do you mean?

W.D.: Is there any intimacy?

J.H.: Every once in awhile...but it's pretty...uh... almost robotic.

W.D.: But...there is some intimacy?

J.H.: Like I said, every once in awhile.

W.D.: And...what does that mean? Days, weeks, months...?

J.H.: Probably once a week, nothing more.

W.D.: In other words, like most other married couples.

J.H.: Well, I don't know about other married couples, but for us, compared to before, once a week is not very often.

W.D.: Again...like most other married couples.

J.H.: You know, I don't have to pay $250 an hour to get this kind of attitude—I can get it for free from my relatives and friends.

W.D.: And they know about your plans to dissolve your marriage?

J.H.: Well, I've never said it in so many words, but I'm sure they won't be shocked.

W.D.: And you don't think any of them would have mentioned their suspicions to your husband?

J.H.: He literally hasn't left the house in weeks, and he never talks to anyone on the phone—he doesn't have a cell phone—so his only communication with the outside world is through me. Besides, he would never believe them.

W.D.: Why is that?

J.H.: He would think I was be incapable of something like a divorce.

W.D.: Because you are too good of a person.

J.H.: Yeah, he says that only fuck-ups—am I allowed to say that in a deposition?—get divorced.

W.D.: And he would never describe you that way?

J.H.: No. I get the impression that he thinks the sun shines out my butt.

W.D.: And, for the record, it does not?

J.H.: Not anymore.

W.D.: You believe that your husband needs help in most aspects of his life?

J.H.: Yeah, unfortunately.

W.D.: And this is without his being aware of any of the plans you have for dissolving your marriage?

J.H.: Uh...yeah...I...uh...guess so.

W.D.: Can we assume then, based solely on your accounts of his problems, that his being served with divorce papers will only exacerbate his problems?

J.H.: Uh....yeah...I...uh...guess so.

W.D.: And you have no difficulty with the possibility of such a result?

J.H.: Well, I...uh...don't want to...uh...see that happen to Timmy, but I don't know how I can...uh...avoid it.

W.D.: Are you certain that—?

J.H.: Look, I don't want to see Timmy get hurt, but something has to change. I can't go on like this. He can—he will.

Every day is a new day for him. He told me so. He just doesn't remember much of anything about yesterday. I do. I remember everything. I can't forget and he can't remember. Who do you think will suffer more?

W.D.: You do understand that if your husband's problems are as serious as you indicate, and especially if there is a potential for their becoming even worse because of the divorce, there is a distinct possibility that you, as the primary source of income in your marriage ,will be charged, as a condition of your divorce, with providing a continuing financial contribution to his care and well-being.

J.H.: I thought the government would take care of that.

W.D.: Well, again, if your husband's difficulties are as severe and ongoing as you have described, there certainly is every likelihood that he would qualify for SSI—

J.H.: What is that?

W.D.: Supplemental Security Income. It is a monthly payment from the Social Security Administration, not unlike the monthly checks people get after they retire.

J.H.: Is it a lot of money?

W.D.: It is generally not enough to replicate one's current lifestyle.

J.H.: The government will give him as little as possible?

W.D.: That would be a harsh assessment—not inaccurate, but harsh. With your relative youth and ability to make significant income for years to come, it would be likely to expect the judge and the government to enforce your participation in the financial

maintenance of your husband's well-being.
J.H.: For how long?
W.D.: Well, it would not be unreasonable to assume that it would last for most of your adult life, until retirement. But your husband might also be assigned a portion, perhaps a significant portion, of your monthly Social Security payment.
J.H.: Is there...any way to avoid this?
W.D.: And yet still proceed with the divorce?
J.H.: Yeah.
W.D.: It is unlikely. The government is not generous when perceived deep pockets are involved.
J.H.: I'm screwed.
W.D.: There are no winners in a divorce action. A divorce is an admission of failure.
J.H. Mr. Delaney, I already have a mother.

You know, the strange thing is, I can't find any record of the divorce. It all happened before my memory completely disappeared, so I remember going to court, and there was a hearing, but it's like a blur when I think about it, and, in fact, as I remember the whole situation, I was the only person on my side of the court room (I didn't get a lawyer because I kept thinking Judy would come to her senses and call the whole thing off), not that I expected my mother to be there and support me—dream on—but I would've thought there was at least one person in the world who might have had the slightest of interest in my situation, although I'll be the first to admit that I hadn't cultivated many, or any, friends since I had gotten married—your wife is supposed to be your best friend, right?—and staying locked up in my house all the time for that last year didn't make any new friends, and the guys I had known from running were mostly retired by then or into coaching and were, in any case, way too busy to have anything to do with me, a situation I noticed seem to coincide almost completely with my bombing out at the Olympic Trials, as if I had not only failed to make the US Olympic team, but I had also failed to make anybody's team, and, now that I think about it, from the moment I was brought back to life there on the track at the Trials, my relationship with the rest of the world—up to and most definitely including my wife— seemed to change, and not for the better, and it was almost as if the one thing that had been my stock-in-trade with the rest of the world, being a great runner, had turned out to be bogus, and so I was essentially starting at zero—as in zero friends and zero credibility—with few prospects, since running was all I did and running was all anyone knew about me, which was mostly my fault, because I had pretty much shoved running down the throat of anybody who knew me and had been doing so since my freshman year in high school, always making certain to get the latest information in running magazines, wearing running shoes for every social activity, including my Confirmation at Blessed Sacrament Church and the senior prom at the Beverly Hills Hotel, all my t-shirts having running slogans or logos on them, always using a track bag for luggage and, well, you get the idea—I was a walking billboard for running—and everyone knew what to talk to me about, and that was all that I ever talked about, even in my English Lit. classes at UCLA—I did a paper on "The Loneliness of the Long Distance Runner", an obscure British film from the early '60's, having to explain what the film was about (a British long-distance runner trains and trains and trains and then, after leading in the big race, stops just before the finish and lets everyone pass him) and what possible relevance it could have to the works of Thomas Hardy (I somehow managed to weave "Jude the Obscure" into the discussion with just enough élan to get away with it)—and so, basically, I *was* running; for everyone who met me discussions started and ended with that, not that I didn't know what else was going on in the world, but when someone is wearing running shorts, a singlet, running shoes and a visor while shopping at the market, it is not too difficult to figure out where the conversation is going to lead, which I was only too happy to oblige by entertaining one and all with anecdotes about either my races, my training, my nutrition tips or whatever else I had on my mind at the time that I thought was so utterly fascinating and was positive that this enthusiasm was shared by everyone I met, to the point that I must have been, now that I think about it, the most boring and predictable person to have a discussion with, unless the other person was also a runner, in which case I would up the ante by bringing out the heavy artillery with every bit of runners' gossip and rumors I had encountered in the last few weeks, pretending to listen to what the other person was saying when, in fact, I was just waiting for my turn to talk again, and then bombarding the listener—*they* were always listening, right?—with so much information, coming at them so fast, that they would not have a chance to take charge of the conversation, which, if you think about it, was pretty much the way I ran my races, just putting it all up there and daring anyone to challenge me and, make no mistake about it, conversation was a competition with me, one that I took almost as seriously as what happened on the track, because the goal in both situations was not merely to participate but to win, and to so completely dominate—and demonstrate that domination *to*—the other person or persons that they would become subdued and almost passive, nodding and following along as I directed the conversation in much the same way that the runners behind me in a race would follow my lead, reacting to my maneuvers and hoping to stay with me but without any hope of surpassing me, and even when someone else would manage to get in a few words in a conversation, similar to a runner challenging me for the lead in a race, I would control the discussion by asking questions that would take both of us in whichever direction I wanted, and then asking another question before the person had completely answered the previous one but had given me enough information to move on to something else, the important thing being not what they said but the fact that I was generating the discussion even if they were doing the talking, much the same as in a race when I would get right up on a runner's shoulder if he had somehow taken the lead from me in a race, and make him react to me, by pretending to challenge him or changing my pace, so that I was controlling the situation even though he was leading, and, yes, I know that this was all very ego-driven and self-centered, but it was also very enjoyable, because I was conscious of what I was doing, either in races or conversations, and sometimes would throw completely unexpected detours into the mix—a question completely off-subject or a sudden sprint around a curve—just to see how the other person would handle it and also, of course, to demonstrate to them, whether they realized it or not, that while they might be doing all the talking or leading the race, I was the one in charge of the situation, which is, I am sure, what came back to bite me in the ass when I suddenly nose-dived at the Olympic Trials, and even more so when I started being a no-show at track meets and even training sessions, with the result being that for people who probably didn't care for me that much or maybe couldn't even stand me, but tolerated me, it was now perfectly all right to ignore me, because at the Olympic Trials I had been exposed as a fraud as a runner, and at the divorce hearings I was being exposed as a fraud as a human being, someone who could not control the two main things in his life, running and being married, and I really couldn't blame them if they did that because, well, besides my running and my wife, they saw nothing else of consequence in my life. (I used to have friends—all runners. Dom Brown and Bobby Winlock were fun. Another guy, Wilson Reilly, was a pest, hanging around on and off the track. I pulled him along to more good clockings than I could count. He came in second behind me at the NCAAs, finished hard, got a 3:42.9 and dropped like a sack of potatoes. He claimed it was the same as a 3:59.9 mile—you add 17 seconds to your 1500 meters time—but the only way he could have covered those extra yards was in the back of an ambulance. Off the track, he also followed me around. I think he had a thing for Judy. I'm surprised he didn't contact her when we broke up. He was an electronics geek, so now he's probably living in his parents' basement, planning to use his computers to take over the world.)

I realize that this all comes across as something I studied in a psych course at UCLA called a " persecution complex", and, yeah, I would plead guilty to that. Actually, I think there's also some paranoia thrown into the mix. It's not on the surface, but there's always been an undercurrent in my life of the fear that there is someone or something observing my life, that there is a force out there trying to control my life. Whether it is for good or bad is almost irrelevant. What is most important is that it would be out of my hands—the decisions would be made for me. Hell, for all I know, it might've happened—it might be happening right now. I don't see anything in my notes or tapes about untoward events affecting my life and, today, I feel real good, look pretty good and generally have a positive attitude, but there is still the feeling in my subconscious that, somewhere out there, there is an energy with which I have to contend. Being a runner, and especially one who will take the lead and wait for anyone to catch me, any kind of paranoia would sort of be part of the game, and when I have a serious lead in a serious race, I am concentrating as much on what those behind me might be doing as I am on my own actions. It's the difference between trying to win and trying not to lose. In both instances, you want to finish first, but your approach is completely different. When your thoughts are all positive, winning is what you think about, trying to think of ways to get better; when the negatives predominate, the fear of losing is the driving force and you spend most of your time just trying not to screw things up. I think it is obvious that how a person handles any competitive situation says a great deal about their approach to life. There might not seem to be much difference between the attitude of winning—*I'm better than they are*—and the fear of losing—*I'm not going to let them defeat me*—but actually the gap between them is huge. I can remember my first winning 660 junior varsity race, looking at the other runners—I think some of them were basketball and soccer players out there for conditioning— and being terrified at the thought that any of these guys, or maybe all of them, might finish ahead of me, and what that would mean for all the self-esteem I had built up in myself over the years of running at the beach. I could not let that happen. I did not win the race so much as I did not lose the race. Big difference. When you win, you feel elated; when you don't lose, you feel relieved—until the next race, when it starts all over again. The problem with this—well, actually, there's lots of problem with this, but we'll focus on the main one here—is that unless you are completely superior in every race, you are going to lose, and probably with some regularity: some days you just don't have it in you, some days you are just taking the race easy, as a glorified training run, while the others are dead serious, and some days there are runners who are simply better than you. Why the Olympic Trials was such a killer for me was that none of those conditions were present: I did have it in me, I was not taking it easy, and, to be blunt about it, I was the superior runner. They didn't defeat me—I did it to myself. To me, losing when you are the best, know you're the best, and are in the process of proving you are the best, is almost beyond comprehension. It challenges how you feel about yourself in particular and life in general. Was I really a fraud? Was that what Judy was thinking, standing over me on the track, almost screaming at me, asking what had happened? An even more important question: Was that what I was thinking as I lie there on the track? Guys were pumping my chest, working my lungs to get me breathing, but I wasn't even all that worried about dying. My little out-of-body experience was part of the reason, but mostly it was the fact that I knew what had just happened: I had lost when I was the best, the fastest runner in the race. The fact that it was the Olympic Trials and I had failed to finish in the top three and qualify for the U.S. team might've made it more sobering, but I really believe I would have been almost as distraught if this had happened at that mile race in Fresno I was telling you about earlier. If I had crashed to the ground in that race with a half of a lap to go, and staggered in fifth, as I did at the Trials, I think I would have been devastated. Competition is competition. The rewards in some competitions may be greater than in some others but, to me, the greatest reward, the greatest prize, in finishing first, defeating everyone else. (You'll notice I didn't say the greatest prize was winning; I said the greatest prize was defeating everyone else in the race. Understand?) To me, in a race or in life, when you are the best, and are demonstrating that you are the best but, for some reason, do not prevail, that is a catastrophe. Yes, I understand the idea that we learn more from losing than winning—nobody asks questions when they win, but everybody asks questions when they lose—but that only happens later, reflecting on the loss at a future point in time. At the time it happens, losing, for me, is a shock. I am not out there to lose. If I thought I was going to lose, I wouldn't have competed. I cannot ever remember me entering a mile that I did not expect to win, and I cannot ever remember feeling anything but complete rejection if I did lose—rejection of my effort, rejection of my value as a runner and even, unfortunately, as a human being. Yeah, I know that is completely out of line with any rational approach to life, but when competition is your life, the only true validation is finishing on top, defeating everyone else. If that sounds personal, that's because it is. I would humiliate good friends on the track, running them into the ground, because on the track they were not friends, they were people who were trying to defeat me, trying to subvert my worth as a person. I left those feelings on the track—a variation on the old cliché of the monster linebacker on the football field being the nicest guy in the world off the field—but that was primarily because of my success on the track. How would I have treated them, and myself, if I hadn't been successful as a runner? It's a moot question. If I hadn't been successful as a runner, I wouldn't have remained a runner. I couldn't have handled constant defeat, no matter how sterling an effort I had given.

I could never have been Merv Lincoln.

In the late Fifties, according to what my father told me and what I read in some old magazines, the dominant miler in the world was Herb Elliot, from Australia. I forget right now what his best time was—a world record in the 3:54's, I think—but he was the premier miler from about 1958 to 1962…undefeated. He was, according to magazines at the time, a machine, and his training sessions were legendary. He had a trainer, an old guy who still ran, named Percy Cerutty, who devised a training regimen that was pretty much unheard of at the time, with Elliot running a ton of miles a months. (Cerutty would urge his runners to go faster and harder—"…it's only pain…" was his mantra.) Anyway, Elliot was regularly churning out sub-four minute times when that was not as common as now. Merv Lincoln was a fellow Australian and also an excellent runner, but he wasn't Herb Elliot. What he became was Herb Elliot's shadow. Whenever he competed against Elliot, which was often, he never won, almost always finishing second, but rarely lost by very much. If Elliot won in 3:58.2, Lincoln would finish second in 3:58.6, or something similar. (Interestingly, if Lincoln was running without Elliot, he would usually win, but not so often under four minutes.) I could never have been able to endure that. Lincoln was quite firmly the second-best miler in the world (an English runner, Derek Ibbotson, I believe, actually had the world record for awhile, but was inconsistent) and his times were outstanding, and without Elliot there, he would have been the main man in the mile. But Herb Elliot was there, and Merv Lincoln, for all his running talent, was just part of the supporting cast. As far as I can tell, Merv Lincoln handled it well, and he certainly was a great runner, but he wasn't Herb Elliot, and Herb Elliot is who they remember. I have much admiration for Merv Lincoln, but I cannot for a second identify with him. I could never have been Merv Lincoln.

Dear Mom and Dad;
I really don't need the guilt trip you are trying to lay on me. I don't mean to sound harsh, and I know you think you have my best interests at heart but, believe me, you have no idea about what is happening. First of all, I never filed the final divorce papers. I went back and got it changed to a legal separation. I haven't told Tim yet, and I don't know when I will, or if I will. He has finally been able to accept our being apart, and the last time I went out to see him, he was much more relaxed. To tell him what is going on would only stir him up. He might be happy that we're not divorced, but I know him well enough to know that the idea that he has no control over this situation, that I am doing everything, would both sadden and anger him. He knows he has very little control over his life. This would just reinforce that idea. I can't do that to him. It is better to leave it the way it is. He has accepted the divorce as a fact of his life. He is distressed about it, but at least he's not angry anymore. He's started running again, and was even talking about that

track he was going to put around the house. That's a good sign.

I'm pretty good at reading your mind, Mom, and you're probably thinking right now that you don't care about Tim, you care about me. I'm okay. Sorry I haven't been home for awhile. There's just too many things to do with Tim and the legal stuff, plus running a business. And no, I am not seeing anyone else, nor will I be. That's one of the reasons I didn't file the divorce papers. I want to be married. I want to be married to Tim. I can't tell you why. Tim told me something once that I didn't understand then, but I do now: if you can explain why you love someone, you probably don't. I know that after all the depositions and legal hearings, filing the papers was just a formality, but I couldn't go through with it. I sat one entire night, until dawn, just staring at those divorce papers. All I had to do was pick them up and head to court and it would be all over. But, I couldn't touch them. It was like they were on fire.

I know you want nothing but happiness for me. Am I happy? I don't know, but I'm content, and I'll settle for that right now. Will Tim get better? I doubt it, but that doesn't mean he will get worse, at least not for now. When I visit him, we have a good time together, just about the best times I've had with him in years. Every time I go out there, he asks me to stay. I never do, but I always want to come back again. He doesn't need a wife so much right now as he needs a mother. I try to function as a little of both.

Why am I doing all this? I have no idea. I don't expect you to understand (I don't completely understand it myself) but I do expect you to accept it. "For better or worse" is what this is all about. I realized that it's more than just words, it's a commitment. It's not easy, but it's not impossible. So, I guess what I'm saying is, give me some credit. It isn't great, but it isn't bad…and neither am I.

Love,
Jude

PS: I appreciate your telling me that Paul is still available. Tell him not to wait up.

I remember reading, when I was first starting to be successful as a runner, that *Sports Illustrated* had once posed a question to a number of Olympic-quality athletes, asking them if they would take a substance that would allow them to win a gold medal, even if there was the distinct possibility that such a substance could kill them a few years later. Supposedly, over half of the respondents said that they would take such a chance to win a gold medal, despite subsequent risks to their well-being. Since I never read the actual article itself, I'm paraphrasing, and I understand that the article has attained almost urban-legend type status, which means to me that there might be a little embellishing going on. But, even so, it is still a legitimate question that serious competitors could ask themselves: Would they do it?

Would I?

No…not a chance.

As far as I can recall, I've never ingested anything (other than an occasional cup of coffee for the caffeine) to boost my performance. I don't have much about this on my tapes and in my notes, but my impression is that in the last few years, basically since my memory went south, all kinds of things have been happening on the enhancing-drug scene. I just remember the big thing when I was starting to succeed was all about Lasse Viren. He was a distance runner from Finland who won the 5,000 and 10,000 meters in the

Olympics, disappeared for four years, then suddenly reappeared at the next Olympics and won both races again. (I'm oversimplifying here a little, but not too much.) The assumption, which was strongly hinted-at but never proven, was that Viren and his people used a blood transfer system which, as I understand it, would take some of his blood, store it for awhile, then pump it back into him just before the Olympics. Don't ask me why, but this stored blood, when introduced back into his body, would increase his endurance, I think, by better utilizing the oxygen in his blood, with the result being that a guy who did nothing between Olympics was on the top step of the podium twice picking up gold medals. Of course, Viren wasn't just some guy off the street. He obviously had talent, and in the films I've seen of him running, his stride is excellent, and he looks to be a strong finisher. Basically, the guy was an athlete. The question is, and, I guess will always be, was he *that* good? In asking the question, you are not only impugning his credentials as an athlete, but also as a human being, as a moral person (I think Viren was a policeman). It goes to the heart of who the person actually is. I could never live with myself if I knew I wasn't completely responsible for any success I might have. I probably wouldn't have collapsed at the Trials if I had been taking something, whatever was available at the time, to increase my endurance, but it would have been a dagger to my soul. There is also something a little less altruistic to worry about: the possible consequences for your tainted victory (should it ever be discovered), not only for yourself but also for anyone with whom you interacted on the track, such as a teammate on a relay. (One of my notes mentions a Marion Jones, who lost all her gold medals for failing a drug test and also caused the other members of her winning relay team to lose theirs.)

It's the old story: Sin in haste, repent in leisure....

The steroid thing really isn't a problem in distance running—nobody's trying to bulk up—and some of the other performance-enhancing protocols are also not relevant to track. But, others are. Without a strict question of legality or prohibition by a sports body, it can get very murky. Caffeine is a stimulant. Is overloading with caffeine, through coffee or soft drinks or whatever, a problem? You'd probably have to guzzle a quart to make a difference, and dragging your butt around the track with that much liquid sloshing around in your stomach would be more conducive to heaving than a personal best, but a strategic cup of coffee, especially for someone who does not normally drink it, could certainly be a stimulant. It would be legal, but would it be cool? I don't know. There are lots of other aids to one's performance that seem almost passive compared to the more exotic—and forbidden—chemical compounds continually being formulated, but they can still generate a better performance. Creatine is a good example. It's an amino acid—no problem there—and perfectly legal in and out of sports. It can make you stronger and, if taken wisely in small doses to avoid weight gains, can definitely give you an edge. I tried it once, years ago when I was spending a lot of time in the gym, and I increased my weight lifting poundage by about 25% within about two weeks. Problem is, I got so worked up about being stronger and actually adding a little muscle—milers tend to exhibit a concentration-camp physique—that I digressed from my training regimen, hitting it hard in the gym and going through the motions on the track. Running a 4:08 and finishing fifth in a race brought me back to reality real quick. Before the race, everyone was complementing me on how buff I looked. After the race, everybody was asking me what was wrong. The creatine got dumped almost immediately, going to the gym became a chore once again, but my training on the track got better, and three weeks later I ran a 3:55.2. It was sad to see the muscles disappear—I got a couple pictures of me flexing—but you gotta know what's important. So, when I said just above that I would not want performance-enhancing drugs to artificially induce a better time, I wasn't just being idealistic. Going the drug route is a major distraction, both mentally and physically. I remember when the creatine was first starting to kick in, I would be doing the bench press at the gym and lifting twenty pounds heavier than normal, with no problem whatsoever, and I almost started laughing, saying to myself, "Do I know you?" It was as if another, stronger person had taken over my body.

The closest thing I can compare it to is the one time I took LSD with a couple of my friends from UCLA. All sorts of things were going on in my mind that were completely unfamiliar to me (although one feeling was familiar, as I went out for a short walk by myself while still on the acid and got the definite feeling that I was being followed, and even though there was no one on the street, the paranoia was heavy, and that I did understand). I felt different, acted different—was different—but it was still me. Sort of. I suppose that is the attraction of mind-altering drugs for many people, but for me it was uncomfortable to the highest degree possible, and I could barely function as a normal person. My friends and I decided to go out and mingle with the crowds in Westwood while on acid. Big mistake. Besides the rampant paranoia, I found myself struggling so hard to act normal when nothing about me at that particular time was normal. I'm sure I looked like a robot. I know I felt like one. My most vivid memory of that night is sitting at a counter in a Denny's (being on acid in a Denny's at three in the morning—is that a vision of hell or what?) staring at a piece of steak on my fork and saying to myself, with as firm a conviction as I have ever had in my life, that if I tried to eat that piece of meat I would choke to death. That was not a great meal. We did at least have enough wits left about us to decide against going over to the track at Drake Stadium on the UCLA campus and seeing what kind of a mile time I could run while completely stoned. I passed on the one chance in my life to have a Doc Ellis moment—Doc Ellis was a pitcher for the Pittsburgh Pirates who, one day during the 1970 season, didn't realize he was scheduled to pitch, took some LSD, then found out it was his turn in the rotation, and proceeded to throw a no-hitter despite experiencing hallucinations on the mound that would have done Hunter S. Thompson proud—but I also probably passed on the chance of being busted by the campus police, relieved of my scholarship and thrown out of school.

Anyway, I always try to study the faces of people filmed performing incredible feats of athletic prowess who were subsequently found to be juiced, to see their expression or attitude as they exceed their wildest expectations and know inside exactly why they are exceeding their wildest expectations. It is probably like pretending to be shocked at your surprise party when you knew all along what was going to happen. There has to be some guilt in there somewhere, with either a very big or maybe a very small g.

Despite my condemnation of any drugs that elevate performance, I can think of one particular time in my life when I would have gobbled them up by the handful, if only to render me unconscious. For reasons that now escape me, I once upon a time decided to run a marathon. I have no idea why, although it might have had something to do with the rampant propaganda in the track media at the time that the marathon was the only true indicator of what kind of a runner a person was. The fact that I was gullible to this bullshit shows how susceptible I was at the time to any idea that I was less than a cutting–edge runner. Understand, this was a short while after I tanked at the Olympic Trials, so I was not exactly a font of confidence to begin with, and then all these articles in *Runner's World* and other assorted running magazines seemed to concentrate on marathons, to the exclusion of all other running events—even the shorter road races—with the implication being that you could not be considered a real runner unless you ran marathons and everyone else was just a pussy who did not have the balls to put it all on the line for 26.2 miles, the interesting thing being they didn't talk about marathon performances—winning times, splits, etc.—as much as they did about the basic idea that running constantly for two, three, four or more hours was somehow a test of a person's character and willingness to push oneself to the limit, again the implication being that running shorter distances—and, by this line of reasoning, a mile race was not much different from the sprints—was something of a cop-out, primarily because to run a marathon one has to put in lots of mileage on a weekly basis for a prolonged period of time in order to be ready for just one race, as if this excessive devotion of time and energy to preparing for the running of just one particular race, however long that race might be, was the primary indicator of how completely committed a runner was to the sport, whether or not the person had the proper training for a marathon, the proper motivation for running the marathon or, in general, if they had any business running a marathon in the first place, although all these considerations fell by the wayside when you would see someone wearing a t-shirt proclaiming "I Finished the (fill in the blank) Marathon!", as if the ultimate goal was participation, and whether or not your performance justified the effort was irrelevant, because, for all we know, that person could have walked most of the distance, might have stopped along the way for a burger and a beer or whatever, but they finished, and that was all that really mattered, wasn't it? Here we have running reduced to its lowest common denominator.

I remember running a road race in Palm Springs to help get ready for the marathon. It was the Palm Springs Tram Road Challenge, and only about 3.6 miles long, so I thought it would be a good chance to do some fast, short distance work as part of my marathon training. The main problem here—there were several—was that I was not overly familiar with Palm Springs, probably because I had never been there before. "Tram Road" should have been a clue, since trams tend to be in hilly areas (a tram goes to the top of a hill or mountain, right?) and "Challenge" should have set off alarms, but the fact that I had even considered running a marathon, much less started rigorously training for one, is a pretty good indication of how seriously my rational thought process had been compromised, and so I just paid attention to the length of the race and the time and date of it, ignoring all the other details and, yes, the devil is most definitely in the details, because the Palm Springs Tram Road Challenge is only 3.6 miles, but it is basically straight uphill, except for one brief section where there is a slight downgrade, the point here being that nothing was flat for recovery during the entire length of the course, and the elevation climb of the Palms Springs Tram Road is approximately 2500 feet, which, over just 3.6 miles, is a serious ascent, especially if you are a miler, because what the hell would a miler be doing running up a seriously steep road except to destroy the calves and quads that he has finely tuned lo these many years through arduous work on the track, where every step is measured and taken into account, as opposed to some dumb-ass road race, where the quality of the ground upon which said runner will trod is probably of dubious quality and most certainly uneven, in contrast to the expensive and finely-maintained all-weather tracks that a top-flight miler trains on daily and where there is comfort in every stride and, most important, no deviation whatsoever in elevation, a first-class track (the only kind on which I would train) being flatter than the earth envisioned by Christopher Columbus' critics, and now I was subjecting myself to surfaces that were constantly traveled upon by cars, trucks and buses, some with leaking transmissions and engines, all of them leaving rubber on the road and bearing down on the road with their weight, as well as the sun beating down on the pavement every day, leaving a running surface that even if it was brand-new could severely damage the carefully-maintained legs of a champion middle-distance runner.

So, anyway, I get to Palm Springs—the Tram Road is just before you enter Palm Springs proper—and I see all the cars and the people, and then I see the road heading up the hill. *Oh, shit.*

There was not much I could do, since I had been planning this as a distance sprint workout for about a month, and I had nothing else to take its place. I reluctantly got out of my car and started to stretch, never taking my eyes off that fucking hill. My mood was sullen, to say the least, whereas everyone else, a couple hundred people, seemed to be very chippy. It was the usual road race crowd: a few class runners, a few plodders, lots of in-betweens, and no good-looking women. There must be a law or something that no attractive women can compete in road races, because they almost never do. (Of course, there are always a few law-breakers.) In track and field, we have lots of beautiful women, and not just the sprinters, but in road races most of the women look like they're answering a casting call for extras on *Star Trek*.

Four of the women were notable not for their attractiveness, or lack thereof. They were blond, tiny, and jogged around like machines as they prepared for the race. These were serious runners, and they all stretched and worked out together before the race. One of them went to a pile of warm-up clothes and put on a sweatshirt. I don't remember exactly what was on the shirt, but one of the words was "Moscow", and I moved just close enough to hear them talking in a language that sounded either Baltic or Slavic or somewhere else that was about eight thousand miles away, but I couldn't figure out what they were doing at some crappy little hill road race until I noticed an ESPN truck in the distance and then a couple guys with big video cameras and wearing ESPN caps, milling with the crowd and cameras focusing on the four women runners. Apparently, either the four women were a big deal, or the race was a big deal—or both—which meant that this was more than just a workout for me. I had this idea in the back of my mind that everyone here knew of my collapse at the Olympic Trials, although, if they did they were managing to hide their curiosity and concern incredibly well. (Could it be that these road racers really had no interest in any running that wasn't their own, that running a race was, for them, a personal achievement and nothing more, and they could just as easily have been bowling or throwing darts? *Nah.*)

We all eventually lined up for the start, and I put myself in the second line, just behind the four Russian women. I noticed that my arms were thicker than their legs. As soon as the gun went off, I also noticed those four pair of skinny little legs hauling ass up the steep grade just beyond the starting line while I, flat-earth runner that I was, huffed and puffed up the same grade that was like Everest to me and obviously a plateau for them. I was in about eighth place after the first half-mile, and as I looked back at the other struggling behind me, I saw that we had already risen about five hundred feet above the desert floor. The Russian women, along with a couple of guys, had already disappeared around the next bend, beyond which I could only assume lurked even more vertical challenges to me and my already-aching legs. I actually slowed down for a moment or two, seriously contemplating dropping out of the race, jogging back down to my car and getting the hell out of there, when I noticed an ESPN cameraman on the back of a motorcycle on the side of the pack of runners right behind me. If I dropped out of the race and slipped back down to my car, I would have been on *Sports Center* for the next week, with them dredging up my Olympic Trials failure and building on it—"...he couldn't finish the 1500 meters at the Olympic Trials, and now he can't even finish a simple road race. Is Tim Hardman finished?—so I just gritted my teeth and moved on. The run itself (it's hard to call it a race, since those who ran the best were those with the highest threshold for pain) was a joke. I stopped every quarter of a mile or so, to rest my weary quads, then relied on my sprint training experience and leg work in the gym to propel me to the next stop. I would fly by a few people, then rest as they dragged by me, then I would sprint past them again. After awhile, I got into the rhythm and the steep grade didn't bother me that much, and at the finish I was only about fifty-five seconds behind the Russian women (that sounds pretty close, but it was actually about three hundred yards). Realizing that I only wanted this as a workout, I ripped off my number before I got to the finish, then avoided the timer, and walked my way back down to the bottom of the hill, so that I would remain anonymous. It worked. There was no mention about me in any of the reports of the race. There was also no feeling in my legs. They had gone numb. I spent the next day crawling around the house on my hands and knees while Judy comforted me with reminders every fifteen or twenty minutes all day long that she had warned me not to do the race. A day or two later, I was back running again, same as before, none the worse for the experience but, unfortunately, none the better, either. I should have stopped right there, realizing that long-distance road racing was not for me. Instead, I went for a twelve-mile run through Westwood and Brentwood. My legs were no longer numb; the same could not be said for my brain.

And so it went until the day of the marathon. It was the Western Hemisphere Marathon, run in Culver City every year since the 1930's. With lots of tradition, but not much money, there was an absence of big names. I'll tell you how devoid the field was of well-known runners—I was one of the main attractions. Of course, there was no way of knowing—well, I probably could have found out rather quickly, but did not want to know—whether the interest was because of my success as a runner, or a morbid curiosity, seeing how I had fallen at the Olympic Trials and wondering if I might fall a little further, sort of like Johnny Unitas when he hobbled along with the San Diego Chargers at the end of his career. The public and press get weepy when a legend tries to push it just a little too far, but they also cannot look away. (Not that I considered myself a legend, but, you know....) And there was some press there: a guy from the daily paper in Santa Monica, whatever it's called, and an intern from the *L.A. Times*. There was also a woman reporter from some local cable channel—this was when a lot of cable television was still local and basically amateur-night—who knew nothing about marathons, or running, but knew that the wind and mist were ruining her hair.

Standing there at the starting line, I looked around me. It

was depressing. The guys who were obviously any good looked like they weighed about 125 pounds, with bony shoulders that a fashion model would kill for. Marathon running is fine, I guess, if you don't mind looking like Barney Fife. There were ten good runners; the rest of the field were obviously plodders with varying degrees of running ability. The gun went off and within two minutes, I was looking for the first of the aid stations, not because I needed any assistance but because I had devised a strategy, after reading several articles about what to do during a first-time marathon, of stopping for a few moments at every aid station along the way, making the race a series of shorter runs, rather than a long seemingly interminable one. I figured I could go five or six miles before stopping the first time, but, within a couple minutes of the start, I was ready for a break. I had jumped in front and was leading, but that was mostly because I had forgotten I was running a marathon. My basic instincts had taken over: when I hear the gun go off, I haul ass outta there, which is okay for a mile, not so great for a marathon. I hit the first half-mile in the marathon at about 1:58, which I probably could've kept up for another mile or so and then would have collapsed in a heap from which there would have been no resuscitation a la the Olympic Trials. So, I tapered off a bit (actually, I started walking real fast) to let the runners who otherwise would be leading catch up with me and even, in the spirit of goodwill and sportsmanship, let a couple of them pass me momentarily, before speeding up and passing them again, letting them know that I was a real runner, not some candy-ass marathoner who gradually moves ahead or falls behind so subtly that it only becomes obvious after the fact. Real runners, (those who perform on a track) go balls to the walls when they want to make a move, elbows out wider than Wilt Chamberlain on a defensive rebound, daring anyone to get in the way, unlike some pussy road-racer tippy-toeing past the runner in front of him and hoping that no offense is taken. There is one thing you need to understand:

A marathon is garbage running.

Marathons are races designed to see who can run slowly the fastest. (Props to sportscaster Bob Costa who, during the Seoul Olympics, made a comment about race walking, saying that a contest to see who could walk the fastest was like a contest to see who can whisper the loudest. He subsequently got a lot of shit for this comment from race walkers, although it was never clarified whether they were upset because he made the remark or because it was true.) Yes, running a race of 26.2 miles at an average pace of, say, 4 minutes and 55 seconds is impressive, but only in the context of the distance. A 4:55 mile is still a 4:55 mile. Fourteen-year-olds do them all the time.

The mile is the last honest race. (In truth, the sixty-yard dash is the only honest race, because that is the longest distance a human can run at top speed. After 60 yards, the winner at any distance is whoever slows down the least.) Anything beyond a mile is a compromise. Look, when little kids start out racing each other, they race to the corner, a sprint. The ones who win stay at that length, while the ones who lose move to longer races, maybe to the corner and back. And the ones who lose at that race each other around the block, and so on. The point is, nobody, unless they're getting paid a lot of money to do it, runs any farther than they have to. Why would a quarter-miler, who runs forty-four seconds for a quarter-mile, run a half-mile and a minute longer? Do the math. What it comes down to in running is this: If you can't run fast, run far. If I could run a world-class half-mile, why on earth would I put out the extra effort, both in the race and in training, to run a mile? People who run (and win) marathons—again, assuming money is not a factor—mostly do so because they can't run a fabulous 10,000 meters. Champion 3000-meter steeplechase athletes are capable of running a good 5000 meters, but probably not fast enough for them to win many races.

When I needed a few cheap laughs, I used to go out to an all-comers track meet, usually run at a local college on a Saturday night with only family and friends of the competitors in attendance, and watch the half-mile. Almost everyone in that race was, at one time or another, a quarter-miler who, for various reasons usually involving lack of speed, had moved up to the half-mile. They were not happy about this, and you could see it on their face as they lined up for the start of this race, because the half-mile is the toughest race there is. The mile is more strenuous (and glamorous) but you can make a serious mistake in a mile and, if you have the chops, still manage to come out on top, but the half-mile does not allow for mistakes like getting boxed in on the backstretch or going six-wide around the third curve. The half-mile is tough and will eat you alive, even if you win. And these guys lined up for the start all know this, and they also all know that they are really quarter-milers who just got a few bad breaks and are now stuck running the toughest race of all. You don't believe they believe they are really quarter-milers? Watch the start. The gun will go off, and because they all start together, it is a mad scramble to lead at the first turn, and the leaders are hitting the first 220 at about 23.5, with the others right behind. The first quarter will come in at between 48 and 50 seconds, with their beautiful quarter-miler stride still evident. But, after rounding the third turn, the real world starts to creep in, strides start to shorten, shoulders start to slump, and chests start to heave. The more talented (or delusional) manage to tough it out to the final curve, but that last 110 is generally a funeral procession, and the winner is not the runner who finishes the fastest but, as I said, the one who slows down the least. After the race, they all lean over each other, and it is difficult to tell the winner from the also-rans,

because they all look beaten, and in a sense they all are, because none of them is doing what they want to do and they are not having a very good time doing it. And they will do it again at the next meet. (Understand, I am talking about second-tier half-milers. The elite 880 guys are a different species altogether who can run a great mile, if they want to. They don't...probably too much work. You never run farther than you have to.)

When I said that the mile is the last honest race, by "last" I mean "longest". Any race beyond a mile is, as I said, a compromise for those who do not have sufficient speed to run shorter. A half-miler is faster than a miler, a quarter-miler faster than a half-miler, etc., but to run a fast mile—a 3:56, for example—is to average 59 seconds each quarter mile. That is very fast—about 15 miles per hour. (Try running alongside a car at 15 mph and see how long you last.) So, as I muddled my way through the Western Hemisphere Marathon, stopping indeed at every aid station, chatting up the locals and then passing almost everyone, I really had the attitude that by running a marathon I was slumming. All I wanted was to have it over as soon as possible. The most obvious way to achieve that, of course, was to run faster. But, at mile thirteen, I started having flashbacks to the Palm Springs Tram Road Challenge and, more importantly, how I felt in the days following that race. By mile fifteen, I had decided that I would just go through the motions for the last eleven or so miles. What happened, of course—remember me saying Bill Bowerman told his sprinters to relax, and they subsequently ran their fastest times?—was that I started inching up on everyone, and I could've made a plausible run at the leaders if I hadn't insisted on stopping at the last two aid stations. But I did...and still finished with a pretty decent time of 2:22.30, and got fourth. I knew that if I trained really hard for the next six months, I could improve my time by about seven or eight minutes and come close to winning a marathon some day.

Who would care?

Certainly, not me.

After the race, I had to endure a forced communal spirit that marathoners apparently feel compelled to share with each other, much like survivors of a terrible disaster, as well as interviews with the two newspaper guys and the cable television lady with the bad hair. Both the runners and the reporters were terribly sincere about all of this, and it was all I could do to keep from laughing. I kept thinking: *Do you people really think this is serious running? Do you know what it's like to have thousands of people screaming in your face for you to win? Do you know what it's like to have your wife screaming in your face because you didn't win?* I didn't want to appear to be condescending—I *was* being condescending, I just didn't want to appear that way—so I just smiled when I was supposed to, shook hands when I was supposed to, and otherwise kept my mouth shut.

It was not easy.

My attitude toward the entire experience was basically to say to myself on the way home that "...now I've run a marathon and I never have to do it again."

And I never have.

TRANSCRIPT

Station: KCCC-TV
Channel: 76
Reporter: Martha Weingarten

Martha Weingarten: We are here today for the running of the Western Hemisphere Marathon, a tradition here in Culver City since the 1930's. KCCC-TV, as Culver City's only cable television channel, is proud to broadcast this event. The weather today is good for runners of the marathon, cool and overcast with a slight breeze, but not so good for a reporter who has to cover a fashion show directly after this race. But, we journalists all make do. Today's race is—oh, they've already started! I was going to say that today's race has plenty of local athletes, including Tim Hardman, who used to run for UCLA and lives right by here in Venice. We will go back to our studios for a special feature and then rejoin the race....

MW: I'm here at the aid station at mile six, expecting to catch a glimpse of the runners as they rush by, but, instead, I actually have one of them standing here, drinking some water. According to my entry sheet, this is number 5, Tim Hardman, who I mentioned to you earlier in the broadcast. Excuse me, have you dropped out of the race already?
Tim Hardman: No.
MW: Are you tired? You don't even seem to be breathing heavy.
TH: No...just taking a break.
MW: Can you do that in a marathon? Do they have time-outs? I thought you had to keep running.

TH: Uh, no...there are no time-outs in running. But, you know, you can stop anytime you want. There's no penalty, although everybody passes you by while you're standing still.

MW: Isn't that a problem?

TH: Well, it would be if they were much better runners than me, but they're not.

MW: You sound very confident.

TH: Confidence has nothing to do with it. I've seen these guys running for six miles now. I haven't seen anything special.

MW: So you think you'll win?

TH: Well, I always expect to win, but this is new territory for me—I'm a miler.

MW: Isn't that—?

TH: Hey, I gotta go...rest time is over.

MW: Well, that was interesting, ladies and gentlemen, sort of like stopping a football player in the middle of a touchdown run to have a chat. He didn't look very tired, but they've only run six miles. *Only?* I haven't run six miles in my entire life. Meanwhile, here we have some shots of the runners warming up before the race....

MW: We're here at the aid station at mile fourteen, and here we have Tim Hardman again, just as he promised before.

TH: Yeah, that's me...Mr. Dependable.

MW: You've run fourteen miles and you can still make jokes?

TH: Well, the marathon is sort of a joke.

MW: What do you mean? The Western Hemisphere Marathon is the oldest road race on the West Coast. It—

TH: Sorry, I didn't mean this race…I was just talking about marathons in general.

MW: What do you mean?

TH: Well, I'm a track guy, and road races all seem kind of amateur. I've been trying to figure out why I'm running in this race

MW: Why are you running in this race?

TH: I have no idea. I just know that I spent so much time and trained so many miles for it.

MW: How do you feel?

TH: I feel like I'm throwing good miles after bad.

MW: No, I mean…how do you feel so far?

TH: Mostly, I'm bored out of my mind. I should've brought something with me to read…take care….

MW: There he goes again, ladies and gentlemen. What little research I've done told me Tim Hardman speaks his mind. He certainly does, doesn't he? Maybe we can catch up to him later in the race, since he doesn't seem much concerned with the way things are going….

MW: At mile twenty-four, you've stopped again?

TH: Yeah.

MW: How is everything?

TH: Pretty good, actually. I've been passing a few guys. I think I'm about fifth. I was getting ready to catch the guy in fourth when I stopped here.

MW: Why would you stop if you were ready to pass someone? Won't he get farther away?

TH: No problem. I'm a track and field guy, he's a road racer…I'll reel him in.

MW: So, you think this strategy of stopping for a few moments at ever aid station is working out for you?

TH: Well, did you see the guy I'm trying to catch?

MW: Yes.

TH: Was he huffing and puffing?

MW: He looked tired.

TH: Do I?

MW: No...but, don't you—?

TH: See you at the finish.....

MW: Well, this year's Western Hemisphere Marathon is now history. Diego Mara was the winner, with a time of two hours, fourteen minutes and five seconds. He and the second and third place finishers have all disappeared, but we do have the fourth-place finisher, who should look familiar to anyone who has been watching our coverage. Tim Hardman, are you pleased with your performance?

TH: I'm pleased that it's over.

MW: Are you happy with fourth place?

TH: Yeah, surprisingly enough, I am. I'm used to winning, I can't remember the last time I finished fourth in anything.

MW: I thought you finished fifth in the Olympic—?

TH: I always expect to win, but this was new for me. I wanted to experience it

MW: And what was it like?

TH: It was like what you would expect running through Culver City for two hours and twenty-two minutes on a cold morning to be...boring. Two hours and twenty-two minutes of my life that I can never get back.

MW: But you accomplished something, didn't you?

TH: Not really.
MW: Something good must have come out of this.
TH: Well...I got to talk to you.

At least I didn't get sucked into trying the triathlon. I don't doubt for a second that swimming, cycling and running in the same event is a considerable achievement. It is. Whether it is worth the effort is another story.

It's a moot point for me, personally, mostly because my swimming prowess is limited to a weak breaststroke. I have never been able to come even close to mastering the freestyle stroke. I suppose I could learn it, but I'm fairly positive I would never reach a level of ability that would justify the incredible commitment of time for training that swimming requires, not to mention that swimming for more than a few minutes has got to be one of the most tedious activities on the face of the earth (swimmers call it zen-like; *zen* is a code word for "boring'), especially when the benefits from swimming are taken into the mix. Swimming is mostly just a good cardio workout, so your body quickly gets used to that level of activity and will need more and more swimming for continued development. But, that's about it. Nothing else happens. There's no resistance, so you're not building any muscle. (The great physique that most swimmers seem to have comes from lifting weights in the gym, not from swimming.) And any substantial swim training program will burn up a shitload of calories, which means you have to eat a ton of carbs, a habit that is probably not going to be very easy to break if you stop swimming..

And running after cycling is a special skill, too. I tried it a couple times, running after riding a bike a few miles. My legs were like jelly, as if I had not been ambulatory for the last six months, so, again, I am not dismissing the ability of someone to go immediately from a competitive bike ride to a competitive run. It is impressive. However, so is Keith Richard's ability to stay awake for nine days and nights in a row. Most of us can't do that, either, but I don't think we'll be seeing Keef's picture on the cover of *Sports Illustrated* anytime soon. That something is extremely difficult to undertake and complete does not qualify it as important.

Challenges in life are always worthwhile, but what counts is not the degree of difficulty but what is accomplished.

Basically, what's the point of these sports?

Extreme sporting events, such as marathons, triathlons, whatever-athons, are all monuments to mediocrity. The Ironman Triathlon is a perfect example of this. Put together a decent two-mile swim and 120 mile bike ride and finish up with a so-so marathon and and you've got a good chance of winning. (I know a guy who ran a 2:49 marathon in an Ironman, which was a fabulous time for a triathlon. However, a 2:49 will not get you in the top 300 finishers in any major marathon.) Nobody sets world records, or comes even remotely close to doing so, in any individual event in a triathlon. It's basically impossible, because it would ruin the athlete and because these are not potential record-setting athletes. They are superbly-trained, well-conditioned, incredibly-dedicated people who can spread their above-average skills over three demanding events to the greatest possible effect. But, with one or two notable exceptions, enter any of them into a competition limited to just one of those events featuring world-class athletes, and they will finish well back in the pack.

Look, there's nothing wrong with any of these extreme sports as long as we understand that they are the penultimate athletic expression of the jack-of-all-trades-master-of-none concept. I don't begrudge the athletes in a triathlon whatever they've accomplished. We should just keep it in perspective.

I'm even going to lump the holiest of holies—the decathlon—into this "monument to mediocrity" grouping. Again, these are wonderful athletes, impressive physical specimens, but I am not aware of any decathlete ever coming close to setting a world record in any of the ten individual events that comprise the decathlon. (I know there won't be any competing tonight, even though all ten events are separately on the schedule.) The winner of the Olympic decathlon competition is always declared the "world's greatest athlete". He is not...but, he may be *one* of them. (I think professional basketball players are the world's greatest athletes. They combine awesome physical skills with hand-eye coordination that is world-class, and they do it almost every night, not several times a year, with a grace and finesse unheard of in previous generations for people of their size and strength.)

I've always thought the main reason that the decathlon is regarded as a killer athletic undertaking is not so much the ten varied and demanding events, although they are that, as it is the time consumed to complete the decathlon: five events each day, for two days. We've all seen these guys dragging their sagging bodies around the track four times for the last event, the 1500 meters, and the complete exhaustion they all experience when it is over. I think that's more the result of having to hang around for about ten hours each day waiting to compete in each event rather than the events themselves. I'm pretty confident that if a decathlon was scheduled where a group of eight athletes at a time moved on from one event to the other, without having to wait for the entire field to complete each event, they could probably wrap the whole thing up in one day—maybe six hours—or, if that proved physically impossible because of the demanding nature of the varied events, they could break it down into two three-hour days. There would not be the attendant waiting around to compete that takes up most of the athletes' time on the days of competition, and I think the performances would also be much better.

I mentioned this theory once to Dan...uh...not Dan O'Brien, but the other Dan who competed against him in the decathlon and went to the Olympics when O'Brien bombed out in the Olympic Trials. (Golly, I wonder what that felt like?) Anyway, I told him that I thought the most draining part of the decathlon was not the events so much as the waiting around and the stress involved. I don't actually remember his reply, but I imagine I would have if he had vehemently disputed this notion, so I'm guessing he more or less agreed with it.

Cycling is the one sport I have some real problems respecting. I suppose my basic attitude toward cycling could be summarized thusly: It must be nice to be able to sit down while you're exercising. I just have a really difficult time treating cycling as a serious sport. (Not to mention that you have to ride forever to get a decent workout. A one-hour run is a great workout; anything less than three hours on a bike is a waste of time) I always remember reading the comment Oscar Levant made about ballet in the early 1950's. (Oscar

Levant was a great wit, actor and pianist—not necessarily in that order—who was a close friend of George Gershwin. I took a music appreciation class at UCLA on Gershwin but ended up appreciating Oscar Levant more. Imagine Groucho Marx without the slapstick, or moustache, but with biting, sarcastic wit and serious classical music chops.) Oscar Levant once said that ballet was baseball for homosexuals. (Actually, he said "fairies." It was the Fifties, you know.) I have the same opinion of cycling as it relates to running. Cyclists wear those butch helmets, brightly-colored jerseys, skin-tight shorts and shoes that look like ballet slippers. Why don't they just put on a *tutu* and make it official?

Cyclists always make the point that riding a bike for six hours straight (nice choice of words, eh?) is tough. Doing anything physical for six hours in a row is hard. Typing for six hours non-stop is tiring, too, but I don't think anyone says typing is a sport. I've come across a lot of people who have stopped running and started riding because running was too hard on their body, but I've never met anyone who stopped cycling and started running because cycling was too tough. I read an article about Lance Armstrong (I guess he won a bunch of Tour de France races; I have some articles about them that I've kept for some reason or other. The only thing I remember about Lance Armstrong was that he was part of the support group when Greg LaMond won the Tour twice in the 1990s.) Armstrong ran the New York Marathon a while after winning his seventh Tour de France in a row. After the race, which he ran in 2:59, he said it was the toughest physical thing he had ever done. So, basically, Lance Armstrong was saying that running over the flat streets of the New York for three hours was harder than riding a bike up and down the French countryside for three weeks. I think that tells you all anyone needs to know about the relative merits of cycling and running. I read that Armstrong only has one testicle, losing the other one to cancer. That means he still has one more than most cyclists.

I always liked encountering cyclists when I was running, especially if we were going up a hill. (Not that I used to run hills much, but every once in a while, mostly to remind myself why I didn't run up hills.) If you have any serious running ability—and I do—it's not very difficult to keep up with or even pass most cyclists up a hill. They'd be struggling along, huffing and puffing, while I'd nonchalantly glide alongside and start a conversation, not talking about anything in particular but just trying to convey to them that even though I am getting more out of this workout than they are, I am also having a better time, and I would usually manage to inject my standard comment about how nice it must be to be able to sit down while exercising, which always got me a few glares, although a couple of the guys might laugh if they were honest enough about it, and then I would tell them that they should put a little TV on the handlebars and maybe a mini-fridge on the frame and then they could be really comfortable. I would smile and wait for a reply, but there was never one forthcoming, so we would move along in silence, side-by-side for a few yards, before I'd look over at them, wave and say I had to get going, and kick it into another speed as I pulled away from them, always looking around at just the right moment with my final comment: "Have a nice ride, girls."

I'm sorry, but cycling is a pussy sport.

(And I'm not going to even get into what seems to happen to male cyclists and the damage to their reproductive capabilities as a result of their perineum (look it up) being pushed down against that hard-ass bicycle seat for hour after crotch-crushing hour. I just think of it as population control among the trolls of the athletic community.)

If I've offended any cyclists...please accept my apologies, ladies.

from:
EdwardWoodward<edwdwd@yahoo.com
to: Morgan <Fisher@SportsIllustrated.com/mf

Morgan: I received an interesting communication from a Judith Hardman yesterday. She was the wife of Tim Hardman, the runner who collapsed and almost died at the Olympic Trials. We had a fairly long talk on the phone and, at first, I thought she was just the typical ex-wife of a once semi-famous jock trying to cash in because the support payments stopped or something like that, but it got more interesting the more we talked. She never picked up the divorce papers so, legally, they are not divorced, just separated. But he doesn't know that, which is only one of a list of things he doesn't know. Hardman is living by himself out in the desert in some shack, and he's got a whole lifestyle thing going on with his running, and from what she says he's as jacked-up as he ever was about the mile, and he trains every fucking day, according to her. This guy is stone serious, even though he's never run in a race for years, and he really thinks he still has it. I don't want to go too literary on you, Morg, but this sounds to me like Robinson Jeffers on spikes. (You might want to Wikipedia that reference.)

You've got a long lead-in to the Olympic Trials, and I know how your mind works and that you're probably already relegating this story to the "Where Are They Now?" files, but, from what she told me, there is a lot more to this than just nostalgia. Mentally, the guy has some problems. His father died from Alzheimer's and he seems to have a very early onset of the first stages, with a complete short-term memory loss. He cannot remember anything that has happened in about the last six or seven years, so he depends on written notes and some funky old video camera from the 80's to get him from day to day. But, she says that, physically, he's a stud, probably in the best shape of his life, and she says she's seen him run some times that are close to what they're getting in stadiums today, and he's doing it without competition. Plus, she says he's not whacko, that he's perfectly rational on a day-to-day basis, and that if you met him, you wouldn't know there was a problem, but if you met him the next day, it would be as if he had never seen you before.

I really think we have something here. She told me I was the first person she had contacted about this, because of my work on the Lance Armstrong thing, and that nobody knows or cares about what is going on with this guy. I talked to Lou at the agency and he's waiting for your call. I think we could really have something here. I'm even willing to cut you guys some slack on an advance and the per diem. I really want this, and I'm willing to give you guys first shot at this because of the way you treated me when nobody else would touch me. Get in touch with Lou, and let's get busy!
Ed

When they called me earlier today to tell me when they were going to be picking me up, whoever it was on the phone sounded and acted like he was talking to a six year-old, telling me three times when someone would be there for me, as if I am a complete idiot and can't do anything for myself. Look, I'm the first person to admit that my day-to-day regimen is a little tenuous (without the notes and tapes, it would be a whole lot of tenuous) but I'm not a moron. I really don't need anyone treating me as if I am ready to fall apart. I now understand why some people with handicaps really get aggravated when they feel they are being condescended to. Within the structure of any given day, I get along just fine.

My days have a pre-set plan: pretty much the same every day. One thing I do not do is start off the day with a big breakfast. Breakfast is not the most important meal of the day, and all these people who say that you need a big breakfast to start the day are out of their mind, saying you need a full meal on account of your stomach being empty; it is empty because the food has been digested and the energy generated by that food is ready to be utilized, but, instead, these people want you to fill up your stomach again, so that you have the calories from last night's meal (plus any snacks) and now you're adding a whole new set of calories from your breakfast on top of everything you already have, and so by the time you set out for work you've got two meal's worth of calories in your system and you probably don't burn many calories at work (sitting at a desk only burns 100 calories an hour), then you have a break and suck down snacks, probably followed by a lunch that has a boatload of calories, then back to your desk, and so on, and people don't understand why they cannot lose weight. The main reason is that breakfast is bullshit. Lunch is the most important meal of the day, because the energy from that meal is what is going to start working for you later when you hopefully do something energetic and cardio-centric before dinner, which should also be light, and the basic guidelines you should follow for your meals is what us Catholics use during the two days of fasting—Ash Wednesday and Good Friday—in Lent, which is to have your two smaller meals, in this case breakfast and dinner, not be bigger, in total, than your main meal (lunch) and I would say that dinner should be two-thirds of that smaller-meals equation and breakfast only one-third (a large banana and a big glass of skim milk, maybe with some chocolate protein powder in it, works for me) and to those people who protest that no one can function all morning, even if just sitting at a desk for four hours, on merely a piece of fruit and some milk, I would say that every Sunday morning there are marathons commencing all across the United States, and I would guarantee that almost no one out of the thousands starting those marathons (not to mention 5 and 10 k runs, bike races, and whatever else) has a full breakfast in their stomach, and maybe did not even eat or drink anything at all since the previous evening, and yet they are going to engage in constant activity for, on average, the next three and a half to four hours, burning about 3600 calories during that time, without any ill effects from the lack of a full breakfast, and to any suggestions that these people are highly-trained athletes, I would answer that the front runners in a marathon may be highly-trained athletes, but anyone who runs a four-hour marathon is basically a plodder with a high threshold for boredom, who may sit at a desk for the rest of the week with a full stomach, burning about a hundred calories an hour and wondering why he trains for marathons and still can't lose any weight, and the culprit is not his training, but his breakfast.

Later in the morning, I do some   physical activity, usually shooting hoops on a portable basketball set-up I have by the side of the house, which is an important part of my exercise regimen because I do it for about twenty minutes at a constant pace, running after the ball non-stop, so that by the end my heart rate is significantly elevated—a target for a tough cardio workout is to take your age and subtract it from 220, the result being the number of beats per minute your heart should be pumping; mine is in the mid 170's, and I have gotten closer to that with my basketball workout than I ever have in running, and I think that is because of all the quick stops and starts in shooting and chasing a basketball, whereas running tends to be more fluid—and there is also the idea that shooting baskets is fun, which means you are tricking your brain into thinking you are just having a good time when, in fact, you are having a serious cardio workout that has lots of running without ever setting foot on the track. After that, I have a big glass of skin milk and an energy bar, rest for a little while, take care of whatever needs to be done around the house and then have a serious lunch (enough protein for muscle growth, more than enough carbs for energy, and a crap desert for the soul). After eating, I do some reading, take a nap, then go out and do my running workout for the day, after which I will do some do some body-weight exercises such as push-ups and pull-ups during the season and weight-lifting during the off-season. (I only do legs during the off-season: I put my car in neutral and lean back against the front of it and push it with my legs—never my arms—the length of my dirt driveway, then get behind the back of the car and push it the same way back to its original spot. When I finish, both my quads and my heart are thumping like the drum solo on *Wipeout*.) I do my weight-training after running, because I already have my pulse rate up high and the weight training allows me to continue it at an elevated stage without having to run too much and over-train. (Working out after running also preserves whatever cuts I get from my weight-training, whereas running after lifting would smooth them down. Vanity? Probably.) Then I take a shower, have a light dinner, walk around or shoot some more hoops (to keep the metabolism up), read something, maybe play a little guitar, and then crash. Not a bad life. One might think that to do the same thing every day would be boring, but since I can never remember anything, it is always fresh. I know what I've done because of my notes from the day before, which is the only way I could pyramid my training—building on what I've done the day before—and so I act as if (and pretend to myself) that this is all part of one long process when, in fact, every day is isolated from every other day. I will tape my most serious running workout of the week, usually going down to the local high school (which has a decent track for the high desert, which is not exactly a beehive of athletic activity) late Sunday morning or early Sunday afternoon, after Mass, and do 440s, 880s, sprints or whatever I have been pointing toward that week, and then go home and analyze the tapes to see how my form and stride look and if I was running relaxed (remember Bill Bowerman?). For awhile, I tried to run barefoot, which is I something I used to do when I ran on my cross country team at Venice High School, because our cross country course was at a park that was all grass, and I've never forgotten the feel of cool grass on my soles as I ran (I've also never forgotten stepping on pebbles that were hidden in the grass) and even though there's not much of any grass in the desert, running on the football field at the high school brought back pretty good memories. If tonight goes all right, then I think I might plan on trying to eventually run a mile barefoot, and I think it would be incredibly cool if I could run barefoot at a regular big-time meet like the girl from South Africa at the 1984 LA Olympics or the Ethiopian in the marathon at the 1960 Olympics in Rome whose names escape me right now but whose example I would love to follow, not just because of the nostalgia factor, but also because running barefoot is actually better for you and makes you run correctly, whereas running shoes allow runners to cheat by landing on their heel and then rocking forward as their foot hits the ground, something no one would ever do if they were barefoot because, one, it would hurt too much and, two, cause heel injuries, so you would have to run properly, landing on the front half of your foot and pushing off on the ball of your foot as you take the next stride, and I have a minute or two on tape of me running barefoot on the football field in the grass and my form is impeccable and so is my smile, because that is the way you are supposed to run, and while I understand it would probably cripple the world economy if people stopped buying running shoes and ran barefoot, everyone should at least try it, because if they do they will fall in love with running all over again, just like I did.

You might have noticed that when I mentioned all the things I do during the day, there was no mention of television. There are two things I do not have in my house: a television and a mirror. Well, that's not actually true—there are a television and mirror somewhere on the premises, but I use them so infrequently that neither is a part of my life. The reasons, for me, are fairly simple.

Television is a problem for me because so much of what is on television—especially weekly dramas and comedies—relies on continuity, which is the one thing that my life does not have. Even the news broadcasts generally refer to what happened on previous days to put what they are talking about into perspective, which makes sense for most people, but for me is sort of like re-inventing the wheel on a daily basis. Sports, too, fits into this category, unless we are talking about individual events, rather than a conference or playoff series, and even then you have to know something about what the participants have done before to make it all relevant. (The Super Bowl, for example, is just another game to me unless it has been fully explained how these teams got to this point. I can watch a track meet and appreciate the performances, but I probably will know little or nothing about any of the runners.) On some sports broadcasts, they will bring the viewers up to speed on the consequences of what is being contested, otherwise it is boring to constantly research before watching any sporting event on television. I used to go to bars and have some guy who'd had a few beers fill me in on the information I needed to know. But, for the most part, television is a very small part of my life, so now the TV sits on a shelf somewhere in the garage. I know where it is, and if I really want to, I can bring it out since, as far as I can tell, it works fine. A special occasion would be a really important sporting event or if I see a movie listed in the newspaper that sounds interesting. Movies are okay, unless it is a sequel or something like that.

Not using the TV mostly has to do with practicality, but my reasons for not having a mirror in the house are more altruistic. First of all, I do, as I said before, have a mirror, which wass stashed away under the bathroom sink. It's small and the mercury or whatever it is that gives the reflective image is starting to wear away a little, but I can still make out what I look like. But I rarely use it. Like I said earlier, I have a pretty good opinion of myself: nice hair, good teeth, tight waist, a few muscles in the right places. All of that has already been established, so I decided, according to my notes, to let it go at that. It's too easy, especially when you live by yourself, and especially when you like yourself as much as I like me, to spend an inordinate amount of time checking yourself out, making certain everything looks perfect. So, instead, I just have a medium-size floodlight behind me on one wall of the bathroom and a bare wall over the sink, onto which I project my shadow, which allows me to make certain my hair doesn't make me look like Alfalfa in the Our Gang Comedies, and if my posture is okay. Other than that, what do you really need a mirror for? It was under the sink, if I really needed it, but that was rarely the case.

And, yes, I realize that the video camera can sometimes function as a mirror, but the camera is usually only on me if I'm doing something active, during which time I rarely look my best. When I make video notes to myself, I'm generally off-camera, doing a voice-over, focusing the camera on what I'm talking about if that's possible.

The interesting thing to me, and something I only realized and made note of a couple months ago, is that the two things in my life that I have restricted—the television and the mirror—are both visual items. That may simply be coincidence, but I don't think so, because the visual in my life is what reminds me that I have no independent concept of what has happened yesterday, or the day before that, and so on. Ideas are abstract, but visuals are not, which is probably why I read so much. I read some fiction, but mostly history, partly because I really enjoy history but primarily because it tends to re-tell events that I know or have heard of and can relate to. I just finished reading a book, according to my notes, on the First World War, a conflict which for me, like most people, is a complete mystery in terms of why it happened, how it happened, and how it ended. I know, like everyone else, that the reason the war started was because of the assassination of the Archduke Ferdinand but I've never understood why that was the cause. (In some ways, I still don't.) The book is very long and full of facts, and, if you can get past having to read about graphic accounts of thousands of men being slaughtered on the battlefield day-after-day for no apparent reason, it is also endlessly fascinating: one thing I learned, for example, was that at Verdun and the Somme there were entire settlements behind the allied lines that catered to the soldiers who were off-duty; soldiers served four days at the front, four days in reserve, and had four days R and R at the camp that had been set up behind their lines and which featured cafes, bars, women, and whatever else, so, if you managed to survive four days at the front—and hundreds of thousands didn't (England lost an entire generation of men)—you could probably cruise through your reserve time on automatic pilot and then go wild for four days before going back to hell. Pretty amazing, eh? I never knew that.

Of course, the truly ironic (or cynical) among you would probably suggest that I would really only need one book or magazine, which I could read over and over everyday, since I wouldn't remember reading it. As a matter of fact, I must confess that I have done that on occasion. For instance, if I really enjoyed a book, such as the World War I book, I might leave myself a note indicating that yes, I have already read it—look, I'm not gonna treat myself like an idiot—but it's so good that I should read it again. I remember seeing a *Seinfeld* episode a long time ago where Jerry wonders why people read the same book over again, sarcastically remarking that if you read Moby Dick again, the ending changes and Ahab and the whale become good friends. Actually, I have a pretty good-sized library, with little notes to myself on the front pages, sort of like a book review. Remember my saying how I started a daily journal when I was at UCLA but then got rid of it because it just seemed too self-involved? Well, these little reviews in the front of my books are the closest I have come to a journal since then. I might make mention of what was happening to me at the time of my reading the book, in general what my life was like, little things like that. It's sort of a cheat, but it's also kind of helpful, another way of letting me know how things have or haven't changed for me.

Newspapers are cool, because they are immediate. Anything that is published every day does not have much too of an overview (that's what magazines are for), taking everything pretty much a day at a time which, of course, is what my life is all about. Newspapers are my reference point for the rest of the world, and are just so enjoyable to read. The *LA Times* doesn't deliver out here in the rural areas, but I used to try to get into town every few days and pick up a copy, and I had a guy at a liquor store who would save me back copies from days that I missed. I'd clip out articles I wanted to keep. Newspapers are history that I can read as it unfolds. I have read a few articles that have mourned the closing of some newspapers, the down-sizing of others, and the basic fear that computers will eventually replace newspapers as the main source of information. Man, I hope not. Without newspapers, I might as well live in a cave.

Radio is important to me, too. I have an entertainment center, a really old one, that includes a record player, a cassette player and recorder—I record some of my notes on there—and also has an AM-FM radio. I sometimes get news from the radio, but I prefer the newspaper for that, because I can hold it in my hands. Mostly, I use the radio for music. I have a decent record and cassette collection (no CD's; don't like 'em, don't need 'em) but there are still plenty of things I like to hear on the radio. I usually listen to the classic rock stations because I can relate to all the songs. Besides, that's about all we get, since it's mostly people over forty out there, with demographics determining playlists. Hearing a song from my youth is a great pleasure. I'm sure that's true for most people, but it takes on a special significance for me because all I have is the immediate present and the distant past. For some people, nostalgia is quaint. For me, it's an emotional lifeline. (I've heard something called "indie rock" a few times. It seems to me to have three main features: no guitar riffs, no guitar solos, and some yuppie singing through his nose.)

But I don't play music nearly as much as I used to. I enjoy the silence. In the high desert, it is pretty quiet most of the time, except for dogs barking—everybody seems to own two big dogs, which would always bark at me as I ran past them. The thing that got me is that I rarely saw any interaction between these dogs and their owners. The dogs were always stuck out in a barren back yard, surrounded by an ugly-ass chain link fence. It's as if they were just pieces of furniture. I think the dogs were just barking at me for any interaction with a human being, however brief it might be.

But, other than the dogs, it's very quiet out there. At night, you can hear a pin drop a mile away. So, to suddenly have Led Zeppelin pounding away, even inside your house, seems a little contrary to the whole vibe of the area. And, the quiet is very nice. I'm not afraid of my thoughts. I don't need background music. Something I didn't realize until I started keeping it quiet in the house is that time is more important and more immediate now, because when I had music going all the time, it was generally songs that I knew and was sometimes only subliminally listening to, helping to make the time go by. Of course, that is the whole idea with music in stores—to make you forget where you are and what you are doing and just act without thinking. But, with no music, I really pay attention to what is going on around the house and in my life. My life is no longer a fast-paced movie with a soundtrack but a story which I can savor and enjoy at my leisure.

I have not been able to transfer this new-found solitude to my car, however. Turning on the radio or popping in a cassette is almost Pavlovian with me as soon as I turn on the engine. Occasionally, I've tried to turn off the music and drive in silence, but that usually lasts for about twenty seconds and then I'm cranking the tunes back up again. Silent driving, unless I've got some intense internal debate going on with myself, is not illuminating, it's just boring.

I don't drive a car...I drive a Corvette. It's a '74—a 454 with a 4-barrel carb and a 4-speed (lots of 4's, eh?)—the last Sting-Ray, I think. I bought it with some shoe money I got from Nike, plus trading in my old Jag. The shoe thing never happened, but I got to keep the money, so I bought the Vette.

It was old then and is older now, but not old enough to be a classic...just old enough to be old. (Judy always hated that car. I got it while we were dating, but didn't tell her until after I bought it. I think she was under the impression we were going to use that shoe money as a down payment on a house when we got married.) If I park next to a new Mercedes, my old Vette will get all the attention. In ten years, the Mercedes will just be another car, but a Corvette will always be a Corvette. I've met guys who had tons of money tell me they'd always wanted to have a Corvette—guys who could probably pay cash for a new one—but they never did.

I have a theory about that: There is no justification for owning a Corvette. It's completely impractical, with only two seats and almost zero luggage space. You will probably need a second car, and another one if you have a family. Some people, even those with lots of money, are not prepared to make that commitment.

It has nothing to with money.

It has everything to do with balls.

My problem with driving the Corvette is that I know I'm driving a Corvette, and my attitude towards other drivers is, essentially, "Get the hell out of the way—this is a Corvette!" Seeing me in their rear view mirror as I look like I'm preparing to drive right up their ass—the '74 has a vicious-looking front hood that is perfect for an automotive rectal examination—tends to make almost all drivers change to a slower lane. I do it all the time, I guess, but since I can never remember if I've done it before, every time seems like the first time, which is just as thrilling as it sounds. Sometimes I'll be driving, minding my own business, and someone will pull up next to me and give me a drop-dead stare. I can only assume that on some previous occasion my car looked like it was going to mount his and he got out of the way. In those situations, I just wave and give my biggest smile. It all works out. After all, I'm driving a Corvette, and they're not.

The one thing I do not do is speeding. I don't mind pulling a few g's going around a tight corner at 55 or 60 miles per hour (I love centrifugal force) but I avoid pedal-to-the metal most of the time. If you drive fast, you get used to it real quick, and you either have to push it up to some ridiculous speed—and if you should blow a tire or something, you and your car will be doing cartwheels down the highway before you realize there is anything wrong, because you have had absolutely no training on how to deal with this type of situation—or you will have to back off, and I guarantee that 70 will feel like 30. You can also get a ticket. Try dealing with a police officer or a traffic court judge when you have no memory whatsoever of what has happened before today. One or two evasive or dodgy answers can open up an entirely new line of questioning (let's just say it all worked out, but not quickly). The way I speed is that most of the roads out here in the high desert are at a 70 mph speed limit. If I'm waiting at a traffic light, when it changes to green, I jump on it and almost red-line it in first gear—only the '74's with a 454 have a four-speed—and push it into second just below the speed limit, then I back off. So, technically, I haven't exceeded the speed limit, although I have been told that the California Highway Patrol does not look favorably upon jack-rabbit starts.

Actually, I don't drive the Vette too much. It inhales gasoline at a prodigious rate—the '74 is a Series 3 (C3) Corvette, the first model of which came out in 1968, so we are talking state-of-the-art early-60's technology here, when gas was about eight cents a gallon—and I can't afford that on a continuing basis, so I only use it every once in awhile, but that makes it very special. Those drives on a long desert highway, cruising along listening to the Zep or Nirvana— that's my time machine. It's like nothing has changed. I videotaped me once on one of those drives. *Total bliss*. I was almost crying as I talked on the tape. Cruising down a desert road in my Vette is not better than sex, but it's close.

Judy and I started going out to the high desert a couple years after we got married, because it was so completely different from West L.A. (not as nice, of course, but different); we found this little place to rent near Landers (an area famous for earthquakes) for weekends and when the guy who owned it died, his wife sold it to us cheap, so we started going out there all the time and I got to know the area really well and since nothing has really changed out there between now and then, my memory from way back when allows me to move around as if nothing is different when, in fact, almost everything in my life has changed, the only constant being that I'm still a runner, but, other than that nothing is the same—no wife, no family, no memory—but no one knows that because no one would think to ask (I really doubt anybody out there spends much time paying attention to the world of track and field). When we used to go out there, Judy would pretty much stay locked up in the house, just wanting to relax, so I would do all the errands, and I don't even think people knew I was married, or much less cared, because you have to understand a couple things about the desert, one of which is that the people in the desert mind their own business (to the extent of more or less ignoring everyone else), and the other is that there are two basic types of people who live in the desert: those who have already made it and have come to the desert to retire and those who are never going to make it anywhere and the desert is the only place they have left (there is a small group in the middle who service the other two, and you understand here that I'm talking about the small villages and scattered settlements in the desert, not the bigger communities and towns). And if you think that living in the desert is optimal, consider that in the Old Testament, when God got pissed off with the tribes of Israel, He didn't condemn them to wander the beaches for forty years, and He didn't condemn them to wander the mountains for forty years...*He condemned them to wander the desert for forty years*, which I think is a pretty good indication of God's attitude about the desert, and which is why you will find the bottom-feeders of society who live in the high desert go through an entire summer without getting any color—the sun shines there about 350 days a year and nobody's got a tan—because they never go outside except to get in their car and drive somewhere. (Maybe they'll have a red neck from the crappy outdoor job they have, probably the only employment they could secure given their previous work and/or criminal history). People there all say they love the desert, but you never see anyone outside. No one is out walking or tending a garden...there's just houses surrounded by all kinds of crap that they never get rid of. In the city, these people would be called "shut-ins". In the desert, they call themselves "desert rats". They're really just hermits. The desert is the beach for nerds.

I wish I was at the beach. The beach is all about movement...the tide comes in, the tide goes out, waves crash on the shore...in the winter, the storms bring in debris, in the spring, it goes back out...things are changing. In the desert, nothing changes...it's the same every day. It gets me down, and I can't even *remember* yesterday. The desert is the world's biggest vacant lot. People do things at the beach...run, walk, swim. They're tanned...they look healthy...they *are* healthy. People at the beach are studs. People in the desert do nothing...nothing at all. The desert is a still-life painting...and so are the people who live there. I wish I lived at the beach. I could still train. I did it before. (That's how I got started, remember?). I tried to call my mother once to ask her if I could stay there. I guess she changed her number.

The Soles That Try Men's Times

Mitch Wheeler's Track World:
Tim Hardman: Past Present

June 10 of this year was an incredibly slow news day. Nobody famous died, nobody famous got married, and nobody famous got sent into drug rehab. The Associated Press was so desperate for something to put across their wires that they must have started raiding obituaries, looking for anything or anyone with even the slightest connection to something newsworthy. Thus it was that the news of Richard Hardman's passing came across my desk.

Who is...who was Richard Hardman? I was asking myself the same question when I read the obituary and saw the name of Timothy Hardman, Richard's son and sole surviving carrier of the Hardman name.

Still doesn't ring a bell? Oh, come on, it hasn't been that long ago since Tim Hardman blazed around the track for three and a half screaming laps in the 1500 finals at the Olympic Trials before collapsing in a heap. He managed to get up and run to the finish line, but the damage had already been done, and he finished fifth.

Oh, you're probably saying to yourself, *that* Tim Hardman, as in... whatever-happened-to-Tim Hardman? The 24/7 news cycle has really destroyed our recollection of the recent past, although I am certain that Hardman's collapse will be played over and over again as this year's Olympic Trials commence in six weeks.

So, without belaboring the obvious too much, where exactly has Tim Hardman been? And how would I possibly be able to find him and get the answer, since he seems to have fallen off the face of the earth, at least in terms of newsworthiness? A few phone calls got me the information that he was living out in the high desert, incommunicado, and it was explained to me that my interest in him would be passed along and, at his convenience, he might—might—give me a call from a pay phone somewhere out there, since he seems to be one of the few people in the Western Hemisphere, or any hemisphere, without a mobile phone.

But the call did come, and it wasn't at three in the morning, it was in the middle of the afternoon, but it could just have easily been in the middle of the Twilight Zone. It was a fairly surrealistic conversation. I am not certain where he has been for last few years, but I got the feeling he has yet to completely return.

There was a certain ethereal quality to his voice that it made it seem as though he was relaying my questions to the real Tim Hardman and then giving me back the response.

So, where exactly has he been for the last few years?

"Oh, everywhere and nowhere."

See what I mean?

Does he think often about what happened at the Olympic Trials?

"Well, it crosses my mind every now and then, but not as much as you might think. My memory seems to be short-circuiting."

So, he doesn't remember what happened that well?

"Oh, no, it's burned into my memory—what I was feeling, what I was thinking...all of it. But what happened in the days and months...and years afterward...gets a little blurry."

I asked him if he was still running.

"Yeah...somewhat. I'm running, but not everyday and not with any particular goal in mind. I've got a project planned that might change everything."

And what was the project?

"Well, we've got a house out here on five acres, set back from the road, and I got the idea of putting a quarter-mile track around it, so I could have my own training facility. It would be a lot of work, and I really haven't gotten beyond some preliminary planning stages...."

"So, you still want to compete?"

"Oh, sure...sometime. It's all in the future right now. Nothing is happening at the moment."

"You said 'we'. Is your wife there, too?

There was a pause long enough to make me think the connection had gone dead, but then he finally spoke.

"Uh...no...we're...uh...not together. It's been..."

His voice trailed off and again I thought the connection was dead, but then he spoke.

"...difficult. It's changed everything in my life."

There followed another long pause, and I spoke up, trying to keep the conversation going. I mentioned that I had seen the obituary about his father, not exactly a breath of fresh air to the discussion, but I needed something to keep it going.

"Uh, yeah...that, too. I was surprised that he died, but not shocked. I guess he could have died anytime in the last couple years, so his death wasn't a shock, but I was surprised because he didn't seem any different than he had for a long time."

"Had you seen him recently?"

Another long pause.

"Uh...no. I really had no way. I mean, I've got my car out here, but there was no way I could drive all the way into LA and back again."

"But you did go to the funeral?"

"Yeah...sure. I couldn't miss that. He was a great guy. When I was a kid, he used to take me to track meets and talk about famous runners he had seen when he was my age. He's a lot of the reason I became a runner. And he was a lot of fun, too. It was really sad to see him lying there in the hospital bed, just sort of staring into space."

"What was the funeral like?" I know, a stupid question, but I was grabbing at straws in the wind.

"Like any other funeral, I guess, where it was expected. Everyone was sad but, like me, nobody was shocked. A lot of people said that he was in a better place. I don't think like that."

I was afraid the conversation would end, but then he spoke up.

"I felt more alone at that funeral than I ever have in my life, even out here in the desert all by myself. My wife wasn't there—that was the first time I had gone to a family function without her. She sent a card and some flowers. And my mother wasn't there, either."

My ears perked up at that.

"Your mother wasn't at your father's funeral?"

"No." There was a long pause. "She has some kind of aversion to seeing dead people, I guess."

Even her husband?

"Yeah, I guess so. She just stayed at home and got everything ready for the reception afterwards."

"Were there many people there?"

"Not as many as I expected, and some of them who were there I had never met before. Some guy named Ross Backer sort of seemed to be in charge of everything, because my mother looked a little tired. It looked like she didn't want me to bother her...so, I didn't."

That didn't seem a very promising subject, so I tried to be light and breezy.

Did he visit any of his old haunts, like UCLA, or any of his old friends when he was in town?

"No, I just got in my car and drove back home right after the funeral."

"So, you were able to—?"

"Hey, look, I gotta go. It was good talking to you."

And then the connection went dead. Is his career dead, too? He almost did, but it looks now as if he never will.

--Andy Franklin

So, the high desert allows me to go back to a time when I was like everybody else and to live as if nothing has changed at all. I've made a couple of improvements to the property, the most important, by far, being something that I wanted to do for a long, long time: put in a running track around the outside of the house. I drew up the plans while Judy and I were still together. I laid all the groundwork, but then my personal life got kind of complicated with the divorce and the MCI and everything, so the track idea pretty much fell by the wayside, but, fortunately, I had written rather copious notes about exactly how I wanted the track to be developed, and so, when I finally moved there for good, even though my short-term memory was shot, I had all these papers that I stumbled on one day that I had forgotten about and which immediately triggered in my mind all the plans that I had been making for the track years before and which still seemed as fresh as the day I drew them up, and you can't imagine the joy I felt when I saw those papers, not only because I really, really wanted that track, but mostly because it was the first time since my memory problems had started that I had a complete connection with some aspect of my past, a real project, not just some attitude, something I could actually work on, something that was a continuation of what I had started long before and which I could follow through on now, making me feel that maybe there still was a chance that what I was enduring was just a temporary situation, as a result of the Olympic Trials and the divorce and everything else, and even if this wasn't the case it was more than ameliorated by the fact that I could finish, in my current compromised state, an idea that I had developed when I was completely whole, and you would not believe how liberating that was to me, and one of the greatest days of my life— I would call it *the* greatest day of the life I am now living— was when I finished the track and took my first lap around it, with my feet feeling as if they barely touched the ground the entire 440 yards (no metric bullshit, remember?) around the loop and not being able to restrain myself from screaming out to no one in particular and to everyone in general, "Top that, motherfuckers!"

It is a very cool track. I spent a whole lot of time on it, which might not be obvious if you just took a look at it, since it runs through the bushes and everything, but to me it is an engineering feat of no small means, if for no other reason than the fact that I am not the type of person who is very good at implementing solid ideas (I don't know if it's the right-side or the left-side of the brain thing, but whichever side it is, that's the side I don't use), and even if I have the best intentions in the world, I generally do not have the intellectual capacity or wherewithal to take an idea for some specific, hands-on project, and turn it into a reality, whereas with abstract ideas, such as writing, I am more capable and comfortable, so for me to take on a project such as this and bring it to fruition is really a bit of a wonder and something I am terribly proud of and would be pleased to show anyone, although I never have, which is probably just as well, since they would only see a slightly-bumpy, slightly-uneven four-feet wide path meandering around the exterior of my house for a quarter of a mile, whereas I would see an engineering marvel, a canvas on which to paint my masterpiece—the mile run—and an affirmation that I still am able to accomplish something besides making it from one day to the next without doing irreparable harm to myself.

The property our house sits on is five acres, and even though all the surrounding acreage is owned by people waiting for the high desert to bring them riches—dream on—there is nobody on either side of me for at least a mile, and even those people are only there for short periods of time. People keep to themselves. I have a suspicion there are also a couple of meth labs around here, since I usually see at least one police car in the area every day, but the last thing those people want to do is attract attention to themselves (not that anyone would notice freaks who never wash or comb their hair, have scabs all over their face and weigh about eighty-five pounds each, right?). I spent a lot of time measuring out exactly how to plot the track. As I said, I had pretty extensive notes from years earlier about exactly how the track was supposed to be laid out, and so, to a certain extent, all I had to do was connect the dots, but some of those dots were very complicated, and when you realize that the decisions you are making now are the ones you will have to live with for a long time to come (which is pretty much, come to think about it, what life in general is all about) then you will take the time and energy to get it absolutely right, which, in this case, meant measuring and re-measuring ad nauseum, which was only lessened by the fact that since every day is a new day for me, I didn't have déjà vu—actually, I never have déjà vu—about doing the same thing over and over and over again to make certain that everything was absolutely right, and because I was doing this with materials and protocols that would not have been high-tech five thousand years ago (unless you consider two sticks and a ball of string for measuring to be high-tech) it was a very time-consuming process, and I think the fact that I could not remember the feeling of having done the same thing the day before, and the day before that, kept me from throwing my hands up in despair and just walking away, which was probably what would have happened in my previous, non-MCI life. (I seem to remember actually starting the first couple measurements for the track a long time ago and being so frustrated and impatient that I threw my measuring tools to the ground and, in fact, *did* walk away, leaving them to lay there until I stumbled across them years later and realized their significance).

Basically, what I did was measure steps around an oval with straight sides and a semi-circle at each end (years ago, by walking around an old 440 track, I had determined that 500 of my steps constituted a quarter of a mile), with my house in the middle, which works out well since the house is set back from the dirt road by about a hundred yards and if I need to suddenly go in the house for something, I don't have to come in from the back 40, plus it also looks kind of cool from an aesthetic point of view to see the house right in the middle of everything, sitting inside the track, because that is really what my life looks like at the moment, my life at home surrounded by running, and so to take an overview of the property gives a very real sense of what my life consists, which is what I guess the whole form-following-function thing is all about, but I don't anticipate I'll have anyone from *Architectural Digest* pounding in my door, wanting the first chance to take pictures of my project, mostly because it looks like crap, although it does exactly what it is supposed to do. I've been trying to figure out a way to have timers at every 110 yards of the track to show me splits for what I am running.

The track (like I said, it's really just a wide path, but calling it a track sounds so much cooler) took about four months from start to finish, mostly because, as I said before, I went over everything so many times to make sure it was properly measured and the proportions were right, with that taking almost as much time as the actually digging of the track itself and, yeah, it was digging, because I wanted it below the surface level of the ground (actually, I wanted it elevated, but the logistics, not to mention the ball-busting labor, involved in moving enough dirt to have an elevated quarter-mile track were so daunting that I realized after about eight shovels full of dirt that it wasn't going to happen) but when you realize after you get a couple inches below the floor of the high-desert that the soil starts to resemble solid rock, then your commitment to the project is immediately questioned, and it became obvious that it was going to be one long, hard slog for any number of reasons, not the least of which was the keeping on the lookout for the Mojave Green, a particularly venomous rattlesnake that I am told makes its home in the area, with the green being not some blarney-stone green from Ireland that would stand out but an olive green that blends in perfectly with the Joshua trees and most of the foliage that dots the area, and whose bite is followed by a helicopter ride post haste to the Loma Linda Medical Center, where they will try to save your ass if you get there in time for the anti-toxins to start working and where you can ride out all the marvelous effects that a bite from a Mojave Green can produce, such as the swelling of the affected areas to elephantitis-like proportions and searing headaches and rushes of pain for a few days. I have never, in all my years spent in the high-desert, actually seen a Mojave Green but I've been been assured by locals they are a threat, with warnings that sometimes are so dramatic that I often get the feeling that what we are dealing with is a high-desert version of a snipe hunt, but just about that time I will suddenly read in the local paper that somebody was bitten by a Mojave Green, usually after doing something really stupid, such as trying to catch one (holy shit!) or sticking one's hand into a collection of rocks for no apparent reason, with the last paragraph of the article always saying that person was expected to live, although that was probably not their first choice.

Anyway, I spent a hell of a lot of time with one eye on what I was digging and the other, more attentive eye on the surrounding area, which did not speed things up at all but did keep my mind at ease. This was all undertaken in the middle of the summer, and even though the high desert does not reach the temperature extremes of the low desert, the sun is relentless, with no shade whatsoever from the Joshua trees, whose relationship to trees in general is about the same as the relationship of camels to horses—vaguely similar, but no one would ever confuse the one with the other. (I subsequently discovered that Mojave Greens tend to get out of the sun during the day, probably lying in the shade, sipping on a cool one, and watching some dumb-ass dig in the midday heat.) I decided to have the surface of my track a foot below the ground level, dumping the dirt on each side to form a barrier against, well, Mojave Greens. There is something *zen* about digging, doing the same thing over and over again. (You remember what *zen* really means, don't you?) That I anticipated. What I did not anticipate was that since I had no day-to-day memory of what I was doing, I did not grow more accustomed to the task at hand, and every day seemed like the first day on the job. My body understood and accepted that I had been doing this day after day, but my mind approached every day as the first one, looking for shortcuts and long breaks. Generally, when it comes to hard work, for most people the mind is willing, because it can cruise along on automatic pilot, but the body, which has to do all the work, is weak. In my case, my body was ready to rumble but my mind was timid, looking for ways to get out of the project. It was very strange, I noted on one of my tapes—I devoted a lot of video time to documenting my work on the track—to be in a situation where your body feels great and your mind is the weak link. When I finished for the day, I would go into the bathroom, look at the shadow on the wall at night and I could see from the curves on my upper arm that my biceps and triceps were getting bigger and more shaped; my shoulders were broader and my delts almost came to a point; from a sideways point of view, my pecs loomed out over my abs. I even grabbed the mirror one time, just to make sure, and then I started laughing, realizing that I was kind of buff, something I had always secretly wanted but not at the sacrifice of my running (remember the creatine?). Then I sensed that I was getting a little too fascinated by myself, so I took the mirror out to the garage and threw it on a top shelf, still accessible, but now probably in the company of a few nasty black widow spiders.

The reason I did all of this work in the summer, the ultimate bad time to start such a job in the desert, was that summer was when I took a break from running. (If you are competing, all the big meets are in the summer and you train, train, train; if you're not, that is when you take it easy.) I wouldn't stop running, but I would stop running every day, or with any great effort. It was mostly for conditioning and to remind myself that I actually enjoy running, that it isn't just a job. Serious running was from October to May, jogging was June to September. (Of course, my jogging may be a little more intense than yours. In case you're wondering why I was doing all this "serious" running if I hadn't competed in a race in a long time, the short answer is that a competitive training schedule kept me in shape. For the long answer, check back later tonight.)

I love my track. It came out pretty well, all things—such as basic ineptitude—considered. It isn't completely flat, but there are no hills or valleys, and I soften up the surface enough running with my spikes that I can run without shoes. The ground sometimes was too hot to run barefoot, so I tried wearing some expensive ($15!) running socks, very tight with a little padding on the ball of the foot and the heel. Perfect. I timed myself in those socks and did a 4:07! It was the greatest, most organic run of my life, every step a soft, comfortable thud as I landed and then pushed away from the ground. I really felt as if I was animal running across the desert, like the rabbits I see all the time. Running without shoes on an all-weather track, however, would take some getting used to, plus the fact that the other runners would undoubtedly spend some time trying to step on my feet with their spikes, but it's something to think about. (Wasn't the Ethiopian who ran barefoot in the marathon at the Olympics in Rome in 1960 named *Bikila*? It just popped into my mind.)

I actually ran a 3:58 on my little track about three months ago. It was late in the day with no breeze, an almost unheard-of combination in the high desert, and I just felt, according to my notes, that I had a special run inside of me. I even taped the whole thing as best I could, showing me at the start and coming around at the end of every lap, to save for posterity. It was hand-timed, and I was carrying a stopwatch as I ran, so there is a chance of deviation in the correct time (maybe I squeezed it off and on while I was running) but I don't know how much and so I think the time is fairly legitimate, which is why I am where I am right now and why I will be where I will be later tonight. A 3:58, even allowing for variations of accuracy in the time, run on a homemade track, without any other runners, is a hell of an accomplishment. What actually happened was I thought I saw a Mojave Green on the backstretch of the first lap and, scared shitless, hauled ass to a 58, decided to take a chance, and on the second lap I realized it was just a bungee cord, and by that time I was on my way to a 1:55 at the half; then I calmed down to a 62 for the third lap and came home with a 61. It was perfect, because I finished at 3:58 with a 2:03 for the second half-mile, and I knew I was capable of doing that last half at least two seconds faster, so I felt I had something going on but I just wasn't sure since I hadn't run for time in a long while. When you are away from competition either against others or just against the clock for a long time, it's tough. Training is training and competition is competition. They are both running, but as different as night and day. Remember how I said that your race strategies determine your training? Well, your training also determines your race, but it cannot predict it, because training is primarily from the neck down, and racing is mostly from the neck up, by which I mean that you process information as the race progresses, and react accordingly, something that cannot be duplicated in training (yeah, I know, you can race against your training partners, but that is not competition, that's cooperation). In horse racing, the term "morning glory" refers to horses that run fabulous times by themselves in the morning workout but then fail to repeat the effort when put in competition with other horses in the afternoon. Well, if the effect of competition can have that type of adverse effect on a horse who, judging from its workouts, has great potential, that effect can exponentially expand when it comes to humans. Remember Merv Lincoln? When Herb Elliot was in the race, he didn't win but he ran a great time. Without Elliott, even though Lincoln usually won, his performance was much less impressive. You train with your body; you race with your brain.

All of which is my way of saying that the 3:58 was a training run and nothing more. The time was not as important as the fact that I could seemingly dial it up whenever I wanted to. And isn't that what is really important in life, not so much what you do as what you know you are capable of doing? I think confidence is almost as decisive as ability. Without confidence, ability is just potential and nothing more. And when you have almost no clue except for a few cryptic notes and maybe a little information on a video tape about how your life is progressing, confidence has to be secured and safe-guarded with as much vigilance as possible. Knowing I could run the 3:58, and even faster, was more important to me at that moment than the actual time. That is for later…maybe later tonight.

TRANSCRIPT

Transcriber: Mary Welton
Interviewer: Edward Woodward
Subject: Judith Hardman

Edward Woodward: Mrs. Hardman, it's good to finally meet you.
Judith Hardman: Nice to meet you.
EW: I'm sorry for the delay in arranging this interview, but *Sports Illustrated* takes a long time to get projects approved.
JH: This will be with *Sports Illustrated*?
EW: Yes…didn't anyone tell you?JH:
JH: No….Oh, that's great…Tim has been reading that since he was a kid.
EW: Does he read it now?
JH: I think so.
EW: Does he…does he know if he reads it?
JH: Well, if he saved an issue or tore out a particular article to save, then he would know. I haven't seen too many copies or articles when I was there, but—
EW: So, you go out there every once in awhile?
JH: Every three weeks.
EW: That often?
JH: Sure, for a few years now. He was out there for a few months by himself before I started going. I had set him up and everything, but didn't go out there until just after his father died.
EW: Did his father dying have anything with your deciding to go out there?

JH: Indirectly. I didn't go to his father's funeral, and I think that was the first family gathering we had not gone to since we got married. I sent a card and some nice flowers, but something in the back of my mind told me that wasn't enough.

EW: And...it wasn't?

JH: I should have been there. I heard about how lost he looked—his damn mother didn't even go to the funeral and wouldn't speak to him at the reception. I heard she had been hanging around with some rich guy. I immediately felt so sorry for Tim, and that's when I realized how much I loved Tim and how much I missed him.

EW: You're certain it wasn't just pity?

JH: Pity doesn't make your heart ache.

EW: Well...that's interesting. But, let's not get ahead of ourselves. I want you to start at the beginning, and tell me everything. I'm not saying it will all be in the article, but we need to get it all down.

JH: Will this be a long article?

EW: I would imagine five or six pages.

JH: Will he get on the cover?

EW: I don't make that decision...they do. But, my experience is, if they think the story warrants that kind of attention, they put it on the cover.

JH: Tim and I were supposed to be on the cover while we were going together.

EW: I read something about that.

JH: Tim was running some great times, so they came out and took a bunch of pictures and interviewed us just like you're doing.

EW: What happened?

JH: Some hockey player scored three goals in three games in a row, and, the same week, his wife had triplets, so....

EW: It must have been a slow news week.

JH: Sure, that's why we were going to be on the cover in the first place. Instead, we just got a one-page article near the back and two small pictures.

EW: You must have been disappointed.

JH: Not as much as our relatives....

EW: Well, I can almost guarantee that will not happen this time, because they are going to fold this in with their coverage of the Olympic Trials in six months and the previews of the Olympics themselves.

JH: This won't be out for six months?

EW: Is that a problem? These things take time. All my other research is finished, but we'll need another interview after this, and then the article has to be written, checked, edited, and re-written. It takes time.

JH: I understand. Will we have to wait until it's published before we get the money?

EW: Please...please don't discuss that with anyone. SI does not pay for anything, and if they knew I was giving you even fifty cents for this story, they would cancel it immediately.

JH: That's about what you're giving us.

EW: Patience, Mrs. Hardman. If this story is as good as you say it is, and if he is still as good as you say he is, the money thing should take care of itself.

JH: Can we get started? I have a client in two hours.

EW: A client?

JH: I'm a financial planner. Didn't you know that? I thought you said you researched everything?

EW: I have. So...you met Tim when you were both students at UCLA?

JH: In an English class. I didn't even know who he was, but I figured he must have been on the track team.

EW: Why is that?

JH: All he ever wore was running stuff.

EW: In class?

JH: Everywhere...in class, on a date, at church....

EW: At church?

JH: Sure. We'd go to Mass on Sundays at St. Paul's in Westwood when we were dating, and he'd wear a track warm-up suit. It wasn't sweaty, and he looked good, but...

EW: So, you knew he was an athlete?

JH: Or, doing a very good impersonation of one. No, I'm joking. I knew he was a runner. He looked like one. I just didn't know how good he was.

EW: You didn't follow track and field?

JH: Who does? It was football and basketball for me. Even now, I don't know or much care about track. The only reason I cared before was because Tim was competing.

EW: How did you find out about him?

JH: I asked a couple girl friends, and one of them gave me a copy of that day's *Daily Bruin* and there he was, all over the sports page.

EW: Did you go to see him run?

JH: It was the last meet of the season, against USC, and it was at the Coliseum, which was SC's home track, and there weren't too many UCLA fans there.

EW: How'd he do?

JH: He won by sixty yards, and broke four minutes for the mile. It wasn't even a school record—a guy named Bob Day ran about two-tenths of a second faster in the Sixties—and I guess everyone expected it from him, so there wasn't much of a commotion. I walked up to him, he was all sweaty, and gave him a big hug. It was the first time we had ever embraced. We hadn't even gone out yet and had only talked in class a couple times, so I wasn't sure he'd even remember who I was.

EW: Did he?

JH: Oh, yeah. He said my giving him a hug was the best thing that had happened to him all day, and he had just beaten SC and run his best time of the year.

EW: You were impressed?

JH: Impressed? I was in love.

EW: Already?

JH: Oh, yeah. Definitely.

EW: Can we switch gears here and talk about Tim's home life? You're looking at your watch…is there a problem?

JH: I have to drive out to Encino for a new client, and if I'm late, he will shit.

EW: Uh…what were Tim's parents like?

JH: I never met his father. By the time Tim and I got together, the father had already been stuck away in a home for a few years.

EW: Stuck away?

JH: Oh, yeah. Tim's mother saw to that. She wasn't going to have a feeb hanging around the house. Those were her exact words.

EW: Tim told you that?

JH: She told me that.

EW: Can you describe Tim's mother for me?

JH: Not if you're going to quote me.

EW: I can paraphrase.

JH: She was the coldest-hearted bitch I have ever met in my life. She had no interest in anyone but herself. She didn't give a damn about anyone else. The first time I met her, within five minutes I wanted to tear her a new one, and that opinion has never changed from that day to this.

EW: And how did Tim feel about her?

JH: He adored her.

EW: Why?

JH: She was his mother. She was his family.

EW: Didn't aunts and uncles come by?

JH: Nobody came by—no one could stand her.

EW: No one but Tim.

JH: He thought the sun shined out her ass, which would have been extremely difficult, because she had her head up there most of the time.

EW: How long has it been since you last saw her?

JH: Not long enough.

EW: Did she—?

JH: Can we talk about something else?

EW: Of course.

JH: Thanks.

EW: So, you and Tim started dating?

JH: It was wonderful. He was so sweet, and a real gentleman. He never tried to make a move on me. In fact, I was usually the instigator. I didn't know if he was too shy or too moral, or both.

EW: Too moral?

JH: Yeah, he's always been a real strict Catholic, which I kind of liked. I'm a good Catholic but... not a great Catholic. Tim is.

EW: So, you were happy with that?

JH: Oh, sure. Football guys and everyone used to come on to me all the time. I love football, but not football players. They're basically a hard-on with shoulder pads.

EW: How did Tim express all this to you?

JH: Well, at first, he didn't. Bu when it looked as if we might get serious, he sat me down and explained the facts of life.

EW: And what were they?

JH: That he had never had sex with a girl and wouldn't until he got married, period. After we were married, that would be another story, but before then, it was hands off.

EW: And that was all right with you?

JH: I had no choice, but he was worth it.

EW: How long did you date?

JH: A year. We got married exactly one year to the day after our first date. That was Tim's idea. I thought it was kind of cute.

EW: A big wedding?

JH: Oh, yeah. We filled St. Paul's in Westwood. My parish church is in Reseda and his is in Westchester, by LAX, but we always went to St Paul's when we were dating, so that seemed the perfect choice. My parents spent a lot of money on the wedding. I just wanted a small wedding with a few friends and family, and use the rest of the money for a down payment on a house, but I'm their only child, so....

EW: What did Tim want?

JH: Tim just wanted to get married.

EW: And—?

JH: ...Tim's mother wore the most ridiculous outfit you've ever seen. I think she was trying to upstage me at my own wedding. I wanted to shove that dress so far down her throat that she'd be shitting rhinestones for a week.

EW: How was it after you got married

JH: Wonderful...the best time of my life. We rented a small bungalow in Venice, overlooking one of the canals. I think Dennis Hopper lived down the street. Tim and I had the best times there. I never wanted it to end...I thought it never would.

EW: Did you want to buy that house?

JH: Sure, but it was too expensive. Tim had gotten some shoe money from Nike before we got married, and I thought that money could be saved for a down payment, but it didn't work out.

EW: So, you just stayed in Venice?

JH: Yeah, it was comfortable. Too comfortable, really. Tim was running good times, getting nice appearance money, I had gotten my degree and started a business…things were going well.

EW: Then things went not so well?

JH: Uh…yeah. It started with the Olympic Trials thing, although there were problems before that.

EW: What kinds of problems?

JH: Well, I guess you could say that Tim's philosophy in life is that anything worth doing is worth over-doing. That's great in love, but not so great in some other things.

EW: Such as?

JH: Such as…everything. He wanted the best wife, the best marriage, the best house, the best mile times, the best stuff…he wanted it all.

EW: And you couldn't handle his selfishness?

JH: Oh, Tim doesn't have a selfish bone in his body. He wanted it all for me…for us. He was confident he could do it.

EW: Could he?

JH: Well, he had the best wife, and the best marriage, and the best mile times…

EW: But, the other things?

JH: They might've happened, but I think the thing with his father was weighing him down. He always said his wedding day was the happiest and saddest day of his life. The happiest because…well, that's obvious…and the saddest because his father wasn't there…he knew his father was just staring at a wall in a hospital room while his son was getting married, and there was nothing either of them could do about it.

EW: He sounds rather melancholy.

JH: Tim? No, he was just facing reality. It didn't drag him down and he kept it in the background, hidden away, until after the Olympic Trials, and then it started coming out. Depression, confusion, isolation.

EW: Gradually?

JH: Oh, yeah…it took awhile. I could see where it was going and tried to stop it, but….

EW: Did you give up trying?

JH: No, I never gave up. I still haven't.

EW: Is he worth it?

JH: Uh….yeah. That's why I didn't finalize the divorce, and why I go to see him every three weeks. Yeah, he's definitely worth it.

EW: You told me before that he doesn't know that the divorce never became final.

JH: What's the point? He's out there by himself.

EW: A cynic might say that since you are still his wife, you could easily, with his condition, get legal control of his finances.

JH: His only finances are about $850 a month from the government.

EW: Which you control?

JH: I make sure he gets the money every month. I don't take any of it, if that's what you mean.

EW: What I meant was, some people might say that you are playing your hand close to the vest in case Tim actually achieves some sort of a comeback.

JH: Well, some people might think that, but, you know the old saying—"Dirty minds see dirty things."

EW: You control his life, don't you?

JH: I have a certain amount of influence on his life, but he does what he wants.

EW: Within the sphere of your control?

JH: Well, if by that you mean that I'm protective, I would agree to that.

EW: Protecting your investment?

JH: I'm not going to comment on that.

EW: You have him isolated out there in the high desert, away from everyone else, and you control his life, don't you?

JH: You remind me of an attorney I did a
deposition with a few years ago.
EW: I'm not trying to cross-examine you,
but I do need to cover all the bases.
JH: You know, the traffic on the 405 this
time of day is terrible. I can't afford to be
late for my appointment. Good day, Mr.
Woodward

So, anyway, even without that time, I would have been
thrilled beyond belief with my track. I really felt a bit like
Robinson Crusoe, there on my little island, with the track
around the house being my beach or border. Lately, I have
only been going out once week or so for groceries and other
necessities, such as the mail, if there is any. The rest of the
time, I am at home, content beyond belief. So, the obvious
question, I guess, is why am I not at home right now? Why
am I here? The closest I can get to a sensible answer is that
there is such a thing as being too comfortable, that you need
some irritation—you know all about the sand in the oyster
shell and the pearl, right?—and because I am a runner, a
competitive runner, whose claims that he only runs for
himself are as bullshit as the writer who says that he only
writes for himself. It may possibly be true, but only if fear is
the dominating force in your life. And when I say fear, I am
not simply talking about the fear of failing, although that can
be incredibly powerful.

Some people are afraid to fail...and some are afraid to
succeed. If you fail...hey, you gave it your best effort,
hopefully, and it didn't work out, no problem, let's move on.
But, if you succeed and are a true competitor instead of a
glory freak there suddenly is the responsibility to prove your
success is justified, that it wasn't just a fluke, and also a
responsibility to try and even surpass your performance the
next time you compete. Quitting while you're on top,
leaving them begging for more, etc., can be legitimate, but I
always suspect there's more to it than that. Jim Brown
notwithstanding, the great ones always want more, even if it
puts their legacy at peril. Ask Michael Jordan.

(Of course, there's also the problem that, no matter how
fabulous an athlete may have been, by the time he reaches an

age at which most men are just starting to hit their stride in their chosen profession, he is ready to retire or has already done so, and he may live another sixty years but will probably be remembered for what he did when he was a young man. In some ways, his life ended a long, long time before he died.)

GOOGLE ANNOUNCES PUSH FOR U.S. TRACK WITH MEET

(AP) Internet giant Google today announced its sponsorship of an annual track and field competition to be held at Stanford University, to be called the Stanford Relays. "We think that U.S. track and field has been overlooked for far too long and is danger of becoming a niche sport, like soccer, popular only every four years with an international competition—the World Cup for soccer and the Olympics for track and field—and the rest of the time suffering from benign neglect," said Wilson Reilly, vice-president in charge of community relations for the company and, not co-incidentally, a middle-distance runner at UCLA before getting a masters degree in computer science at Stanford and moving down the road to Google when the company was just a fledgling enterprise. "We intend, over the next several years, to upgrade *gratis* the facilities at Stanford Stadium, starting with an all-weather track that will be the ultimate racing surface in America, if not the world. Then, we will bring the best athletes from around the world to compete. As a former miler, I can guarantee that the Stanford Mile will be the pre-eminent event at the Stanford Relays. We are going to do this right, and fully anticipate that the results for the American sporting scene in general and American track and field in particular will be positive, immediate and long-lasting." More specific information about the details of Google's involvement are expected to be announced within several weeks.

I imagine a lot of people—probably everyone who's ever heard of me, actually—would be shocked to hear that I'm running some pretty decent times again. It doesn't surprise me, because I always knew what I was capable of, and one of the blessings of having no short-term memory at all is that that there is no inventory of despair or regret to build up in your sub-conscious as you try to move forward with your life, which has really worked out well for me because I know that enough negative things have happened to me over the last ten years or so to really shut down any internal expectations on my part for getting better, either as a runner or as a person, but one of the few positive aspects of this MCI thing (it's hard to believe that there could actually be anything even remotely positive about it) is that while I know that some things have happened to me over the last few years that I wish had never transpired, I don't have any emotional memory of them, so they are just facts and nothing more, and I could just as easily be talking about someone else (in a way, I am) considering the lack of feeling and remorse I have about what has happened to me since the Olympic Trials, and even my divorce is something which I know I should feel bad about, and I do miss my wife, but only in the way that anyone would miss their spouse when they are not together, with the divorce being information I know is unpleasant but cannot actually prove it by my feelings or emotions, and I'll you exactly what it is like because I knew a guy about my Dad's age who told me he was once diagnosed with prostate cancer, and he went in and got some treatment right away and apparently they caught it in time and now he is cancer-free, but the point here is that he never felt any illness whatsoever, never felt the slightest twinge of anything, and his basic line to me was, "They told me I had it, they told me they took care of it, and now they tell me it's gone", but the guy himself has no emotional evidence or scars from what he went through and he told me that people called him a cancer survivor, and he guessed that he was, in the technical sense, because he did have cancer and he did survive it, but the term "cancer survivor" conjures up images of someone at death's door, undergoing chemotherapy and other dreadful treatments, battling for the right to stay alive, and suddenly—and perhaps miraculously—triumphing over cancer at the end and emerging grateful just to be alive, whereas my friend went into the hospital at six in the morning, was put to sleep at seven, had some radioactive seeds injected into his prostate at about eight, woke up at ten, was home by noon, took a couple Advil, had a nap, and by three in the afternoon he was back to normal, and the next day he played eighteen holes, with his friends all calling him a "cancer survivor" when he really had no emotional investment in the procedure at all. Understand? That's they way I feel about my situation: I know unpleasant things have happened, I know they have affected me negatively, and I know my life has been altered in a way that can't be remedied. I know it but I don't feel it, which doesn't mean that I'm numb (sitting alone here at night in the middle of the desert is not my idea of a good time) but only that I can't process the information, which is all it is, nothing more. People always say that knowledge (or information) is power. That's bullshit. Knowledge is trivia, nothing more. Knowledge plus implementation *can* be power, but generally it takes knowledge plus implementation *plus* ability to equal power. (I know how to shatter the world record for the quarter-mile: average 10.5 seconds for each 110 yards; I can try to implement that strategy by running around the track as fast as I can, but if I do not have the ability to average 10.5 seconds for each 110 yards, I will fail, regardless of how much information I have. The *if-you-believe-it-you*-can-*do-it* philosophy of the pop-psychology airheads would be laughable if it didn't have the potential for emotional damage to the bozos who actually believe that nonsense and proceed forthwith.)

This morning I had room service send up a copy of today's *New York Times*, which had a rather lengthy and exhaustive about the Catholic Church and the priest molestations. It was really depressing reading. I had some stuff in my notes about this, but the article laid it all out. It's really difficult to believe that all this happened, but there is just too much evidence, and too many admissions of guilt, to come to any other conclusion. I refer to the perpetrators as SPWHTBCPs—Sexual Predators Who Happened To Be Catholic Priests. But, you can't ignore the environment in which they functioned, and their superiors who allowed the behavior to continue. However, it's difficult for me to keep from appreciating the irony that for so many years the Catholic Church hierarchy was castigated for a perceived negativity toward homosexuals whereas, in actual fact, they were being overly lenient with some of them and, in some cases, criminally compliant. Dorothy Day, one of my heroes (more on her later, I hope) once said the Catholic Church was the cross onto which Christ was nailed, the idea being that the Catholic religion may be sublimely formulated, but it is administered by fallible individuals who sometimes demonstrate their fallibility with depressing regularity. (When I was eleven, I joined The Future Priests Club. I didn't renew my membership, but if they allowed married priests, I would really consider it, or would have before things changed for me.)

What I do not understand is people walking away from the Church because of what has happened. For some, I think it was the excuse they were looking for to leave; others say we don't need any church (or Church) because Jesus said whenever two or three were gathered in His name, He was with them. To me, they are like the people who say you can get a good workout without having to go to a gym (see me through on this analogy, okay?). You can make an argument for that, and health-equipment suppliers make tons of money based on that assumption. However, most of that equipment ends up in a closet, unused, or given away to a thrift shop. You *can* get an excellent workout at home, but you probably won't. A home is for living, and the distractions are numerous. A gym has only one function, to work out; a church has one primary purpose, as a place of prayer and worship. When you go to a gym or a church, you are making a commitment just by being there. You know why you are there. You have no other reason to be there.

People who either pray at home or work out at home are cut from the same cloth and usually do just enough to get by, if they remember to do it at all. The people who only deal with God at home are in as poor shape spiritually as those who work out at home are physically. Both are flabby. (I am amused by people who say they don't need religion because they are "deeply spiritual". This is code for "I'm too lazy to go to church".)

The reason I get a hair up my ass about going to church is the way I was raised. My Dad always made certain that we made it to Mass every Sunday, and to every Holy Day of Obligation. Once he was away, my mother could have slacked off, with all she had to do, and it would have been understandable. But, she didn't, and I've always admired her for that. We may not have always been on time, but we were always there, and I've begun to realize over the last few years how difficult it is to keep your priorities in order. When my Dad was still at home, my mother seemed mostly like some pretty lady who got dressed up all the time, and liked to go to the best restaurants and hotels we could afford. But, when she had to, she did the right thing. She could have veered off course and no one would have blamed her. But, she didn't, showing a depth I didn't know was there.

Religion is an area of life where an inability to remember or be dragged down by the past is a definite positive. As an imperfect but balls-to-the-walls Catholic (I'm sorry, but my attitude is basically: If you ain't Catholic, you ain't shit.), not being dogged by all of your past transgressions makes it a lot easier to look Jesus in the eye. (Those of you who really aren't into religion—until, of course, your mother goes in for open-heart surgery, and then you're down on your fucking knees night and day—can take a five-minute break here, because nothing I have to say here is gonna sound like anything you want to hear.) I cannot remember a time in my life when I did not go to church, when I did not care about religion. I guess it is sort of in my DNA. I can't imagine my life without my religion. When I am dealing with someone who has no religious bent or orientation and I try to look into their soul, I feel like Gertrude Stein: ...I can't see any there *there*.

Religion is important—any religion. (It's just that some, the Christian ones, are more important than others, and one, Catholicism, the original Christian religion, is the most important one of all.) Religion subjugates the ego. At church, when you through the door, you ego goes out the door. If it doesn't, you're wasting your time, just like the Pharisee about whom Jesus talked who would go into the temple and review for God all the things, such as fasting, prayers and giving of alms, that he did on a regular basis to make him the hell of a guy that he obviously thought he was. Jesus, of course, essentially says the Pharisee is full of shit and not fit to carry the jockstrap of the humble beggar in the rear of the temple pleading with the Lord for forgiveness. Religion should be humbling. Most of the hierarchies of any religion, especially Catholicism, don't look particularly humble as they move about in flowing robes during elaborate rituals that to the untrained eye look more like they belong at the halftime of the Super Bowl than a solemn religious service. Personally, I find a lot of the liturgy boring. I am not a big fan of ritual. (I get the feeling that Jesus wasn't, either.) I remember once going to Mass on Holy Saturday evening to fulfill my Sunday Mass obligation. I hope this isn't blasphemous to say, but, basically, the Holy Saturday service seems to me to be the *Inna Gadda Da Vida* of the Catholic liturgy. It just goes on and on and on. I gave it twenty minutes and then decided to come back the next morning for Easter Sunday Mass.

I must confess—we Catholics do that a lot—that the Crucifixion and, to a lesser extent, Easter Sunday, are not the focal points of my devotion to Jesus. I understand their importance, that they are basically the foundation of Christianity. But they do not move me the way just sitting in a church and having a heart-to-heart with the Lord does. I guess I approach Good Friday and Easter Sunday the same way as I do the things that have happened to me in the last few years and what I just finished discussing: I understand

and appreciate all of it, without being as moved as I should be. I'm sure this is a terrible spiritual shortcoming on my part. I really try to get worked up, in the best sense of the term, about all of it, but I always end up treating Jesus as a much wiser and cooler big brother, whom I love with all my heart, for whom I would do anything, and away from whom I never want to be. In my own, staggeringly insufficient way, I hope that is enough.

I always feel terribly sorry for non-Catholics when they worship God. Their intentions can be just as genuine and deeply-felt, but all they have is words—they go to some generic church, hear biblical texts read with great solemnity, listen to a sermon, sing a few up-lifting songs and then go home. The difference between the Catholic Mass and the other churches' service is the difference between making love and reading a romance novel. Catholics get the love and passion and emotion, while the others get Fabio on the cover without a shirt and not much else.

I do a lot of praying during the day...*a lot of praying*, just little bits and pieces while I'm doing other things around the house. For example, there's an ab exercise I do that involves squeezing your palms together, flexing your arms and pecs, sucking in your abs, and holding for a count of ten. Well, instead of counting to ten, I just say a Hail Mary—it takes about the same amount of time and now you're working your body *and* soul. (Actually, what I ended up doing was adding an Our Father at the beginning and a Glory Be at the end, doing ten reps, and you've got a decade of the Rosary.) Sandwiched between two sets of those ab squeezes, I undertake my own set of leg-raise exercises— none of those bullshit crunches or sit-ups, which are mostly excellent for putting a strain on your neck and back—that has given me a serious six-pack on my abs. "The bicycle" is the best ab exercise there is: Keep your back flat and slowly bring a knee up to the opposite elbow, then alternate, as many times as possible, while sucking in your abs; mix that up with any other leg-raising exercises you can come up with (lying flat, bringing your straightened arms and legs to meet up above your mid-section, grabbing your toes and squeezing for a beat, and going back down, about twenty times, is a killer) and you can ignore those people who say diet is the main way to get a six-pack. I don't even call it a six-pack, I call it "the chapel", because to me it looks like a little church with three sets of pews and an aisle down the middle, leading to a little steeple that rises up between the pecs. Cool, huh?

There is one prayer I only use on certain occasions. It is so special to me and its use is so restricted by me that I won't even say the prayer now, for you, or at any time during the day around the house, during work or training. It is a prayer I only say at the beginning of a race, just before the gun goes off. It's a special prayer written by St. Teresa of Avila back in the 1500s. I came across it when I was in Tucson for the NCAA Championships during my last year at UCLA. They had a van take a few of us to a nearby Catholic church for Sunday Mass. As it happened, they were saying a Spanish Mass, and since I neither speak nor write Spanish, I read the English translation in the missalette. During the sermon—*they* now call them "homilies"; *I don't*—I had a choice of either nodding off or looking through the missalette for a few prayers to read while the priest droned on in Spanish. I came across this prayer from St. Teresa and thought it was really cool. It was only six lines, about thirty words, but it really moved me, and I spent the rest of the sermon memorizing it. Later that day, at the finals of the 1500 meters, I remembered that prayer just before the starting gun went off, said the prayer to myself, and ran my best time in three years and won the national championship. Would I have won the race without saying the prayer? Don't know. But I know that I did say the prayer and I did win. So, that tradition—calling it a superstition when prayer is involved seems almost sacrilegious to me—started then and has been with me ever since, and I have done well with it (my final year at UCLA before that prayer had been less successful). In fact, there has only been one time in my running career since I discovered that prayer that I did not use it—the Olympic Trials. We were at our marks, with the gun ready to go off, and I was leaning forward too much and almost had a false start, but I caught myself in time; however, just then the gun went off and I had no chance to say my prayer. One of my most vivid memories of that race is not the fast pace or my collapsing. One thing that I remember most from the race itself was my continuing wonder as to how I was able to be running those fabulous splits for each lap without having said my special St. Teresa prayer. I remember distinctly being elated with my times as I ran around the track and simultaneously dejected that it was happening without any help from my prayer. Was it really just a superstition? I actually had that thought floating across my mind as I ran the backstretch of the last lap. Suddenly, I found myself on the ground—when you collapse as suddenly as I did, you are already down before you realize anything has happened (there is no movie slow-motion in real life, you know)—and my first thought was not to wonder what was going on, but to say to myself, "Sorry, St. Teresa…my bad." I was almost laughing to myself as I said it, acknowledging a gotcha from God. If you have ever seen the extreme close-up on video tape of me as I get up on my feet and start running again, trying to catch the guys who passed me while I was down, you can actually see a little smile on my face. Commentators have said it was a grimace, but, no, it was a smile. I knew…you ignore prayer at your own peril.

L.A. DAILY NEWS

WHATEVER HAPPENED TO TRACK AND FIELD?

I was at Drake Stadium on the UCLA campus last Saturday for the annual USC-UCLA track meet. It was a beautiful late spring day, high 70's, not a cloud in the sky, the stands full of anxious family and friends of the competitors, the Bruins and Trojans in their colorful track suits and racing uniforms bounding around the track as they prepared for the contest, excitement in the air.

It was so depressing that I had to leave.

The USC-UCLA track meet used to be one of the most important competitions not just in Los Angeles, not just in America, but in the world. It was held at the Colisseum, which made it seem world-class. In those glory days of Southern California track and field, the Bruins and Trojans each fielded a team that, had it been entered in the Olympics as a nation, would have finished in the top six. The athletes were that good. The USC 440-yard relay team held the world record for that event. Times, distances and heights posted in this one collegiate track and field meet routinely were among the best performances in the world for their particular year. In those days, the US-USSR track meet always got more press, but the USC-UCLA meet was better (and the rivalry was also nastier).

So, what happened? How did this crosstown mega-meet dwindle down to a competition in which no one but friends and family of the competitors have any real interest?

Two reasons: Money...and diversity.

With regard to money, I can summarize this with two words: Allyson Felix. Ms. Felix, the best lady sprinter to come out of L.A. in a long time, with the Olympic medals to prove it, attended USC. But, you will not find her name in any of the Trojan record books, or even on any of the rosters for the USC track teams while she was at the school.

Why? Because she never competed for USC. She turned pro right out of high school, signing a contract with Nike that included her tuition for four years at USC but precluded her being an athlete for USC. I wonder how much gnashing of teeth there was on the Trojan campus when one of the best female sprinters in the world was among them but not with them.

Money is beginning to do to collegiate track and field what it has already done to college basketball— make it irrelevant.

The diversity I mentioned has nothing to do with equality. Well, that's not exactly true. It does deal with equality, but in athletic rather than social terms. The best high school track athletes in America, including those here in the LA area, do not automatically, or sometimes even at all, consider USC or UCLA as their collegiate destination. Arkansas, Florida, Baylor, LSU and a few other major universities now have track programs that far over-shadow the Bruins and Trojans. Is that good for track and field in America? Of course. Is it good for track and field in southern California? Of course not.

But, there is more to it than that. Youngsters don't gravitate toward track and field like they used to. Sprinters become halfbacks, distance runners become soccer players, and high-jumpers become power forwards. I wonder if there is even anyone out there anymore with the talent and the drive that is necessary to succeed, who is training, putting in the long hours, trying to get to the peak of form. Track is a lonely sport. When you win, all the glory is yours, and when you lose, all of that is yours, too. The only thing track teams share is the bus ride to and from the meet. Everything away from the bus is about the individual, even the relays, since only one person is running at a time.

Is there someone out there who can bring back the glory to track and field? Is there anyone out there willing to do whatever it takes, no matter how hard and demanding the work, to extract every bit of talent that they have? Is everything about being on a team? Where is the individual?

--Roger Allen

There are some very good and very simple reasons why I am running times that I might have expected ten years ago but not now: one is that since I don't remember yesterday, running is always fresh, as if I'm coming off a break with new challenges and, as I've said about a hundred times so far, serious, competitive running is as much mental as it is physical (I talked about "morning glories", didn't I?), because when you get to a certain level of competition in running, or any competitive sport, everybody is good, everybody was an All-Star back home, so that physical ability by itself, unless you just have the most complete genetic package possible, will not be enough by itself to allow you to prevail most of the time (I always remember reading when I was at UCLA about a guy on the football team who was All-Everything back home in San Diego but was having trouble making the first team at UCLA; one of the coaches said the problem was that in high school this guy was the best athlete on the field, and sheer athletic superiority allowed him to cover any mistakes he made, but, in college, everybody on the team was the best athlete on the field in high school. Understand?)

The other reason is that I have dropped about eight pounds—5% of my total body weight—over the last six months. Less weight means more speed. For example, in an automobile, dropping 100 hundred pounds from a car's weight is like adding ten horsepower. You haven't made the car more powerful, but it has less weight to pull. The same principle applies to humans. Your body has become lighter and more efficient (as long as you have kept your strength). It all has to do with physics, which I know nothing about. All I know is that I'm running faster...which is all I am interested in.

I have been basically the same weight for fifteen years. I've never had any particular diet and my only secret foods are neither unusual nor secret: frozen green peas, which I cook with most of my meals and eat frozen as a snack (2/3 of a cup has only 70 calories, but 5 grams of protein; I usually have a few two-pound bags in the freezer—they're also the best for an ice compress on an injury), raisin bran, a big bowl of which I'll have for dinner once or twice a week (filling, sweet and good for you), and bananas whenever I'm hungry between meals, because of their carbs and also because they are a little hard to digest, which gives your stomach something to do besides begging for more food. During the running season, my meals would be high in the carbs that gave me the energy to plow through my workouts, and during my off season, when I hit the gym, I would bump up the proteins, to build muscle, and eat tons of fruit, but cut down on the carbs. Nothing earth-shaking...just common nutritional sense. (I think vegetarianism is bullshit. I can always spot a vegetarian—they usually have dark rings around their eyes because they don't get enough iron. Most vegetarians look like raccoons.) The one constant in my diet has always been skim milk, gallons of it.

(Lest you think that my nutritional habits are as pure as the driven snow, I should mention—*confess* would be a better word—that my favorite food is butter. You may not think that butter is a food, but it is if you eat it with a knife and fork. And I would drink cream with every meal if I could get away with it—whipped cream is paradise. The skim milk I drink has double the calcium of regular skim milk, and tastes like whole milk. I have dairy issues, which I am just barely able to manage with self-discipline. If I ever become lactose-intolerant, they might as well shoot me.)

My weight rarely varied more than a pound or two during the year, and that was a very good thing, since the last thing your body needs is surprises, and I can give you a very good story of just what I'm talking about: when I was at UCLA, just jogging around the track one day during the off-season but still looking like a stud (my running form has been described more than once as "classic") a really muscular guy who had been dragging his butt around the track came over and started talking to me and it turned out that he was a boxer and a heavyweight contender (I forget his name now; he soon bombed out, partly for reasons that I am about to explain) and he complimented me on my running, saying that I looked like a pro and he wanted to change his training methods, starting with his running, and wanted to know if I could come up with a running program right away because he wanted to change his regimen as soon as possible, and when I asked him when his next fight was, he told me it was in a week, and, after regaining my composure, I told him that no one, in any sport, under any circumstances, changes their routine so soon before a competitive event, that such a shift was insane—well, I didn't actually say "insane", but I think I conveyed the notion that an abrupt change a week before a fight was spectacularly stupid and would be disastrous if implemented—and he just got a serious and seriously unhappy look on his face as he shuffled off to quickly finish his laps and his career.

The point here is that you don't mess with your body, especially if you have been having success with it, and especially just before a competition. I remember reading about a triathlon guy who, five days before an Ironman, suddenly decided to go on an all-fruit diet. The guy, as I remember, left most of his stomach lining out on the course.

As I said, a significant weight loss gives you less weight to pull around but it can also mean less strength if you're not careful, and strength is what you need on that last lap. Besides, strength is speed. I actually got a little stronger while I was losing the weight, the result of having more energy to do an extra set or two of reps (your last set is always the toughest and, thus, the most productive.) So, how did I lose the weight? Well, as with most great discoveries, chance has a lot to do with it. According to my notes, I'd been getting up in the middle of the night and going to the bathroom. Part of getting older, I guess. Anyway, apparently it was difficult for me sometimes to go back to sleep right away. If I just said my evening prayers (*You* say your evening prayers, don't you?) and closed my eyes, there was a good chance I'd drift off asleep, usually in mid-prayer, but if something is on my mind and starts to wander, it can be hours before I get back to sleep, which is no real problem because I don't have any schedule to keep, but trying to sleep and being unable to is not a very productive or satisfying use of time. So, anyway, I finally started walking around, to see if that worked. It didn't, but my strolling around the inside and exterior of my house in the middle of the night started to morph into a power-walk, long strides and full-arm swings, like some SS Stormtrooper. (Don't underestimate that arm movement. It's a great cardio workout. Classical music conductors all seem to live a long, long time, and the only exercise they get is swinging their arms all day directing orchestras.) Walking inside my small house by following a route in and out of rooms, down the hall, in and out of the kitchen, and back-and-forth on the driveway, I measured with my steps a walk of about a quarter of a mile. It felt good, and I actually did tire myself out. But fast walking, as you might remember from my earlier comments, is not something I particularly embrace, so I guess I started to throw a little jog into the mix, like into the kitchen, down the hall and out to the driveway.

Then the jog became a series of fast walks and short sprints, and I had a mile-and-a-half interval running program set up in and around the house. You might be saying to yourself, why didn't I just run the path I built around my house instead? Here's where it gets really interesting. (Well, it gets really interesting to me. For all I know, your eyes may be glazing over by now.) I tried running around the track instead, but it wasn't as effective. How do I know? I had lost two pounds over three weeks of running in and outside the house. When I spent a couple weeks running a mile and a half around the track in the middle of the night instead of in the house, the weight came back. Why? Because the house run was comprised of short bursts of energy, whereas the run on the track was at a measured pace. Couldn't I do that on the track? It's very difficult to do ten-yard sprints on a track, but fits in perfectly down the hall and out the door. Besides, running on the track defeats the whole purpose of the middle-of-the-night workout, which is just a complement to my regular, daytime workout. Do a quick, fifteen minute workout, change underwear and go back to bed. My weight is down (mostly, I think, because I was amping up my metabolism in the middle of the night, when it expected to be resting) and my muscles are up. And let me tell you exactly how effective these little workouts are: We had heavy rains there the last winter, and I couldn't run outside for six days. The only training I did was inside the house for those six days. My weight stayed the same. So, why don't I just train like that all the time, and skip the track completely? Well, when they start running races in my house, I will. Until that time, the track is where I prepare for races, but my house runs are part of that. They may be an important part of the reason why I am here tonight. You wouldn't think that a little fifteen-minute workout in the middle of the night would be enough to make a difference, but sometimes life comes down to the smallest things making the biggest impact, doesn't it?

WEDDINGS

HARDMAN-ROSSBACKER

Delilah Ann Hardman and Myron Jay Rossbacker were married in the garden of the Beverly Hills Hotel on September 14. Rabbi Sheldon M. Weinstein officiated at the ceremony. Ms. Hardman, whose late husband, Richard Hardman, died earlier this year, wore an original Oscar de la Renta wedding gown. Mr. Rossbacker, who owns several recycling plants in Utah and Arizona, was dressed in traditional Jewish wedding garb. A sit-down dinner at Mr. Chow's for two hundred guests followed the ceremony. Mr. Rossbacker's three daughters by two previous marriages served as bridesmaids. The bride's son, Timothy, was not in attendance. Afterwards, the couple left for a cruise around the world. When they return, they will live at Mr. Rossbacker's home in Bel-Air. He also has houses in Hawaii and Vail, Colorado, and a condominium in New York City.

I was flipping around on the TV here in the hotel room and finally settled on ESPN Classic, because they usually show something that I can remember happening. And, sure enough, they came through. It was the first game of the Dodgers-Athletics World Series in 1988, when Kirk Gibson hit that home run while barely able to stand up in the batter's box. I am not really a baseball guy. It's a little too boring for me and hard to get worked up about a single game, but the World Series is another story. (Baseball is sort of a *gestalt* sport, the whole being greater than the sum of its parts. It seems beautiful to look at, with the stadiums and the freshly-mowed lawns, the players and their sometimes-acrobatic efforts to get the ball, and all the tradition; in reality, the stadiums are usually old and uncomfortable or new and antiseptic, the players spend most of their time standing around doing nothing, and the game is so tied up with the past that it refuses to accept any changes. Volleyball is another *gestalt* sport. Beach volleyball is two players in skimpy swimwear with lots of sand and action, but the girls look chunky, the sand gets up your butt, and the action is boring, it not being very difficult to hit the ball where someone ain't when there's only two defenders—indoor volleyball is slightly better, except that almost every point seems to be scored on a spike. Imagine a basketball game where almost all of the scoring is from slam dunks. Judy, of course, had a somewhat different point of view.)

One of the things about baseball is that there is no time limit. They play until someone wins. It is also the only major sport in which a competitor can order a pizza, sit down and have a beer with it during his team's at-bat, and still be part of the contest. (I remember reading that, during the 1986 World Series, Keith Hernandez of the Mets was sitting in the clubhouse, watching the game on TV in his underwear, sucking down a cool one, thinking the game was over, when Bill Buckner gave the Mets new life. Hernandez put his pants back on and got back into the game. It's a great story, and may even be true. It *could* be true—baseball is that kind of sport.)

What all of this has to do with running is that it is the direct opposite of track and field, because decisions in track have to be made in the eye of the storm, so to speak—*Holy shit, that guy never makes a move on the third lap…what the hell am I supposed to do now?*—and so you have to make a split-second decision, based on information which has only just now presented itself to you and which may or may not be an indication of a completely unexpected set of circumstances but you must assume, until it is proven otherwise (usually only after the race is over), that what you see is real and not just a bluff. This all has to be done immediately.

Getting back to Kirk Gibson, as magnificent as his home run was, and I think it may be the single greatest moment not only in Los Angeles but also American sports history, there was a measured calmness to the situation that any runner envies. Watching the replay on television—and you have to watch at least the last two innings to emotionally re-visit the moment—everything looks pretty crazy, but, actually, Gibson was back in the clubhouse, hitting a t-ball setup when he decided to go to bat, not standing out in center field in the middle of everything. The reason he hit the home run was because he was able to control his emotions and marshal whatever strength and energy he had left—and, remember, that home run did not come off Eckersley's first or second pitch; it was a long, draining at-bat. Isn't that what life is all about, talking a long, hard look at what is going on, making an educated guess based mostly on facts but also with some emotion thrown into the mix, and going for it?

Running is the complete opposite. There is no emotion until the race is over. No one high-fives after a fast first-lap, no one pounds their chest if the split at the half is outstanding, you don't see the Icky Shuffle after a fabulous third lap, and the only thing you feel after the race is relief. Everything else comes later.

I wish my life was like a baseball game, full of individual decisions carefully thought out and taken with a careful consideration of the past. Baseball pitchers have notes, written or mental, stored away on every batter they will face in every game they pitch. Life should be like that. Failure should occur not because of being unprepared but because of poor execution. Starting pitchers only play every four or five days, so they can bask in their success for awhile; a loss, however, is also lived with for the next four or five days. (That the suicide rate among baseball pitchers is so low—Donnie Moore notwithstanding—is, I think, one of the great mysteries of the modern world.)

But the main reason I wish my life was like baseball, and why I envy baseball players, is that they know what failure feels like and yet they press on. The best baseball team of all-time probably lost at least thirty times during their season. The greatest hitter (not slugger, but *hitter*) of all time, Ted Williams, during his greatest season, in which he batted .406, was only successful slightly over forty percent of the time. Any batter who can be consistent at the plate one-third—*one-third!*—of the time, will win the batting title almost every year, and yet he will have failed two-thirds of his times at bat. And still they smile. Baseball players never let the futility of their battle to succeed get them down. There is always the next at-bat, the next game, the next season. And with even a modicum of success, they can last a long time. That is what I want my life to be, to never give up. There is a Mendoza Line in life. I stare it in the face every morning.

And there's something really strange about this whole memory thing that I forgot to mention: I don't automatically lose my memory as soon a I drift off to sleep. There seems to be some kind of cutoff point for when my memory disappears. For example, if I take a nap in the middle of the day for an hour or so, no problem—when I wake up, I still remember everything that has happened that day. Same thing at night. If I nod off for a couple hours, maybe even three at the most, before waking, I still have retention of what happened the day before. That's why my little night-time workouts are so cool, because I make them as a natural follow-up to what I did that day; if, for example, I did sprint work or interval training, then I might emphasize slower walking and 10-yard bursts down the hall or out the front door, something like that, whereas if my daytime workout was longer and more controlled, I might do the walking faster and the runs not so explosive; if I really sleep a long time during the day or at night before waking up, like four or five hours, which happens on occasion, it's a clean slate, and I'm starting from scratch, although I've got instruction sheets posted all over the house to tell me what I'm supposed to be doing, so it's not like I'm wandering around in a daze, and I believe that this really has to do with REM—the sleep condition, not the band—which I think stands for Rapid Eye Movement and which basically delineates when you drift off into the heaviest sleep, or the deepest unconsciousness, and that's when my memory disappears, with the situation being that the more well-rested I am, from having a long and deep sleep, the better the chance that my memories of the day before have evaporated, whereas if I am groggy and need more sleep, I probably remember what was happening before I went to sleep, and you might think that if I only slept for a couple hours at a time, I could retain quite a lot of memory and, yes, theoretically, that is true—I could even do the thing that Kramer tried on *Seinfeld* by emulating Leonardo da Vinci and only sleeping for fifteen minutes at a time, and probably with the same result, being in a constant fog—but life is not lived in theories, so the prospect of staying awake for excessive periods of time to retain memories of daily activities is just not worth the effort and sacrifice needed to retain them, since my life, by design, does not vary much from day to day (Sundays excepted). And, staggering around the house all day half-asleep is not my idea of a good time, not to mention that my workouts suffered, which basically brought that experiment to a swift and conclusive end.

So, as far as I can tell, it's the level of unconsciousness that determines whether or not I lose all remembrance of what went before. I tried cheating on this once, sleeping on the sofa at night, since I have this theory that your body thinks of a bed as *the* place for real sleep, and other pieces of furniture such as chairs, loveseats and sofas are merely resting spots, so that if you can only get, for example, three hours sleep before you have to get up and do something big—like having to go to the airport—it is much better to get that three hours on a sofa or loveseat, where your body thinks it has taken a serious nap and you feel rejuvenated, than on a bed, where after sleeping only three hours and then stopping, your body, expecting to be in bed for the long haul, feels cheated and will punish you accordingly. Well, that idea worked and it didn't work. I *did* manage to fool my body by getting less than a full night's rest on the sofa and still retaining some, but not all, of what happened the day before, but I also spent most of the day with a sore back, probably because our sofa isn't really a sofa in the conventional sense but a futon (and a cheap one) and I seem to recall once reading a description of a futon as an uncomfortable sofa that converts into an uncomfortable bed. Amen to that.

So, the bottom line here is the deeper the sleep, the more memory loss, but the deeper the sleep, the better the sleep, and the better I feel all day, which allows me to train at my highest possible level of efficiency, which is really pretty much what my life is all about right now, so remembering what happened yesterday, assuming that it is even worth remembering, is less important to me than being able to function at the highest level as a runner.

But…what about all that whining and bitching I did awhile back about being so vulnerable and stranded on an island and…blah…blah…blah? Well, those are all legitimate concerns, and I really did mean everything I said but, let's get real, would I rather be completely normal and not still have my running career—which probably would have been over by now if it had continued on its planned projectory (of course, I'd also be the world record holder with the resultant fame and riches that would accompany such a feat)—or be somewhat damaged goods with possible new frontiers in front of me? Basically, at this exact moment in time, would I rather be you or…me?

Next question….

TRANSCRIPT

Transcriber: Mary Welton
Interviewer: Edward Woodward
Subject: Judith Hardman

Edward Woodward: Mrs. Hardman...uh, can I call you Judith?
Judith Hardman: Sure.
EW: Judith, I hope you don't still harbor any ill feelings towards me from our last interview.
JH: I probably over-reacted. I was under a lot of stress to sign up that new client....
EW Did you get him?
JH: No.
EW: Oh, sorry....Well, I wasn't trying to demonize you in our last interview, but—
JH: Some people I know give me a shitload of grief over the fact that I still keep hanging on to Tim, as if I'm a Svengali or something...like I must have some really dark ulterior motives.
EW: Well, to get right to the point, why are you still attached to him and yet he lives alone?
JH: I want what's best for him.
EW: And what is best for him?
JH: Me...having me protect him.
EW: From what?
JH: From everything.
EW: And you know what to do?
JH: Well, I try my best. I'm doing the best I can...what else can I do?
EW: Have you made mistakes?
JH: Probably...but that's how you learn, by your mistakes.
EW: No harm...no foul?

JH: He is my husband…I am doing what I think is best for him.

EW: Why?

JH: Because he needs protection.

EW: From what?

JH: Didn't you just ask me that?

EW: Well, I—

JH: Tim is out there in the desert in his own little dream world and is doing very well as long as no one intrudes on that world. I have people out there who contact me if anything unusual is going on. I have the police drive by his house every day—do you know how difficult it was to convince the sheriff to send a car out there in the middle of nowhere to check on one person? I am out there every three weeks making certain that he is not a danger to himself, that everything is good.

EW: Is he mentally ill?

JH: No, just the earliest stages of Alzheimer's. There is no dementia…yet.

EW: Do you think there will be?

JH: Eventually, but it could be years.

EW: How do you know?

JH: He had a thorough physical about six months ago, CAT scans, MRIs, everything.

EW: He agreed to that?

JH: Of course. He signed the papers.

EW: He knew what he was doing?

JH: He knew what was happening…he just doesn't remember any of it.

EW: I thought he took notes and videotaped himself every day to document important things in his life.

JH: He does.

EW: Then, how does he not remember something as exhaustive and intensive as the physical exam you described?

JH: Well…I…edit his notes and tapes.

EW: You *what*?

JH: I...selectively go through his notes and tapes and take out whatever information or subjects that I think will be a distraction for him.

EW: Isn't that illegal?

JH: Not according to my attorney.

EW: You have an attorney working on this?

JH: Looking after Tim from a distance has its challenges. I sometimes need help and guidance.

EW: Have you tried your conscience?

JH: Look, Mr. Woodward, I am not expecting you to agree with me, I just expect you to report everything accurately. You, and everyone else, can make up your own mind. I have no problem with what I am doing.

EW: How do you edit his tapes? I assume that he guards them very carefully.

JH: He does...when he is awake.

EW: You wait until he is asleep?

JH: We sleep together.

EW: Meaning...?

JH: Meaning exactly what you think it means.

EW: *Really?*

JH: Tim's memory may not function as before, but his body has total recall. It remembers exactly what to do and how to do it...and do it very well.

EW: You're protected against pregnancy?

JH: Well, we...I...use the rhythm method, that's why I only go out there every three weeks. Works perfect. We're Catholic, you know.

EW: Without getting intrusive...is once every three weeks enough?

JH: You are getting intrusive, but, yes, it's enough, believe me...more than enough. He's still an athlete in training, with lots of energy...and a great body.

EW: I think we're veering off the subject.

JH: That's okay. I want you to understand that I'm his wife and he is my husband, and we act...just like any married couple.

EW: Or...any married couple where the wife makes all the decisions without telling her husband what is happening?

JH: That might describe more marriages than you think.

EW: Well...perhaps, but most husbands aren't as susceptible to manipulation as your husband.

JH: *Manipulation*...that's a very strong word...almost nasty.

EW: Let me rephrase that: Your husband lives in a controlled environment, and the control is yours.

JH: I would agree that all the external control is mine, but the internal control, what he does everyday in his own world, is his.

EW: When you visit every three weeks, who decides what will happen during the visit?

JH: This isn't a visit from one of his relatives. I'm his wife, not his grandmother. We act like husband and wife. Like the old days.

EW: Even though he thinks you two are divorced?

JH: In a way, that makes it better...like we're cheating. We giggle and laugh a lot.

EW: Doing what?

JH: Doing everything—having lunch together, going for a walk...

EW: Having sex?

JH: You're really hung on up on the sex thing, aren't you?

EW: And you aren't?

JH: Nope.

EW: Would you go out there as often if you knew there was no prospect of sex?

JH: Of course....but I probably wouldn't be driving as fast to get there.

EW: Would you describe a typical visit?

JH: Well, I get there around noon—I leave LA around nine and it takes about three hours. He's always surprised—"Great to see you...I love you so much!" are what he always says when he sees me, the same nine words every time. We probably—just about always—end up in the bedroom within fifteen minutes of my arriving.

EW: Whose idea is that?

JH: It just happens. We're husband and wife, remember? Then we lie there and reminisce about when we first got married, things like that. Eventually, we get up and have a nice lunch with some things I bought at Nate'n Als in Beverly Hills on the way out there.

EW: Nate n' Als...that's a little pricey.

JH: Once every three weeks, I can afford it. So, then we just sit and talk about things.

EW: What things?

JH: Mostly about us.

EW: He wants you back?

JH: Always...and I always say it will happen, just not right now.

EW: And...will it?

JH: You're really pushing it, aren't you? Is this for *Sports Illustrated* or *The National Enquirer*? Okay...yes, we will get back together...someday.

EW: That sounds like a definite maybe.

JH: May I get back to my description of a typical visit?

EW: Yes...please.

JH: Maybe we'll go for a ride in his Corvette.

EW: He has a *Corvette*?

JH: Yeah...an old one. It's his pride and joy. I can't stand that car.

EW: Why is that?

JH: It's a long story…costs me a fortune to keep it running. When he takes it to the mechanic out there, the guy fixes it, tells Tim it was nothing, and then sends me some humongous bill.

EW: He doesn't know anything about that?

JH: No. So, then, about four or five, he gets ready for a workout, and will probably do a time trial to show me how well he is running.

EW: Is he?

JH: Oh, yeah. I don't want to give you any of his times, but he is making amazing progress.

EW: What does "amazing progress" mean? Is he getting back to the way he was?

JH: No, it means he's moving towards where he always wanted to go.

EW: And where is that?

JH: Where no one has ever been before. He wants to run faster than anyone ever has…faster than anyone ever will.

EW: That seems terribly dramatic…or melodramatic.

JH: Well…I'll let that take care of itself.… After the workout, he'll shower—if I'm in the mood, and I usually am, I'll shower with him—then we'll have a light dinner with something he makes, like a soup or salad, and then just sit and talk and cuddle or whatever and then go to bed.

EW: And more sex?

JH: Edward, you really have a one-track mind.

EW: Everything I have read about you and Tim says that there was no sex until you got married. Considering what an active sex life you two have even now under rather difficult, to say the least, circumstances, is that true or not?

JH: Well…yes and no.

EW: What does that mean?

JH: Is this off the record?

EW: If it has to be.

JH: It does.

EW: Agreed....

JH: When we were engaged, I explained to Tim that while I agreed in principle with the no-sex-until-married idea, I expected to be married to him for the rest of my life, and I wanted to know what I was in for...

EW: Sexually?

JH: Yes.

EW: How did he respond?

JH: He agreed...sort of.

EW: I still don't understand what that means.

JH: He agreed to do enough to convince me...to take care of me, but not himself.

EW: Did he convince you?

JH: He was very convincing. He talked the talk and then he walked the walk...removed all my doubts.

EW: He was the best?

JUH: He was the *only*....

EW: Really?

JH: Really. He probably thought there were others. I used to ride horses a lot when I was younger, which took care of some things, if you know what I mean.

EW: You never told him he was the first?

JH: He never asked. Tim is pretty much in the present all the time; he's always said he doesn't worry about what he can't control.

EW: And is he still—?

JH: Yes, Edward...he is still the only one. That's part of the reason I never filed the divorce papers, so I would still be his wife, and give myself an excuse for not looking around.

EW: You needed an excuse?

JH: I'm not a statue. I've had a few weak moments, but I'd just look at my ring and it would pass. It's very important to me that I have stayed faithful to Tim. *Very* important.

EW: I just find it interesting that you never told him he was the only one.

JH: He's knows that he's the only one now and that's all he cares about.

EW: You must have been—

JH: So, back to the story...that was on a Sunday morning, and right afterwards he rushed us over to St. Paul's, making sure not to get hit by a car or something on the way—dying with a mortal sin, you know—for the ten o'clock Mass and we both went to Confession, got Communion, had a nice breakfast at IHOP afterwards, and I never saw him naked again until our wedding night.

EW: ...when he finished where he left off?

JH: Yes, he did...several times.

EW: Is the sex important to you??

JH: Edward, you really are pushing the sex angle. Sex is important to me because it is important to Tim.

EW: It's not that important to you?

JH: Not that important. Doing it with him...doing anything with him...is what's important. If he had two toilets in his bathroom, we'd *shit* together.

EW: Could you do without sex?

JH: That's exactly what I do until I go out there again the next time. No problem...So, anyway, we go bed, and afterward he falls into a deep sleep—he puts out almost as much energy during sex as he does when he's running—and that's when I get up and do my work.

EW: What work is that?

JH: I view and edit his tapes. He's got a real primitive recorder and his camera work is all herky-jerky, so I can edit stuff out and cut and paste and no one could tell anything has been taken out. Then, I check his notes. He also has a secret set of notes that he keeps in his underwear. I take anything that has information that I think he doesn't need to know.

EW: And then you leave in the middle of the night, and he wakes the next morning with no memory of what happened between you two?

JH: Yes.

EW: You drive out there every few weeks, manipulate him into doing what you want, including sex, then erase whatever evidence there is of previous events which are not to your liking....

JH: You make me sound so cold-hearted. You're confusing me with his mother. Unlike her, everything I do for Tim is out of love.

EW: According to you.

JH: I suppose...but who knows Tim best? Who knows best what he needs?

EW: Are you trying to become his mother?

JH: No...just his protector and his wife.

EW: In that order?

JH: Either way.

EW: But, he doesn't know any of this, especially that you are both still married to each other.

JH: So, what do you want me to do, move out there with him and completely disrupt his world? His running would suffer. I would be a distraction.

EW: A distraction, I dare say, he would be happy to encounter.

JH: Only until it negatively affected his running. He would have to choose...me or the running.

EW: Which do you think he would choose?

JH: I don't honestly know…but I do knthat whichever one he chose, he would be unhappy.

EW: Because…?

JH: Because he wants both…very much. Right now, that cannot happen.

EW: And why is that?

JH: Because right now his running and his marriage are mutually exclusive—he couldn't support both. He will always have me, but the window on his being able to run world-class times is shrinking. I can wait, if I have to….his running cannot.

EW: That's very noble of you.

JH: Nobility has nothing to do with it. Sometimes you have to take one for the team. My time will come. This is his time. Look…Tim has a life most people, including me, would kill for. He has no worries or responsibilities; he does whatever he wants whenever he wants. He takes life one day at a time…I wish I could.

EW: He has no choice.

JH: All that matters is that he's happy.

EW: You know that for a fact?

JH: I do.

EW: He has told you that?

JH: He has.

EW: …when you were with him.

JH: Well…yeah.

EW: Does he ever ask you to stay there with him, rather than returning to LA?

JH: Every time I visit.

EW: Does he remember this?

JH: No.

EW: Why?

JH: It would complicate things.

EW: What things?

JH: The plans I have for him.

EW: What plans are those?

JH: Plans for his comeback. He is running better than ever. He just needs to be gradually brought back into the world he left.

EW: Have you discussed this with him?

JH: Many times.

EW: Was he agreeable with these plans?

JH: Yes, he gets very excited every time we talk about them.

EW: Does he remember these discussions?

JH: No.

EW: Because...?

JH: Because it would serve no purpose at the moment.

EW: Are you helping or hurting him?

JH: I would do anything—*anything*—to help Tim. I'm going out there next week. Would you like to meet Tim?

EW: Absolutely. What will we do?

JH: We'll just have a nice little visit. You can ask him any questions you want, and he'll answer you honestly and sometimes humorously—Tim can be very funny.

EW: And he won't remember any of it?

JH: What would that accomplish? It would be nothing but a disruption for him. If he knew even the slightest bit of information about a planned comeback, it would ruin everything. Tim is a great guy, and I love him very much, but his relationship with reality is not one of his strengths. He would over-train, over-think, and try to over-achieve. There is such a thing as too much information.

EW: And, with your husband, you think that any information is too much information?

JH: At the moment, yes...but, meet me out there next week and see for yourself. You'll view this situation differently then.

EW: I will?

JH: Guaranteed.

There is one part of my life that I do not understand, one area of my life I have no clue whatsoever as to what is happening or if anything is happening. It is all a mystery to me. That dark and hidden part of my life is...sex. There is no information anywhere...none at all. I have a reputation of being a one-woman man and only having that woman after I was married to her. I never had sex with Judy until after we were married, and Judy is the only person I have ever had sex with, but, to be honest, I am using the *Bill Clinton* definition of sex. I did have sexual experiences with other girls before I met Judy—never, ever, after I started going out with her—but it was never sexual intercourse. Usually, like Bill, it was a blow job. Not every girl...but enough. (And never with the same girl more than once.) What usually happened was, I'd meet some girl on a Saturday night— never on a Friday, because our meets were always on a Saturday—and we would hang around Westwood Village with thousands of people all over the place, and she might or might not come back to my place. If she did, nothing would happen that night, because I would say that I was too tired from the meet that day and walking around the Village all night, which made make sense, but that we'd do something in the morning, and I said it in such a way that I didn't sound like I was trying to take advantage of anyone—and I really wasn't, you know; if anything, it was just the opposite—so the next morning, about 8:30 or so, we'd be in bed, making out and it was easy to get them to go down on me, and at just the right time I would ask in a soft voice if it was okay if I came, and they never said no (probably because nobody asked first, or in such a nice voice) and then I asked them if they wanted me to do them, and they always did, and I'd always give them an extra one, just to be nice, and as soon as the second one was finished, it would be about 9:30, and I would suddenly shout that I had to be somewhere at ten and she had to leave right away, which did not endear me to them (which was okay), but the main thing was that I got them the hell out of there in about ten minutes, which meant I had twenty minutes to get where I was supposed to be, and where I was supposed to be was the 10:00 Mass at St. Paul's, and they used to hear Confession, so I would get to the church right on time or a couple minutes late, say a couple prayers and then get in line at one of the confessionals, confess my sins (the blow job, the two finger-jobs and whatever other lesser peccadilloes I had committed since my last Confession) get my penance (usually a couple decades of the rosary, which I would recite during the sermon so I could go to Communion), receive Communion and be back in Jesus' good graces, whereas less than two hours before I had had some girl sucking me off as hard as she could and, yeah, I knew this was really a candy-ass situation, but every time I went to Confession I really believed—*really believed*—that it would never happen again, and I firmly and truly resolved that it would never happen again. And, actually, I became more devout in my dedication to Jesus, begging for forgiveness and vowing never to sin again, rather than being complacent, which would have probably been my attitude if nothing had happened with the girl. I had to get worse to get better. The fact that this could become cyclical did not detract from the idea that I became the most pious right after being the most sinful...and, I must say, I enjoyed both situations tremendously.

And if nothing did happen with the girl, which was just as often, then I would go to the Newman Center for Mass. That they did not have Confession during Mass was not a problem because, other than the occasional blow job and finger-jobs, I led a pretty moral life, and could say my prayers with a clear conscience. When I said that I never had sex with anyone but Judy I was telling the truth because, like Bill Clinton, I believed that "sex" meant sexual intercourse, and everything else was just fooling around, but with Judy there was never any "fooling around" although I got the distinct impression that if I wanted to boink her brains out that would have been fine with her, but if I didn't want to do anything, that was okay, too, and that was very important to me because the main thing to me, both with the other girls and with Judy was that I was in control of the situation and that even though I may have deferred to girls in some things, I was the one who decided what we did, when we did it and how many times we did it, so that even if they were the main benefactors of what was going on, it all revolved around me (pretty much like what I described earlier about the way I controlled a conversation even when the other person was doing the talking, by the timing and subject matter of my questions, right?) not because I'm necessarily a control freak, although I'm not necessarily *not* a control freak, but more as a result of the attitude I have towards sex and, more particularly, the role of men and women in sex, an attitude that I will be the first to admit is so unenlightened as to almost be offensive, a real souvenir of the Fifties that I guess I must have picked up from my father when he told me the facts of life, an attitude which believes that sex is something that men do to women or that women do for men (the idea that sex could be a cooperative effort emotionally as well as physically never occurred to me), which seems to me to only be about a half-step above the idea that women just exist for men, and I really feel ashamed to have harbored such feelings although apparently not ashamed enough to have ever made any credible attempt to change them and, in fact, on occasion tried to justify my outlook in this regard by comparing my own attitude with that of all the vulgar slang people use about sex, all of which seems to be male-centric (not to mention incredibly homophobic and misogynistic) such as in the terms "getting fucked" and "getting screwed" (who gets "fucked" or "screwed" by men?...women and homosexuals, right?) both of which seem to imply that being the receptive partner in sexual intercourse is a dreadfully undesirable position to have ("getting the shaft" seems more benign, until you realize the "shaft" is an erect penis), and calling someone a "cocksucker" or saying that something "sucks" relegates the person sucking to the lowest of the low, the idea being that anyone who would put a man's genitalia in their mouth (meaning, a woman or a homosexual, right?) is pathetic; in fact, the only slang sexual term I can think of that doesn't have the man as the almighty and his partner as sexual cannon fodder is "motherfucker", and even there the impression is that the man, wrong though he may be, is still in charge, and to me what this all comes down to—because, after all, people who will admit to being incredibly enlightened about the sexual roles of men and women use these male-centric words constantly and without any consideration of what they really mean—is that there are two standards for behavior in the world, one for sex and one for everything else, the implication being that if a person can somehow, even if in only the most obtuse way, connect what they are doing with sex, all bets are off. I used to test this theory with the girls mentioned above that I would bring back to my place, when we would be lying in bed on Sunday morning, not yet having done anything, and I would be certain to have a piece of hard candy on my nightstand, and I would put it in my mouth for a minute or so and then ask them if they wanted it, to which they would invariably shake their head (eww, all those germs!) and then within ten minutes they would be blowing me (and compliantly swallowing whatever issued forth), but only after I had first gone to the bathroom and taken a piss; they would go right down and do whatever I said, pretend it was an ice cream cone, let me put it down their throat until they almost choked—anything—and it didn't enhance the pleasure for me, but I was curious to see how far I could get them to go just because it was sex, while I would be watching them and saying to myself that I would kill myself before I would do any of that stuff (and then asking them to do it a little longer) and it just never ceased to amaze me what you can away with, and what people will be happy to oblige doing for you if it involves sex, even if there is nothing positive in it for them, presumably because we have become so brainwashed about sex that most of us will temporarily suspend our better judgment—or any judgment at all, for that matter—and go with the flow. For certain types of personalities, it has been ever thus, but now it seems almost pandemic. Anyway, bottom-line, I met some great girls, got some wonderful blow jobs, and didn't get hit by a bus before I made it to Confession, so it all worked out. Timing is everything.

When we got engaged, I told Judy exactly how it was going to be before and after we got married because, as I said, it seemed to me at the time that Judy could go either way—lots of sex or no sex—and I just wanted to clarify the situation. Even more important was the idea that I would be the one who would be deciding that, which seemed only fair to me, since she seemed rather ambivalent about sex before marriage and I most certainly was not. That put me in complete control. I wasn't really concerned that she would get upset about this, because she wanted to get married. So did I, but I also wanted to establish the ground rules, as it were, for sex before we ever got started, the basic idea of which was that I was in charge. I know this is going to sound terrible, and even now, all these years later, I still cringe when I think about it, and when I told her how it was going to be, I all but held my breath. I simply crossed my fingers and said—and, understand, this is someone who, other than the aforementioned blow jobs and finger jobs, had almost no sexual experience and even less sexual *gravitas*—that her job was sexually to "do as you're told". Those were my exact words, and I was waiting for her to explode or implode or whatever, but all she did was smile and say, "Okay." She sounded kind of cheerful about it. She seemingly had no problem with it, and this was one of those situations where the good news and the bad news are the same thing, the good news being that she understood she was to be subservient to me in everything sexual, and the bad news was that she had agreed to be subservient to me in everything sexual, which only served to expand my already Neanderthal attitude toward the male and female roles in sex exponentially. Of course, there is always the possibility that she had faith in me that I was not a complete asshole and would not subject her to demeaning and humiliating sexual situations for nothing more than my own personal gratification. (Or, at least, not very often.) Most of all, as I said, it established that I was in charge. And I kept my word in both respects. We did not have sex until our wedding night. And on our wedding night, and from then on, we had lots of it, and I made certain that she did exactly as she was told.

And everything I said before about people doing everything for sex is even more pronounced when passionate love is brought into the mix. It was so thrilling to have someone who was as beautiful as Judy do whatever I wanted to do sexually without any hassle that the control factor was almost as exciting as the sex itself. My biggest sexual fantasy has never involved threesomes, foursomes, or even anything visual, but, rather, the idea of sexual control and surrender, the extreme of which would be a girl having sex with a guy she doesn't like to get something that she does. Just the basic idea of a woman turning herself completely over to a man and letting him do whatever he wants with her body is an incredible fantasy turn-on for me. (We're talking about a situation here, not real people, understand?) It is all about control, and it is creepy, I know. Sorry.

My life at that time centered on three things: running, religion and relations (sexual, that is)…my body, my soul andmind (you must have picked up by now that, for me, sex was as much about the mental as it was the physical, right? Just like running.) And they tended to bleed over into each other. Running was almost a religion for me. It was a spiritual experience as much as a physical one. Days when I did not run or, at least, do something that was connected with my running, were incomplete days for me, and I did not feel whole; religion would have a prominence in my day from the time I got up and said my morning prayers, right up until I went to bed and said my evening prayers, with the in-between hopefully being guided by the motivations that led me to be religious in the first place; and sex was important because it was a mixture of all three—body, soul and mind. Some of you might quibble and say there that there is nothing about love in there, but all three of these considerations—running, religion, and sex—were infused with love (love of running, love of God, and love of my wife) and none would have been in my life without love.

Sex got mixed in with running, too. (I understand that this must make me look as if I am, or was, obsessed with sex, which isn't really the case, although I will admit that with sex, for me it was all or nothing: I either completely immersed myself in it or I left it alone. Judy acquiesced.) This happened when I would transfer my running mentality from the track to the bed. When Judy and I were going to have sex, whether it was spontaneous or planned, I always asked the question, "Do you want to make love or do you want to screw?" Sort of implied was that with the former, she was going to have a really good time, and with the latter (which Judy chose more often than you might think) I was going to have a really good time. That didn't mean that in either situation someone was not going to have a good time. What it did mean, other than the fact that I was in control, was that one of us was the focus of attention and the other one went along with it. If we were making love, I would do everything I could for Judy to enjoy it as much as possible, and as many times as possible. If we were screwing, I would do whatever I wanted as long as it didn't negatively impact her.

"Transferring my running mentality from the track to the bed" means that I took the aggressiveness and determination that I had on the track and combined them in sexual congress with Judy.

One time, I videotaped us having sex. (Someone had loaned me a camera for a couple days.) To my great shame, I did not tell her about it. It was incredibly exciting to me as I did it, knowing what I was getting away with, and incredibly depressing for me when I watched the video later, realizing what I had done. The guilt was overwhelming. In my mind, I had made Judy look vulnerable and like a fool, two things she could never be. And, the truth be told, the video was a little bit boring. It was a bit like watching grass grow—albeit very sexy grass. I had remembered it as being more exciting than it seemed on the tape. Judy looked beautiful, of course, and as I try to recall it now, I find myself wondering why the tape didn't do what it was supposed to do—you know, blow my mind. It did just the opposite. The next few days I fawned over Judy so much that it was almost embarrassing. I was trying to apologize without telling her what I had done. I have never told her. I erased the tape immediately, but the guilt is still there, lurking somewhere in my subconscious. I could never do anything like that again.

So, anyway, as I said before, sex with me was all or nothing, which leads me to believe, since I have no information about my sex life (or if I have even had one for the last six or seven years) that nothing has been going on. Something could have happened—six years is a long time—but there's nothing about it in my notes or tapes. See, here's what I don't understand: If I haven't had any sex for the last six years or so, why aren't there any...uh...stains on my underwear? Before I met Judy or got involved with those other girls, nocturnal emissions—wet dreams—were one of the highlights of my life. I had some of the most incredible fantasies and most incredible orgasms while I was sleeping. I rarely dream (or, rarely remember my dreams, since they say we dream all the time) so, when some incredibly graphic—and incredibly filthy—images would suddenly flash across my dreamscape (sometimes featuring animals or older female relatives) there would almost immediately follow the most pleasurable feeling I have ever had in my life, probably more enjoyable because I had done absolutely no work whatsoever to bring about this avalanche of pleasure and because it was completely innocent even though prominently featured in these dreams were acts that would have had me jailed in some states and executed in certain parts of the world. And that euphoria lasted well beyond the twenty minutes it took me to change all my clothes and bed sheets and wash myself down. I even got fairly good at predicting when a wet dream was going to happen—usually about every three weeks. I guess that was when my prostate would decide to reduce its inventory. Friends would say I seemed to be in a really good mood, and I would smirk to myself, "Tonight's the night!"

But, there is nothing. Have I turned into a eunuch? I have only jerked off about three times in my life (one or two girls did it for me at UCLA on certain occasions, but I don't count those) and not in the last fifteen years, and I am not about to start now even though, since I don't remember anything from day-to-day, it would be pretty difficult to establish a pattern of behavior with this (or anything else, for that matter.) So, even though I have no proof, I will consider my house to be a self-abuse-free zone.

But something must be going on. I'm a healthy guy. Just because my memory is fried, I don't think that has any implications for my reproductive system. I remember one summer, between my junior and senior year at UCLA, I had a sore hamstring that would not heal, so I took about two months off from running and got a part-time job working with the mentally-challenged at a school in Westwood, mostly to keep me from going out of my mind with boredom. The class had about ten students, male and female, all in wheelchairs. Me and another guy would have to change the diapers on the boys, which was really gross at first but by the end I could change a full diaper on a sixteen-year-old boy and eat a sandwich at the same time. And, let me tell you, their brain may have been way behind, but their reproductive system was right on schedule. Look in any biology book: the main purpose of any species is to reproduce itself. A couple of these boys, for whatever they lacked mentally, had equipment that would have made some porn stars feel inadequate. (Even more interesting to me, for different reasons, was the fact that we had a couple of sweet young girls just out of high school helping us change the diapers on these incredibly-hung boys; however, me and the other guy were not allowed to even get near the changing area for the female students, probably because of the well-documented fact that all men are rapists. Instead, the two young girls and two little old ladies had to lift a couple of 250-pound dead-weight girls out of their respective wheelchairs and onto the changing table while the male helpers left the room. After this ordeal, which happened twice a day, the women would complain about back problems. Of course, the alternative was for the males to help, but that would probably have unleashed waves of erotic obsession in us, the girls' rolls of fat and, I'm guessing, more hair between their legs than I had between my ears undoubtedly a trigger for unspeakable desires.) The point here is even if you are substantially worse off than me in the with regard to your intellectual capacity, you will still be equipped well enough that you can perform your species' most important and fundamental task with a high degree of competency. So…how come I'm not?

It would be great to have Judy come out here and sleep over one more time. Those were the best days of my life: my mile times were getting better, my dad was still alive, and the sex with Judy was great and it was often. Some of my best work was done between Judy's legs. I know we're divorced now, and I'm still bitter (when every day is a world unto itself, you don't have much time in which to resolve your problems; overview does not exist). I still wear the ring—my wedding ring, I mean—and think of her as my wife, and having sex with her again would not feel weird to me. Well, maybe a little forbidden—banging the ex, you know?

Not that it would be difficult to get worked up about Judy. I am still in love with her. She comes out here every once in awhile and I have her on my video tapes, and she still looks the same. In my notes, it says that she hasn't re-married and that she isn't seeing anyone. It would just be so good to get behind her, grab that fabulous ass with my hands and pound away. I always used to wonder what she was thinking while I was doing that since, from what I understand, that's not the easiest position for a woman to come, and I would ask her afterwards, and she would just say, "It was nice." When is sex *nice*?

I remember once I grabbed her hips while I was riding her from behind, lifted her off the bed and walked around the room, still going in and out of her with her legs wrapped around my waist, her arms out in front to keep from hitting her head on anything.

Afterwards, I asked, "How was that, Judy?"

"It was nice."

The key to being in control is knowing when you have no business in pressing the issue. For example, I have no clue about Judy's sexual activity before she met me. I don't know and don't want to know. What's the point? What will that information do for me? I suppose if I was as much of a control freak as you probably think I am, I could somehow use her sexual history to my advantage—you know, guilt or something. But I am not going to go anywhere near that. I know she wasn't a virgin when we first had sex together, but beyond that I have no information or desire to know. Like I said...what's the point? People who dwell on the past sometimes do so because they want to control everything, even history. Whatever did take place had and has nothing to do with me, so why would I care? I suppose I could have asked her what she did and who she did it with, and she probably would tell me. What would I or could I do with this information? Nothing. Judy's mentioned some guy named Paul a couple times, so maybe he's the one. Don't know...don't care. It's not because I'm so evenly-balanced emotionally (well, maybe a just a little), but because all I care about is the present. Of course, right now, that's all I have. But even back then, I only concerned myself about the here-and-now when looking for things to worry about. I've known guys who completely stressed out over who their girlfriends did what with before they ever met them. That is a dead-end...a conflict you will never win. Now, if that first guy shows up again, it's a different ballgame, but....

There's two things I don't understand about women and sex. (Actually, there's probably a couple hundred, but there's two I want to discuss right now.) The first one is: How can a girl fake an orgasm and get away with it? Any guy who has been scammed this way has either never given a girl an orgasm, so he has no idea what he's dealing with, or has such a high opinion of his sexual prowess that he assumes every girl he touches gets off. Again, I'm hardly the world's biggest expert on women and sex, since I've only had sex with Judy, but whenever she had an orgasm, which was a decent amount of the time, it was something that could not be faked. When Judy was getting ready to come, the inside of her vagina would put a stranglehold on me that was like a boa constrictor embracing a pig. It's like a vacuum cleaner sucking you in, and you think you're going in and out, but you're not moving that much, because her equipment is not letting go of your ass until it gets everything it wants, which is everything you've got. This is all about biology, and the species is not turning you loose until you have nothing left to give. You'd need a tow truck to pull you out of there once—you're not going anywhere. (Not that you'd want to, of course, but, you get the idea.) And I seriously doubt that any woman could summon up that kind of vaginal power without being aroused. A few heavy moans do not an orgasm make, and any guy who buys into that really has no business being in there in the first place.

The second thing I never understood was why I didn't know anything about girls going to the bathroom right after sex. No one ever told me...never heard of it. I mean, I've seen hundreds of movies, and when there is a scene with sex, everybody just lies there afterwards, looking so peaceful and contented. The first time I did it with Judy, on our wedding night, I roll off of her, pleased with my performance and ready to proclaim my everlasting love all over again, and all I see is Judy hauling ass into the bathroom. But, all those movies which are supposed to be so realistic (which is why they justify having sex and nudity in them in the first place, right?) never show the girl going to the bathroom. How come?

And, another question: What does a woman do when she has sex in a car? Dos she squat by the side of the road? Judy and I have always had sports cars (she used to have a Miata, and now has a BMW Z4), with no room for heavy action, the result being that we have never had sex in a car. I asked Judy about this important question once, but she said she didn't know. (I guess Paul doesn't know either, right?)

If U.S. Track Is Lazarus, What Does That Make Google?

(WSJ) Google's foray into the American sporting climate with its multi-million-dollar commitment to U.S. track and field and sponsorship of the Stanford Relays has commentators and observers wondering if the company is not beginning to exhibit messianic tendencies—or delusions, depending on your point of view. "Returning American track and field to the front page of the sports section would be more impressive than the loaves and fishes," says Art Snyder, once the foremost promoter of American track and field meets on the West Coast but now someone who, like the athletes he continues to feature, has to spend most of the track season in Europe to pursue his chosen field of expertise. "I still do a few meets, but it's nothing like the old days—the Compton Relays, the Colisseum Relays, the Fresno Relays, the Modesto Relays [ed. note: all the meets had *relays* in the title because of the relay events featuring junior college, university and sports club teams which, along with the numerous individual events, gave them a three-ring-circus environment].

Wilson Reilly, the man at Google in charge of all this, is not worried. "We hope to eventually bring track and field back to the front of the American sports scene. Obviously, one event, even one as prestigious as we expect the Stanford Relays to become, cannot in and of itself effect a change, but it can become the catalyst." Reilly, a former mile runner at UCLA (and Stanford MBA) remembers his days as a runner for the Bruins, the crowds at the NCAA Championships and the carnival atmosphere at many of the larger meets. "It was a wonderful time. It would have been more wonderful for me if I had won more races, but I had the misfortune—or fortune, since I think failure teaches us more than success—to be running for UCLA at the same time as Tim Hardman, who always won. I was right there behind him. If he ran a 4:00.2, I ran a 4:02.5, if he ran 3:59, I would get a 4:00.5. Tim dragged me along to my only sub-four minute mile at the NCAAs at Tucson in my junior year. He won in 3:58.9, and I sprinted home for a 3:59.9...just barely under four minutes, but I did it. The next year, with Tim graduated, everyone, including me, expected my times to drop even more, but it didn't happen. Maybe I needed Tim to spur me along. I won everything my senior year, including the NCAAs, but I never got under 4:01.2."

(Reilly subsequently contacted the *Journal* several days after this interview was conducted with a correction, noting that the distance at NCAA Championships was 1500 meters and not a mile, and that his time was actually 3:42.9. "But," he explained, "to get the mile time, you add 17 seconds to the 1500 meter time. Same difference," explained Reilly.)

Does Reilly realistically expect to resurrect American track and field?

"Well, you can have the best organization in the world, and at Google I think we do, but it all comes down to what happens in the arena, so to speak. The athletes competing have to inspire the people."

American athletes?

"Absolutely. We will feature the top-flight foreign athletes, especially in the mile, but it is our hope, our goal, to inspire enough young athletes here in America to incentivize a renaissance in U.S. track and field. And not just one outstanding athlete in every event, but several."

Similar to his symbiotic relationship on the track with Tim Hardman?

"Exactly...it benefited both of us. Strong competition is what makes you better."

That sentiment coming from a Google executive must sound strange to Google's competitors.

So, whatever happened to Tim Hardman?

"I have no idea. I heard he had some problems. I hope he is doing well."

American track and field aficionados can only hope Google's interest in their sport is more enduring and their concern more substantial.

You know, I'm thinking that maybe I shouldn't have talked about Judy and sex. It makes her seem vulnerable. I was just trying to make a point about how she would go with the flow even when it wasn't in her best interests, but there's such a thing as too much information. (That's a phrase Judy used to use all the time. I think what she meant was that too much information can sometimes be confusing.) Judy wasn't a pushover unless she wanted to be one. She could bring a lot of power to the fore any time that she wanted.

I hope I haven't been giving you the wrong picture of Judy. I think she's one of the best people in the world, certainly the finest person I have ever met. She's a lot smarter than me, having a double major in finance and accounting at UCLA while I was just trying to slog my way through dumb-ass English Lit. She always deferred to me,

even when she knew—and so did I, to be perfectly honest—
that her answer to a particular situation was better than mine.
I'm not exactly sure why she did that. Maybe she just
wanted to stay married, and figured that letting her dopey
husband make all the important decisions was the way for us
to stay together. Whatever, it didn't work. But, I don't blame
her for it. It just happened. Well, actually, what happened to
me just happened. And I know I make her seem sort of
insensitive when I told you about her standing over me after
I collapsed on the track at the Olympic Trials and screaming
at me, "What happened?" What I didn't tell you was that the
entire week before the Trials she had been drumming it into
my head to just make the team...just make the team. "It
doesn't matter if you lose by a hundred yards, as long as you
finish in the top three. Just make the team. Make the
Olympic team, Tim." Of course, I ignored her. Her plan—
the correct one—was for me to make the Olympic team,
keep to myself (which wouldn't have been difficult
considering the reputation I had) and then trample
everybody at the Olympics. We both knew I could do it—I
think she might have even had more faith in me than I did—
and then we could write our own ticket. But I wanted to
destroy the world record at the Trials, go to the Olympics
with my name on everybody's lips, and bring home the gold
with another world record, finally getting my—*our*—picture
on the cover of *Sports Illustrated*. Fame and fortune and
more world records would follow, and then I could retire
with a bunch of medals and a bunch of money and we could
buy a great house and have kids and....

You know, I just realized that just about the only thing
in my life I haven't talked about was what it was like when
Judy and I first got married. Isn't that strange? I mean, it was
the best time of my life—we rented a little place in Venice
overlooking one of the canals (I think Dennis Hopper lived
down the street), I was running great, Judy was starting her
business, I was...we were...so much in love it was
incredible, everything was just wonderful—and I haven't
really talked about it at all. I guess when something is
perfect, what else can you say? It was the best. Maybe...
maybe there is something yet to happen, or I think there is
something that's going to come along in my life that will
even be better than before, like me and Judy getting back

together, my running getting better, all the things we planned....

If I had paid more attention to Judy, maybe it would've happened back then. But, as you may have noticed, I tend to over-indulge myself and my ideas (actually, *fantasies* might be a more accurate word). Long-story-short, I'm out here in the desert and nobody knows it and Judy and I are divorced and somebody else has all the records. Even so, I am still running--and very well—and I'm okay. I could do without the money and the records, but I wish I still had Judy. I miss her so much. I know she used to love me. Maybe she still does. She wouldn't go out there every so often if she didn't care, right? Even if she only cares about me and nothing more, I could live with that. The best thing about my day-to-day existence is that I don't have this huge emotional inventory of longing for her and missing her. The worst part is that it is still a day without her. Even though she divorced me when I was at the bottom with everything else that was happening to me, I love her more than I can possibly say. Why? Because she is stone beautiful, incredibly smart and a joy to be around? No...those are the things that make her attractive. What makes me love me her so much and so completely? I have no idea. Wasn't there a song once called "Love is Like Oxygen"? Well...it's true, love is like oxygen. In the song, they say love is like oxygen because you can't live without it. To me, love is like oxygen because it surrounds you, you inhale it and exhale it with every breath, you are submerged in it and yet you don't know what it looks like and can't show it to anyone. You feel its presence; you know it is always there. I've always thought that if someone has to tell you why something is great, it probably isn't; I also think that if someone can tell you why they love someone, they probably don't. Love is experienced, not explained.

to: morganfisher@sportsillustrated.com
from:edwardwoodward<edwdwd@yahoo.com
Morg: Sorry for the delay in getting back to you. This Hardman thing is coming together even better than I ever

imagined. I actually went out there with his wife to meet him. It was a bit surrealistic getting there. She didn't want me to know where he lives, so I had to meet her in the parking lot at Pappy and Harriet's, a funky bar in Pioneertown, the cowboy town just outside Yucca Valley that Roy Rogers built in the Forties as a backdrop for his movies. She drove me from there to the house, taking the most circuitous route possible, through all kinds of desert back roads, to make certain I wouldn't know where I was...and I didn't.

I met Tim Hardman. The guy is great, really social, pretty smart, and can be very funny if he wants to be. He was really happy to be with his wife—he thinks she is his ex-wife—and he spent most of the time just looking at her. Where he lives is a well-kept shack, all by itself in the middle of nowhere. He's got notes to himself all over the place about what has happened to him (losing his memory) and things he needs to do, so he seems to function pretty well as long as there are no intrusions, since most of the instructions he leaves for himself have to do with daily activities which, I get the impression, don't change very much from day to day. He was very candid talking to me about his situation. He knows what is and what is not going on inside his brain, and moves through life accordingly. He would be a great interview, if I could ever pry him away from his wife. The only time we spent together away from her was a few minutes when she went to the bathroom. He told me how much he still loves her. I was going to tell him what was really going on but he talked so fast and with such enthusiasm that it was hard to get a word in and I wasn't certain if I wanted to spoil his world. He confided to me that they were going to have sex later, after I left, and how sometimes he pretends he's running a race while they're doing it. I have no idea why he told me that, but talking to him was like listening to a lonely thirteen year-old speed freak, with the words just pouring out.

She came back into the room, looked at us and demanded to know what we were talking about. When I said that he had done all the talking, she looked relieved. Later, we went outside and he showed me his track he made. It's just some little dirt path, but I'm sure it was a lot of work. He is very proud of it. Then he put on his track spikes and ran a half-mile for us, with his wife timing him. He ran a 1:52—that's back-to-back 56s, by himself—and he looked like he was just going through the motions. It was 92 degrees outside and he barely broke a sweat, and talked to us without losing his breath right after the run. All her talk about his coming back might be legitimate. Doing it in front of a crowd with competition might be harder, but I think there is something going on here.

She drove me back the same convoluted route we took to get there and dropped me off at Pappy and Harriet's. She asked me what I thought. I told her I was impressed. She looked pleased. She waited until I drove off and then headed back to his place, presumably to drain his prostate and empty his brain.

I really believe we have something here that could be a franchise. Since you people have been willing to work with me, I am wondering if we shouldn't have a sit-down with some of your people from Time-Warner to see if we can spread this around. *People* would be perfect for doing a cover on the human element of this story, and they could even follow it up a few weeks later with another cover story about the darker

aspects of all this—manipulation and that sort of thing. *Time* could get something out of this, too. And, you guys own Random House, don't you? I really see a book coming from all of this. I've been keeping a daily journal for the last few weeks and will continue to do so until the story is finished. I think that could be a separate book.

Lou sends his thanks for the last check. In case you think you're the only ones with a financial investment in this, the agency is popping for a few bucks themselves, just to keep everything moving along. I think it will pay off big for all of us. Ed

I almost pulled a Thomas Merton this morning. This hotel room has everything, including a hair dryer attached to the wall in the bathroom. I washed my favorite pair of running socks in the bathroom sink for tonight, and I was using the hair dryer to dry them—an old trick I used in college before Nike started giving me cases of shoes and bags full of socks—and I was running a bath at the same time. While I was holding the dryer in one hand, for some reason I stuck my other hand under the faucet in the bath to see how hot the water was. Boom! I felt a shock run through my body, which knocked me away from the water. I may not have known exactly where my heart was before, but I sure do now, because I think that electrical current went right through it. Runners have larger hearts than most people—the heart is a muscle, right?—and that probably helped me. I don't know if I would've died in any case, but who needs to find out?

Thomas Merton is an important person for me. He was a monk, living in a monastery in rural Kentucky, who was one of the great thinkers of the Catholic Church in the middle of the twentieth century. He was sort of like St. Augustine, you know: not born a Catholic, living a fairly hedonistic life, boinking anything that could walk (there is evidence that he fathered a child without ever being married) but eventually converted. Actually, I haven't read that many of his writings. What I like most about Thomas Merton is Thomas Merton: that he came from where he did and ended up where he did. (In the middle of his spiritual journey, he was hospitalized and fell in love with one of his nurses, but he did not consummate the relationship—and he certainly knew how— or even allow it to continue and disrupt his chosen path of life, which says more to me than all his writings. It was also the example that helped me to persevere when my marriage and my running were both dissolving.)

Merton had written that he envisioned his death as happening peacefully in the backwoods of Kentucky with nobody but a few concerned squirrels looking on. Instead, he was in Thailand, in the mid-60s, attending a seminar on Eastern religions (his ecumenical spirit has somehow eluded me), alone in his room, when he turned on an electric fan that wasn't properly grounded and was electrocuted.

Who says God doesn't have a sense of humor?

I don't know if Thomas Merton ever met Dorothy Day. I wish I had. Like Merton, she was a non-Catholic, who had a common-law marriage and a child during it, and who chose to become a Catholic even though her long-time companion said he would leave her and their child if that happened. It did, and he did, leaving Dorothy as an unwed mother in the 1920s, not a good time for that kind of situation. But Dorothy had an education and connections— she had been tight with Eugene O'Neil, among others, and hung around Greenwich Village in New York—so she survived and prospered, not financially but spiritually. To help the poor, she started the Catholic Worker organization, which wasn't Marxist or radical but was considered so by the Catholic hierarchy in New York City, led by a Cardinal Spellman, who, for all his piety, was a truly reactionary character. As with Merton, what I like most about Dorothy Day is Dorothy Day. She had to constantly deal with negativity in her public and private life—her daughter left the Church—but she never wavered, because it wasn't about her. She was revered from the Thirties until her death in 1980. Many people considered her very pious, almost holy. She had a great line: "Don't marginalize me by calling me a saint." What balls!

When people ask me who my heroes are, I'm certain they expect me to name some famous athlete. My two heroes are Thomas Merton and Dorothy Day, but I would never tell anyone that because, first of all, they wouldn't know who I was talking about and I would have to go into a long explanation which, secondly, would cause them to think I was just trying to be terribly clever. So, I just mumble something or other about there being too many heroes of mine to mention just one or two. Both Merton and Day could have easily dropped out—Merton became world-famous, not an ideal situation for a man supposed to be living as a cloistered monk and one which created constant tension with his superiors; Day had to put up with so much shit that no one would have blamed her for either dropping out or moving to a more receptive area, but she toughed it out, the way a saint would (sorry, Dorothy). They both went balls-to-the-walls for what they believed. You don't have to be Catholic, or even religious, to identify and admire that.

I'm dedicating tonight to Tom and Dorothy.

TRANSCRIPT

Transcriber: Mary Welton
Interviewer: Edward Woodward
Subject: Telephone Call from Judith and Timothy Hardman

Edward Woodward: Judith, before we can continue this call, I will need both your and Timothy's permission to record this conversation.

Judith Hardman: Of course…you have my permission.

Timothy Hardman: Yeah…mine, too.

EW: All right, then…to what do I owe the pleasure of this call?

JH: We have exciting news. Here, Tim, tell him.

TH: I'm going to run in a race…a big-time race!

EW: Where? How did this happen?

TH: Judy, you tell him.

JH: Well, I made a lot of phone calls and sent a few e-mails, and finally made the right connection, and after protracted begging and pleading, I managed to get us an invitation for Tim to run in the Stanford Relays at the end of next month.

EW: Wonderful. What are…what is the Stanford Relays?

JH: Google is sponsoring a new track meet at the Stanford University stadium. I guess Google is just a few miles away from Stanford, and one of the higher-ups is a Stanford grad and a big track and field guy, so he persuaded Google to put up all the money for the meet. They want track to become big in America again, and they want to tie Google into it. They're spending lots of money, and bringing in the best track and field athletes from all over the world. They're offering enough prize money to draw a lot of athletes off the Grand Prix circuit in Europe.

EW: How did you manage to get Tim in?

JH: Well, here, let Tim tell you all about it.

TH: Yeah, Judy really worked some magic here. She got in touch with the meet promoter and director, Art Snyder. Me and Art go back a long way, sometimes not very smoothly, but at least I didn't have to introduce myself. He knows what I used to be able to do, and Judy told him that I can still do it. So, I just had to convince him that I would be able to perform at the level they want.

EW: And he agreed?

TH: Yeah, I'm gonna be on the starting line for the mile…first time in a long time.

EW: That's really great, Tim. I'll certainly be there to document everything.

TH: Judy has been telling me all the great work you have been doing. You know, Mr. Woodward, you should come out here to my place sometime, we could sit just down and have a talk. I could show you the track I built—it's really just a dirt path, but I call it a track because it sounds cooler. Maybe I could run for you, just to show you that I still have it.

EW: Uh…yes…Tim…uh…that would be very good. I'd love to meet you.

TH: Judy wants to talk to you.

EW: Yes, Judith?

JH: Hold on for a second….Tim, could you go out to the car and get my notebooks? Thanks….I wanted him to be out of the room for a minute.

EW: So, you've got your comeback?

JH: Well, sort of…but, not exactly.

EW: What do you mean?

JH: Well, Tim is running the Stanford Mile…but not *all* of it.

EW: What does that mean?

JH: They want a rabbit…someone who will set a fast pace for the first two laps and then step off the track and let the big-name runners take over. They need a world record in one of the events to make the meet successful, to make track big in the U.S. again. They think a world record in the mile would almost guarantee that.

EW: Does Tim know this?

JH: No, of course not. I had to beg and plead with Art…I did everything but promise him sex. He finally agreed, but Tim has to put up a fast half and then get off the track. He has to.

EW: Will he?

JH: Once I explain the situation to him, I think he will. This Stanford Relays thing will give him credibility, then we can move on from there. Art said if Tim gives him what he wants, he'll send Tim over to Europe, where they don't know him, to build up his resume, so to speak, and have him ready for next season back here.

EW: It sounds as though you've got it all planned. When are you going to tell Tim?

JH: As late as possible... probably right before the race. I think he'll handle it okay once it is all explained to him.

EW: Why don't you tell him now, and see what his reaction would be, so you will know what to say next time? You can essentially erase his memory, can't you?

JH: Mr. Woodward, I'm not Doctor Frankenstein. However, that is a very good idea. Oh...here comes Tim....Tim, say goodbye to Mr. Woodward.

TH: Goodbye. I appreciate all you've been doing for us, Mr. Woodward. I hope I get to meet you soon.

EW: Goodbye, Tim. I hope—

JH: Goodbye, Edward. I will be in touch.

I remember running at Stanford a couple times in Pac 10 track meets while I was at UCLA, and I think they had the conference finals there one year. The track was okay, but, from what Judy told me, they've put in a whole new all-weather track, supposed to be the best in the world. Some company named Google—a hell of a name for a company— is spending a shitload of money, I guess, for this meet. I really don't know too much about what's going on. Judy called me about three days ago and told me about the meet. It's the first I had heard of it. Probably just as well, because if I'd known about this for a month or so, I think I might've been freaking out by now because this is going to be my first competition in a long, long time, and it isn't some crappy little all-comers meet like that one in Fresno. This is the big-time, with athletes from all over the world, and I saw in the San Francisco Chronicle this morning that the winner of each event gets a first prize of $10,000, and anybody who sets a world record in their event gets $250,000. I know I could have a good chance at that if everything goes perfect for me. It's been so long since I ran in competition and even though I've had some really good workouts lately—I did three half-miles at 1:52, 1:51 and 1:50 on my track last week, with only a one-lap recovery jog in between—as I've said before, training is training and racing is racing and you shouldn't confuse the two, because in training if you don't get it right, you can do it again, but not in a race, and the mental aspect to running isn't all that strong in training either; football players say that when they get nervous before a big game, especially if they haven't played for awhile, it usually always goes away after the first hit, but in the mile run, it only goes away after the first lap, which can really be a problem if your first lap is terrible because the other guys will nail you, and if you're not used to running behind you will have already lost the race in your mind when there's still three laps to go because the shock to your system will be so strong, and that's why you will see guys in the Olympics run times that are five seconds slower than their best time and finish up the track to guys they beat all the time, because those other races weren't the Olympics, and in the Olympics you run as much with your mind as you do your legs—of course, I've never actually run in the Olympics, but I've talked to guys who have, and they tell me that the pressure can be suffocating, and you're running splits in the qualifying runs that you could run in training while holding your breath, and at the Olympics you are running these garbage times and sucking air like a fat man on a treadmill, wondering what the hell is wrong with you and why all these guys that you know you can beat are pulling away from you—because you've been dreaming about being in the Olympics your entire competitive life and this will probably be your only chance and you have created such enormous pressure for yourself that even if you were running by yourself you would not be convinced that you could win, because you are not just running against the other competitors, you are also running against all your own expectations which, if they are anything like mine, can be so unrealistic that the first indication that you may not perform quite as well as anticipated will be devastating. All the training in the world will not prepare you for that mental hell—only competition, and at the highest level, something I have not been exposed to for a long time, will do that.

On the other hand, I have nothing to lose, since no one expects me to do anything worthwhile and Art Snyder is probably just letting me run as a favor to Judy, who he always liked a lot more than me and who I think has always felt a little sorry for her because she married me. I'm just guessing here, but I can't think of any other reason why they would ask me to run in this race. If I run as well as I think I am able, it will look like a brilliant move and, if I don't, they won't be surprised. My job is to surprise them, and I really think I can and will be disappointed if I don't and—oh, shit, I'm doing all that unrealistic stuff again, aren't I ? I wish one time I could just go out on a track and run a race for the hell of it. Well, actually, I did do that one time, at that race in Fresno. Just showed up, ran, and left: 3:50.7. *Vini...vidi...vici.* I wish it was always that easy. It *should* be that easy. But, I think that they're looking for something faster than a 3:50.7. Running that would probably get the promoters calling, but it won't win tonight, and I always run to win. *Always*.

from: JudithHardman<judeeh@yahoo.com
to:williamdelaney@clarkwilsondelaney.com

Mr. Delaney: I got the check from Art Snyder for the appearance money and put it into my account, so you can deposit the check I wrote you. Don't worry about Art's check. All his money is coming from Google, so there's no worries on that front. However, the story with Tim is a little different. I was out there twice last month. I went out the second time, last week, because I was so excited about everything. Tim was real loving all day until I told him what he was supposed to do for the race, how they want him to drop out after two fast laps, and he completely freaked out. It took me a couple of hours to calm him down, and that was just to stop him from screaming at me. It was the only time in my life that I have ever been afraid of Tim...that I thought he might hit me. Getting him to go to sleep took another two hours. I would say that he raped me except that I let him do it. He put in a blank VHS cartridge and taped it all, saying this would be something I could look at anytime I tried to trick him again. At the worst point, he screamed out that I was just like his mother, never supporting him when he needed it. Afterwards, when he fell asleep, I was shaken but managed to stash that tape away in my bag and edit his other tape which had angry comments about me, calling me all kinds of names and saying that he would never drop out of a race for anyone, that he would rather stop running. I also checked his notes and he had written several things down about it. I took those with me. I got in my car, but I couldn't leave. I sat there, staring at that house in the night. I could have had him arrested or I could have just as easily have gone back in and lie down with him. I didn't do either. I wasn't angry, I wasn't scared, I was sad. It was a very slow drive back to LA, getting there at dawn. I had to decide whether it was a new day, or just another day. I didn't know until I called him two long hours later. He was as cheerful and sweet as ever. I mentioned something about the Stanford Relays and he didn't say anything except that he'd never heard of it before. He didn't remember a thing. I gritted my teeth and decided to try and do the same. I'm okay now, but it took me a little while to calm down. I've been kind of sick, upset stomach and throwing up, which is why I haven't kept in touch. I'm not going to tell Tim about the meet until about three or four days before it happens. I'll just say that I talked to Art Snyder and managed to convince him at the last minute to let Tim run. They've got a room for him at the Hyatt Regency in San Francisco and a van to take him to Stanford. Art has been very cooperative in this, but I think he's expecting more than heartfelt thanks in return. I told him to see how Tim runs and then we'd talk.

What I need from you is to make certain the contract with Art is iron-clad, that if Tim does as he's told, Art will do all the stuff he promised—you know, Europe and all that. Art is real good at fucking you and then forgetting you. I need it in writing and I need it air-tight. This guy knows every trick in the book. I can tell you stories about guys he promised everything to and they ended up having to hitchhike back home. He cares more about money than he does about track and field. He could just as easily be hustling refrigerators.

Is there any movement on getting Tim's asshole mother involved? I promised Woodward an interview with her, but that bitch won't do anything without money up front. From what I hear, her rich husband has deep pockets but short arms, and won't buy her anything. See what you can do with her. Thanks for all your help…Judy

PS: Attorney-client confidentiality, please.

I really think Judy and me are turning a corner. According to my notes, there has been a genuine excitement in her voice, like the way I remember her talking about our future when I graduated from UCLA and it looked as though the sky was the limit, and we used to sit up at night talking about what was going to happen us—it was always *us*, it was never me, and although I was the one who was out in front, the way we talked about it and the way we thought it, the future involved both of us, and I would actually ask for some of her input on how I should train and how I should run my races, even though I must admit I was just doing it to make her feel better and never for a second considered taking any of her advice seriously unless it was something upon which I had already decided myself, and so while you might think I was patronizing her (and maybe I was, without realizing it) by soliciting her advice without having any inclination whatsoever of giving it any additional thought, the idea was that we were in this together, and that was important. There was no chance of us living together until we were married, and I would only see her for a few hours a week because of my training and travel schedule during the season, so whatever time we spent together had to be spent together both physically and emotionally, because I did not want her to feel in the least that this was my show and she was just along for the ride (sort of a groupie, you know) even though that was probably closer to the truth. I really feel that intentions are important, and what I wanted was to make her feel as important a part of the team as I was, which sounds pretty ridiculous, in retrospect, when you consider that I was a champion miler and she was just my fiancé, but that was the way I thought on those days, that I had to take everybody else's feelings into account, especially Judy's, with the result that after every race I would have to endure about an hour of her telling me what I did wrong, what I should have done, and maybe, if there was time, what I did right, with me smiling the whole time and nodding in agreement when I figured it was appropriate, and wishing sometimes that I was a little less moral so I could just take her somewhere and screw her brains out so she would shut the hell up, but knowing that I had created this monster and I was going to have to live with it, which was the case right up to her standing over me on the track at the Olympic Trials and screaming at me, "What happened?—the idea was always the same, that we would just get faster and faster and bigger and bigger and more successful and more successful until we dominated the scene and could dictate our own terms: money, hotels, perks, all the trappings that would come to a world-record holder professional track and field, and we would just suck it all up until we decided to stop, at which time we would retreat to one of the several homes we owned around the world and spend our time raising a beautiful family and indulging ourselves in whatever caught our fancy, and sometimes we would get into very serious and lengthy arguments about subjects such as whether it would be better to raise the children in Hawaii or Malibu, then at the end laughing because we knew it was silly, but also believing that it could happen someday.

(Did I say *monster*? Let's just say she was very free with opinions on one of the few things in the world I knew more about than her. Okay?)

> *Mom and Dad:*
> *I need to tell this to someone, and you're the only people I know who don't know anybody else I know and I'm just going crazy wanting to tell someone and I guess I really should be telling you first, anyways, because you're my parents and...I'm pregnant! I can't believe it. And it's Tim's. I don't know if that makes you happy or not, but I'm happy, so you should be, too. I'm so happy I can't believe it. We have been sleeping together every time I've gone out there—and please don't roll your eyes like that is sick or anything, because it isn't—and I always made sure it*

was during my off-cycle time. But I went out there twice in the same month and that must've done it. I think I subconsciously wanted it, because things are getting better, things are going to happen. I want it all, and I want it all right now. We've got a contract to run in a big race and go to Europe for meets. It's all starting to happen for us, just a few years later than expected, but it'll be sweeter than ever. I would do anything for Tim. Things are finally working out for us, Mom, just the way I knew they would. I understand you still have doubts about Tim and especially about his future, but all I'm worried about is the right now. The future will take care of itself. Tim is running at the Stanford Relays on Saturday night, and I'm going to tell him right after the race. Then we go to Europe for the summer. Please be happy for me.

> *Love,*
> *Jude*

PS: If you and Dad had a computer, you would have known about this a week ago—I would've e-mailed you right away. (And you never answer your phone.) Getting around to writing and mailing a letter takes forever. Think about it...mail from Europe takes even longer.

I was looking at one of my videos of Judy and I noticed something about her that, for some reason, had completely escaped my attention: she still wears her wedding ring. I wear mine because I refuse to accept that it's over between us. I can only speculate on why she still wears hers. It might be because she feels the same way about our relationship as I do. Maybe not. But I think it does speak to the idea that she still has me at her emotional center. She's certainly at mine, and I think about her all the time. Some of the videos I have of her on her visits are cool but, like I keep saying, I don't have any emotional connection with what happened yesterday. To me, they're just facts. I can take comfort in them, they can put my mind at ease, but they don't make sleeping without her any easier. I doubt she goes out on dates or gets asked out on dates when she's wearing the ring. Maybe that's why she wears it, to keep the stalkers away. It makes sense, because a woman as beautiful and wonderful as her would certainly attract the slimeballs. As I said earlier, she told me she's not dating and isn't seeing anyone, and I believe her. There is still a tan line on her ring finger, which says to me that she doesn't just put the ring on when she sees me, but wears it all the time. I'd like to think that all her time spent with me, while we were married but also before we were married, gave her a moral center that is carrying her through life now.

Basically, I guess what I'm trying to say, in my typically verbose way, is that I still see a future for us, that I am the only one for her as she is the only one for me. I know that might sound naïve, but I have nothing to prove otherwise. As I've said, you believe what you want to believe…and that's what I want to believe.

from:
JudithHardman<judeeh@yahoo.com
to:
williamdelaney@clarkwilsondelaney.com

Bill: So far so good. Art Snyder came by the house last night, and he signed the contract, no questions asked, when he left this morning. I guess this is commonly referred to as taking one for the team. I have a feeling I'm going to be taking a few more before this is all over. It is amazing what you will agree to if it gets you what you want.

Tim has no effects from our argument, and doesn't remember a thing. So, as far as he knows, he is running the entire race. I made certain that Art says the same thing to everyone else, including the media and the other runners. Of course, I expect that everything in these emails is covered by attorney-client privilege, but I just want to emphasize that Art, you and me are the only three people who know. I won't divulge anything because it would ruin everything for Tim, and Art certainly won't do anything that makes me unhappy, so it all comes down to you, Bill. I know I can trust you, and I feel silly even mentioning this, but I am, just in case you think that this is not top-secret. It is.

This can be very big. It can be Tim Hardman, Inc. Tim and I deserve it, and if you and Art help, you will deserve some of it, too. Take care...Judy

Getting in the right frame of mind for tonight, I took out an article I copied from the library at UCLA during my freshman year that I always keep with me. It was a story from an early issue of *Sports Illustrated* in the mid-Fifties about Roger Bannister running the first mile under four minutes. The first sentence of the article, which seems kind of quaint now, basically says that running a mile under four minutes requires almost reaching unconsciousness, and the picture of Bannister crossing the finish line in that race makes it look like he was about 95% there. I think a lot of that has to do with the fact that no one had done it before. You always hear stories about somebody or other who supposedly had run under four minutes (Wes Santee, from Kansas, ran a world-record 3:42.2 for 1500 meters in the mid-50's, which works out to a 3:59.9. He was banned for life for receiving money under the table. He should've been the first American to break four-minutes...nothing against Dyrol Burleson, who *was* the first and was a great runner, but....), however, no one was ever documented doing it before Bannister. There were even dire predictions that such a time was humanly impossible. As I said, that all seems rather amusing now, but it was serious stuff then.

Part of the reason it was thought to be impossible was that it was assumed that such a record would have to done as a collective effort, where one runner would go out fast for the first lap or two, then another would take over until the third lap, and somewhere on the backstretch of the fourth and final lap the designated runner would rush to the fore, sprinting around the final curve hoping to break the four-minute barrier without dying because of the effort. Until Bannister, neither happened. All the runners survived, but so did the four-minute mile. Meanwhile, all those runners who set the pace were just spear-carriers, interchangeable parts of no real importance on their own. This attitude has always irritated the hell out of me, treating highly-trained athletes as cannon fodder in some record attempt. Let me tell you something, even the runners who are not top-flight are still important. They are gifted athletes, and were probably All-Everything where they came from, but now, on the largest stage, they rarely win, or matter, except to their coaches and teammates, who rely on them to set the tone and the pace in many of the workouts. I didn't become a world-class miler training by myself. On one your bad days, which might be their best day, they can challenge you and perhaps even beat you. Plus, you are all going through the same workout together, which produces a communal spirit. That is very important, and let me tell you why: In most of the races I have run, and in many of the races I have won, I was in the lead a high percentage of the time. There is something about leading in a race that most people don't realize: it is very quiet in the front. If you are in the middle of four or five guys, such as right after the start or if things aren't going too well during the race, there is the sound of eight or ten spikes hitting the ground rapidly at the same time, the heavy breathing of the other runners, and assorted grunts and other personal noises—I have occasionally dispatched a thunderous fart during a race—whereas when you are in the lead, especially by five or ten yards (which was not unusual for me) it is very quiet. What about the crowd? Assuming there is one, you don't hear the people very much. You have other things on your mind. Leading a race from start to finish looks cool, and it is, but it is also very lonely. Most of the people are waiting for you to fail, to fall back with and behind the others. To them, you are either a show-off or you are just taking unfair advantage of people not as good as you. Me, I was just trying to run as fast as I could for as long as I could and win by as much as I could. That doesn't make for many companions either during the race or afterwards.

So, anyway, you need all your teammates to train with you, to make it seem like a collection of equals even when everyone knows it most certainly is not. Guys who set the pace for a fast race are highly-trained and highly-skilled, just not as much so as the winner. To ask a person who has spent his entire running career to be the best he can be to simply run a couple laps at a pace he cannot sustain for more than that and then get the hell off the track and go back to wherever he came from is to me one of the greatest affronts there is to an athlete. They call them "rabbits" because they run very fast but not very far (the tortoise and the hare, right?). To me, they are the athletic equivalent of the food-taster serving his superiors. He does what he is supposed to do, and if something bad happens to him, it's a damn shame, but no one cares as long as it turns out all right for the man on top. Rabbits are the eunuchs of running. The only thing worse than being one is agreeing to be one.

(While I'm on this subject of disrespect for quality but not *top*-quality runners, let me vent my spleen in this sidebar about something that happens to road racers that really frosts my ass. As you may have surmised from my recollections here, I do not consider road racing to be the equivalent of track in anything except the basic fact that both involve running. To me, road racing embodies a phrase I used before: if you can't run fast, run far. However, I do not like to see good-quality runners dismissed as hacks. The most annoying example of this for me is during a marathon that has enough top-flight runners, male and female, to be televised, and the commentators will generally dismiss the male runners who are running alongside the top lady runners as camera hogs whose only importance in the race is as an irritation. Well, the top female runners will run about a 2:20-2:25, and any guy who can keep up with that, while not a champion, is certain way above-average—hey, I ran a 2:22 that day in Culver City, didn't I?—and does deserve to be treated with respect. I don't lie awake at night thinking about this, but it does bother me.)

from:
williamdelaney@clarkwilsondelaney.com
to: artsnyder@snyderpromos.com

Art: I appreciate your handling of the Hardman contract as expeditiously as you did. Your suggestions were greatly appreciated in arriving at the final wording of the contract. I expect to be in San Francisco at the Hyatt Regency that weekend and would appreciate if we could get together and discuss the other plans that Mrs. Hardman told me that you have for her husband. I will contact you after I arrive...Bill

P.S. I am also intrigued by the personal arrangement you have with Judy. I would like some of that. Or, is this a proprietary thing with you?

According to my notes, the last three weeks have been strange. Not a *bad* strange, but...different. Same thing with my videos. There's stuff on there that I don't usually see.

For example, according to my notes, about three weeks ago I noticed some blood in my urine. It was on a Sunday afternoon, after I had gone to Mass and then went over to the high school to run on their track (it's a lot flatter and smoother than mine). I stopped off after at Del Taco for a chicken soft taco, a regular red burrito and a Cherry Coke (I love those carbs after running hard) and I used their bathroom and I noticed red in my piss. It was sort of the same color as the Cherry Coke but I figured the soda couldn't be running through me that fast, so I hauled ass out of there and got to the nearest Urgent Care as fast a I could, because even though I have a regular doctor who Judy got me up there (and she told me not to go to anybody but him), he's not there on Sunday afternoons and I was starting to freak about the blood in my piss and wanted an answer right away, and when I got to Urgent Care, there were no other people waiting to be helped, so I got in right away, which is why I went there instead of my doctor; I didn't see a doctor, I saw a care practitioner (whatever that means) but he seemed to know what he was talking about and he told me because the blood was darker red, it meant the bleeding was internal, whereas if the blood had been fresh and bright red, that would have meant it was coming from right around my bladder or somewhere in my penis, and I asked him which was worse, figuring that nothing could be worse than having a bleeding cock, but he said the internal bleeding was worse, because it would be harder to diagnose the problem without all kinds of tests and scans and whatever, although he didn't feel that worried because it didn't seem like very much blood, so it might not be much of a problem at all and that I should just observe it for a few days and see if it got worse, in which case I should come back.

Well, it didn't happen again until the following Sunday, so I went back to the same place, saw the same guy, and he basically said the same thing. I asked why it hadn't gone away, and he didn't have an answer, but he told me that if it continued for three or four more days, I should either come back there or see my regular doctor. But he didn't tell me what it was, which was all I really wanted to know. My basic approach to any kind of pain or physical problem is to find out what is happening. If it is something that hurts but isn't going to compromise my conditioning or overall well-being (like shin splints, which can hurt like hell but will not do any permanent damage) then I will just tough it out, but if it is something that can get worse and possibly cause a serious injury, such as with an Achilles tendon, then I will shut down immediately. Pain doesn't bother me; what the pain represents or indicates is what I am always worried about. So, that's why I wanted to know what was going on: should I back off or just deal with it?

What's kind of strange is that I have never had any health problems until this. I have been injury-free the entire time I have been in the high-desert by myself, and I have had some serious training sessions, the kind that when I was a competitive runner would sometimes result in a slight pull or tear of a muscle every once in awhile (nothing serious, and I was always a fast healer) but maybe I have been real lucky up there in the high desert, maybe because we're at 3,500 feet above sea level, which is about two-thirds of a mile, and the altitude has to do with my being injury-free, although I can't imagine what the connection would be.

So, anyway, I got some basic information from the care-practitioner, but nothing else. The Thursday after the second visit, when the guy said I should call if things did not improve, was the same day Judy called and told me about the Stanford Relays. As you might imagine, I was all excited, forgot about everything else, and went out and did a serious run, figuring that would be my last workout before the race, and when I pissed afterwards, there was more red in my urine. Judy had told me drive down to Palm Springs and catch a flight to San Francisco that afternoon, that there would be a ticket waiting for me at the check-in desk. The flight was at four. I finished my run at two, and just barely had time to shower, get dressed and packed and drive to Palm Springs in time for the flight. I could see a doctor somewhere in San Francisco the next day. I went to the bathroom at the airport, to see if there was still a problem, figuring that if it was worse, I would see a doctor right away, but everything was cool—no blood at all. I got on the plane feeling pretty good. The guy at the Urgent Care had said that it probably was nothing, that the body sometimes did things for which there were no explanations. I felt pretty certain that this was the case as I headed for San Francisco and my first competitive race in a long, long time. I was nervous, but it was a good kind of nervous, the type of feeling that I used to have before a big race. It was like being visited by an old friend you hadn't been with in a long time.

I didn't take any notes or get my video camera out the rest of that day, so I can't tell you who picked me up at the airport, drove me to the hotel or got me to my room. I know it wasn't Judy, because when she called she had told me she wouldn't get into San Francisco until the night before the race and that I should call her the morning of the race.

The next morning—yesterday—I slept in pretty good, and had room service send up a really bitchin' breakfast, all kinds of pastries, and some bacon and Eggs Benedict and orange juice and milk. I didn't plan on eating it all at one time, but would just sort of snack on it all day. (You remember my opinion of breakfast, right?) I never run the day before a race—I wouldn't know where to run in downtown San Francisco, anyway—but they have a pretty good gym at the Hyatt Regency, so I went down there in the afternoon to do an arm and chest workout (no legs, of course). I was having a pretty good time, but it seemed kind of strange that no had called me about a drug test or anything else. I knew from when I was running big races before that I would also always get calls from the local press, the promoter and maybe even a couple of the other runners in the race, just sort of shooting the shit, but this time there was nothing. Maybe things have changed . The press doesn't know or care much about me anymore; the promoter, Art Snyder, is not exactly a bosom buddy of mine (we had a falling out after the Olympic Trials; he said I had cost him a lot of money) and I don't know any of the current prominent runners, so maybe that explains everything.

I had a pretty good workout, actually a little more intense than I was used to, since it was the first time I had used real gym equipment in quite awhile. It felt good, and I felt good. I went back to the room, used the toilet, and there was more red than anything else in my urine. I didn't have anyone to contact, so I called the front desk and asked for directions to the nearest medical clinic. Getting dressed quickly, I hurried out of the front lobby of the Hyatt and almost immediately got lost. I finally asked some street person where the nearest medical clinic was and he gave me very explicit directions. They took me right to a clinic—the Free Clinic. It wasn't exactly what I wanted, but, hell, they assured me that there were real doctors there—none of that care-practitioner bullshit—and I would be seen very quickly, and without much paperwork (just give them your name and sit down and wait to be called). A really cool doctor, with hair halfway down his back, listened to my story about my visits to urgent care, got me to give him a sample, and rather quickly gave me a diagnosis: I was bleeding internally. From which organ or artery, he did not know, and they were not equipped to treat me, but he referred me to a doctor I could see the next day. He asked what I did for a living. I said I was runner. He said that could be a problem and cautioned me against strenuous exercise of any type. What would happen? Maybe nothing, he said. Or, maybe whatever was leaking blood would develop into an aneurism with catastrophic results. He put it to me this way: "Nothing at all might happen, or you may blow a major artery, in which case you could be lying on an operating table in the *OR* when it happened and they would still have a very difficult time trying to save you." Those were less than the words of encouragement I had expected. I went to the toilet when I got back to the hotel. Took a piss...clear...no color at all.

Fuck it.

Tim:

> *I'm writing this to you, rather than telling you in person, because you really need to sit down and think about everything I am writing to you about. Honey, I understand that some of what I have to say here is not going to be what you want to hear, or what you expected. What you have to believe, darling, is that it is all for the right reasons and, in the end, it will work out the way we always planned it years ago.*

> *I've been watching you run at your track and looking at your notes about what times you have been running, and that's why I contacted Art Snyder, because I really believe in you, and I really believe that we can finally achieve everything we thought we would have already accomplished by now. I am so proud of the way you have pushed yourself and maintained your focus, never giving up, when you could very easily have turned your back on it all. I know I haven't been with you as much as you wanted the last few years, but I was always thinking of you and taking care of you from a distance. And things are going to change. We are going to be together all the time now. We can either live together out there or we*

can get a place somewhere else. You seem to like the desert, so maybe we could live in Palm Springs, where I would still be able to do my business. It is going to be wonderful, like it was before. But, it all depends on several things.

If we want to get back together, we need to cooperate with Art. I know he is not your favorite person, but he is taking a big chance with us, and he is not asking for that much in return. If you run the way he wants tonight, he is going to take us over to Europe for the rest of the season, and we can compete in several meets there and pick up where we left off before. There is just one thing Art needs you to do to make all these wonderful things happen. It's really not too much to ask for, when you consider all the great things that will happen afterwards as a result.

Art wants you to set a very fast pace for the first two laps. I told him how fast you were running a half-mile on your own little track and he said you could probably run three of four seconds faster than that on the new track they installed for this meet tonight. He'd like about a 1:48, which I think would be easy for you and then we can get ready to leave for Europe in a couple of days and spend the whole summer together over there, like we always planned to do. It will be wonderful.

I can't wait to get started living together again. I already talked to my attorney, and he said we can get rid of the divorce with no problem, that he'd take care of it as a personal favor for us.

You don't need to call me after reading this. I don't want you to be distracted, darling. Just lie down on the bed and take a nap and dream about all the wonderful things we are going to do together after tonight. I can't wait to get started.

I love you more than ever, Tim.

All my love always,
Jude

When I woke up this morning, I felt very relaxed...and very sticky. For the first time in years, I had a wet dream. I wonder why, after all these years? Maybe I had been having them all the time but for some reason never wrote it down. (All that sperm had to be going somewhere, right?) I called Judy before I even got out of bed to go to the toilet, hoping I didn't wake her. It was only about 7:30, but her attorney, a Mr. Delaney, answered. I asked him why he was there so early, and he said there was something he had to take care of. Judy had told me he was doing a lot of work for us, so I thanked him. He said she was in the bathroom, throwing up. I was concerned, but she came on the line and said it was nothing...just stress.

I told her I wanted to come up and see her, but she said that wouldn't be a good idea, although she didn't say why. Maybe she thought I wanted to have sex or something, and was worried that I would wear myself out the morning of the meet. (The wet dream had taken care of that. There has always been a debate among track guys about sex and running. Some guys say you shouldn't have sex before a race, because you are using precious energy, and some say you shouldn't have sex after race, when you are trying to recover and the stress might be too much on your system; the only area of general agreement among all runners on this subject is that you should never have sex *during* a race—you might have a good time, but your time will not be very good.) Judy told me that she would see me at the meet that night and that she had something special to tell me, but it had to be after the race. She made it sound really exciting. (You might think it's kind of strange that my wife and I would not get together even though we were only one floor apart in the hotel and hadn't seen each other in weeks, but on days of important races it has always been my habit to be by myself all day to focus on the race, which was easy when we were dating but more difficult when we were married, especially since big races like this one are almost always on a Saturday and she would be around the house, so I would lock myself in a room and concentrate on how I planned to run, go to the race by myself and not see her until afterwards. It didn't do much for my social life, but when I walked up to the starting line for the race, I was one focused motherfucker.)

Judy told me that she was sending me an envelope with a note of inside of it that she wanted to me to read, that it contained some really important stuff about tonight and about our future. Probably something to do with what she said she was going to tell me about after the race. Anyway, she said she had left the envelope at the front desk and had told them to send it up at noon, so I would have plenty of time to read it before I took my nap. She made it sound real important, repeating herself several times, telling me to get comfortable before I opened the envelope and think about everything that was in it. I asked her if I should call her after I read it, in case she needed an answer or something, but she said no, just read it and then take a nap. Besides, she said, she had a lot of things to do today...she was going to be busy.

It was good to hear Judy's voice. She sounded real tired but she's been under a lot of stress lately, I guess. So, I just called up room service and ordered another humongous breakfast to snack on through the rest of the day. I watched television for an hour or so, then did a few stretching exercises, jumping jacks and that sort of thing. I then went into the bathroom. My urine was mostly a darkish red. When I had gone to the toilet right after talking to Judy on the phone everything was fine, but now I was pissing merlot.

Freaking out, I rushed down the hall, got impatient as I waitied for the elevator, skipped down six flights of stairs to the lobby, ran out the front door and froze. Where the hell was I going? I fumbled in my pocket and pulled out a piece of paper, on which the doctor at the Free Clinic had written the name of the nearest hospital. Well, it didn't actually say hospital. It just had an address on it, which I could barely read. I showed it to a passer-by, who was very kind and understanding, giving me very precise directions and at the same time trying to calm me down. He was only half-successful, as I took off running in the direction he told me at almost at full speed, forgetting that I had a race in nine hours. It was a big hospital—please don't ask me the name—and I spent another fifteen minutes trying to find the emergency room. When I finally did, the waiting area was packed—apparently, a lot of people choose late Saturday morning to become ill or injured—and so I got in line for a few minutes, filled out a form, wrote down "blood in urine", underlined it three times, shoved it back at the clerk, who did not seem impressed, and waited.

And waited...and waited....

from:judithhardman<judeeh@yahoo.com
to:edwardwoodward<edwdwd@yahoo.com

Ed: Everything seems to be set. Art just left my room after expressing to me in no uncertain terms that if Tim does not do as he is told, not only is Europe and everything else gone, but he will also personally drag Tim off the track himself if he does not stop after the second lap. It sounds a little dramatic but I got the message. I sent a long note to Tim explaining what is expected of him, and I gave it to the front desk to send up to his room at noon, so he's got plenty of time to absorb it by himself, with no distractions (such as me). I sugar-coated the message as much as I could.

I've been so busy with everything the last three weeks that I haven't been able to go out and see Tim and check his notes and tapes and see how he's doing. I would hear from him or one of my people out there if there were any problems, so I'm sure that everything is fine with him.

I really appreciate all the things that you have been doing for Tim and me. When I told Art that *SI* was doing a feature on Tim, that's what got Tim invited to the Stanford Relays and set everything else in motion. We couldn't have done it without you. I'm going to be free from three to four this afternoon, if you want to come up to my room for a little while. I have to get ready to leave for the meet at 5:00. Thanks for everything...Jude

At three o'clock, I still had not been seen. (Emergencies always jump to the front of the line, and they were coming in like rats off a ship.) I had calmed down and felt good, went in and used the toilet, and it was clear. How could that be? I thought I was hemorrhaging a few hours ago, and now there was nothing. False alarm, I said to myself, a big smile on my face. I decided to move on with the day. On the way back to the hotel, I passed a Catholic church and noticed the announcement board out front said Confession (sorry...Reconciliation) was from 3:00 to 4:30. It was too good of an opportunity to pass up—everything happens for a reason, right?—so I went inside this big church, in which about ten people were kneeling and praying and a few more were waiting in line at the confessionals (or, *reconciliationals*). I knelt down for a few minutes, said a Hail Mary, Our Father and Act of Contrition, then got up and waited in line. You always wonder what kind of priest you're going to get...Fire and Brimstone or Mr. Rogers.

When you have no memory of any day but today, telling your sins to a priest is almost like an Abbott and Costello routine: "Bless me, Father, for I have sinned, I guess; I don't know how long it has been since my last confession, and I don't know what are my sins."

"Have you committed any sins?"

"I don't remember."

"Are you certain?"

"I think so."

And then I went into the whole routine about my situation and made educated guesses at what I might have done since the last time, saying I couldn't remember and had no evidence of my doing anything sinful, after which the priest, slightly exasperated, said I was a lucky man, which was a description of me I had not heard in a very long time, and told me to say a decade of the rosary on general principle whenever I got around to it. After I said my Act of Contrition, I asked him if he could answer a question for me.

"Of course."

"Is it all right to do something which isn't wrong but which you were told might be harmful for you to do, and you might even die because of it?

The priest paused for a second.

"Are you a soldier?"

I smiled to myself.

"Uh…no."

"Is it guaranteed that you might be harmed doing this?"

"No, I have been warned, but it's possible that nothing bad will happen."

"Are you trusting in the Lord?"

"All my life."

"I think you have your answer."

Yes, I did.

I hurried back to the Hyatt, mumbling my penance along the way, and I was just finishing up with a Glory Be when I entered the lobby and was immediately approached by some guy in a track suit. He was my ride to the track meet and we were late. I said I'd have to go up to my room and get all my stuff, but he told me that had all been taken care of, they had all my things in the van. Spikes, socks, shorts, singlet …all my running gear? Yes, yes, yes, yes and yes. As long as I had my spikes, socks, and shorts, that was all that mattered. Anything I'd forgotten could probably be supplied at the meet. It was time to boogie. My video camera and tapes and notes and everything were still in the room. Judy could pick up everything later if I didn't…uh…you know…

Before I went out and got in the van—they made it sound like they were sending a limo for me, and I was expecting a chauffeur, but instead I got some guy in a sweat suit and a funky old white van—I went to the toilet one more time, in the hotel lobby restroom.

Red.

Not dark red, but definitely not clear. There was no one else in the restroom, so I just stood there looking at myself in the mirror for the longest time as I washed and dried my hands.

"Well, asshole, what happens now?" I said to the reflection in the mirror, trying to stare through it. "Do we take the safe way and pussy out, or is it balls-to-the-walls and fuck everything else?" I could go back to my room, return to the high-desert, do nothing and hope that the situation could be taken care of—maybe they could find out what was happening inside of me and fix it, assuming it could be fixed—or I could get in the van and go do what I had been planning to do, what I have been waiting to do for a long, long time, There were serious implications either route: going back home and not running, existing but not really living, or going to the meet and having the chance to fulfill all my dreams and expectations...if...

Maybe nothing will happen...maybe my body is playing jokes on me. Maybe I will run the time I have been pointing towards my entire career, and Judy will fall in my arms and we'll live happily ever after.

Maybe.

This is what I have wanted...this is how I have wanted it. All I have to do now is go out and do what I know I am capable of doing. It is all down to me. I know I can do it. *I know it.* I am in control. Everything else will take care of itself, right?

There is nothing else to worry about.

If you've done the best you can...what else can you do?

May nothing disturb you,
Nothing frighten you;
All things pass, God never leaves;
Patient endurance obtains all things;
Whoever has God lacks nothing.
God alone is enough.

--St. Teresa of Avila

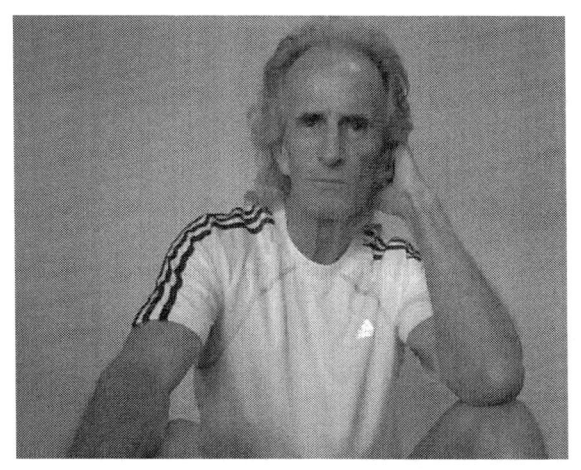

DENNIS AIDEN LOCKHART LIVES IN
SOUTHERN CALIFORNIA WITH
HIS WIFE AND DAUGHTER

trrblyclvr@yahoo;com

Made in the USA
Charleston, SC
09 September 2016